The Von Tood

Or, The History of a Very Distinguished Family

F. Colburn Adams

Alpha Editions

This edition published in 2024

ISBN : 9789364734158

Design and Setting By
Alpha Editions
www.alphaedis.com
Email - info@alphaedis.com

As per information held with us this book is in Public Domain.
This book is a reproduction of an important historical work. Alpha Editions uses the best technology to reproduce historical work in the same manner it was first published to preserve its original nature. Any marks or number seen are left intentionally to preserve its true form.

Contents

PREFACE. ....- 1 -
CHAPTER I. ....- 3 -
CHAPTER II. ....- 7 -
CHAPTER III. ....- 10 -
CHAPTER IV. ....- 12 -
CHAPTER V. ....- 15 -
CHAPTER VI. ....- 21 -
CHAPTER VII. ....- 26 -
CHAPTER IX. ....- 33 -
CHAPTER X. ....- 37 -
CHAPTER XI. ....- 41 -
CHAPTER XII. ....- 47 -
CHAPTER XIII. ....- 52 -
CHAPTER XIV. ....- 59 -
CHAPTER XV. ....- 64 -
CHAPTER XVI. ....- 68 -
CHAPTER XVII. ....- 74 -
CHAPTER XVIII. ....- 83 -
CHAPTER XIX. ....- 88 -
CHAPTER XXI. ....- 97 -
CHAPTER XXII. ....- 103 -
CHAPTER XXIII. ....- 109 -
CHAPTER XXIV. ....- 116 -
CHAPTER XXV. ....- 121 -
CHAPTER XXVI. ....- 127 -
CHAPTER XXVII. ....- 133 -

CHAPTER XXVIII.	- 141 -
CHAPTER XXIX.	- 144 -
CHAPTER XXX.	- 148 -
CHAPTER XXXI.	- 155 -
CHAPTER XXXII.	- 158 -
CHAPTER XXXIII.	- 164 -
CHAPTER XXXIV.	- 173 -
CHAPTER XXXV.	- 176 -
CHAPTER XXXVI.	- 179 -

PREFACE.

I never could see what real usefulness there was in a preface to a work of this kind, and never wrote one without a misgiving that it would do more to confuse than enlighten the reader.

The good people of Nyack will pardon me, I know they will, for taking such an unwarrantable liberty as to locate many of my scenes and characters in and around their flourishing little town. I have no doubt there are persons yet living there who will readily recognize some of my characters, especially those of Hanz and Angeline Toodleburg. That the very distinguished family of Von Toodleburgs, which flourished so extensively in New York at a later period, as described in the second series of this work, will also be recognized by many of my readers I have not a doubt. Nyack should not be held responsible for all the sins of the great Kidd Discovery Company, since some of the leading men engaged in that remarkable enterprise lived on the opposite side of the river, many miles away.

The reader must not think I have drawn too extensively on my imagination for material to create "No Man's Island" and build "Dunman's Cave" with. About eighteen years ago I chanced to have for fellow traveller an odd little man, of the name of Price, (better known as Button Price,) who had been captain of a New Bedford or Nantucket whaleship. He was an earnest, warm-hearted, talkative little man, and one of the strangest bits of humanity it had ever been my good fortune to fall in with. He had lost his ship on what he was pleased to call an unknown island in the Pacific. He applied the word "unknown" for the only reason that I could understand, that he did not know it was there until his ship struck on it. He regarded killing a whale as the highest object a man had to live for, and had no very high respect for the mariner who had never "looked round Cape Horn," or engaged a whale in mortal combat. He was on his way home to report the loss of his ship to his owners. An act of kindness, and finding that I knew something of the sea, and could sympathize with a sailor in misfortune, made us firm friends to the end of our journey.

To this odd little man, then, I am indebted for the story of the old pirate of "No Man's Island," and what took place in "Dunman's Cave;" for it was in just such a place, according to his own account, that he lost his ship. Much of his story, as told to me then, seemed strange and incredible—in truth, the offspring of a brain not well balanced.

Time has shown, however, that there was much more truth in this old whaleman's story than I had given him credit for. "No Man's Island" is somewhat better known to navigators now, though still uninhabited and bearing a different name. "Dunman's Cave," too, has been the scene of more than one shipwreck within six years.

Those who have carefully studied the causes producing "boars," or "tidal waves," as they appear in different parts of the world, and the singular atmospheric phenomena which at times accompany them, will not find it difficult to understand the startling changes which took place in "Dunman's Cave" when the "*Pacific*" was wrecked. They will understand, also, why the "*set*" was so strong at so great a distance from the entrance, and why the "boar" rose to such a height in a narrow gate, or entrance formed by steep rocks, before it broke, and went rushing and roaring onward with irresistible force. They will also understand what produced the noise resembling the sound of a mighty waterfall.

F.C.A.

WASHINGTON, D.C., *January*, 1868.

CHAPTER I.

ANCIENT HEADS OF THE FAMILY.

Not more than a mile from the brisk little town of Nyack, on the Hudson river, and near where the road makes a sharp turn and winds up into the mountain, there lived, in the year 1803, an honest old farmer of the name of Hanz Toodleburg. Hanz was held in high esteem by his neighbors, many of whom persisted in pronouncing his name Toodlebug, and also electing him hog-reef every year, an honor he would invariably decline. He did this, he said, out of respect to the rights of the man last married in the neighborhood. It mattered not to Hanz how his name was pronounced; nor did it ever occur to him that some of his more ambitious descendants might be called on in a court of law to explain the circumstances under which their name was changed. I speak now of things as they were when the old settlers around Nyack were honest and unsuspecting, before Fulton had astonished them with his steamboat, or those extravagant New Yorkers had invaded the town, building castles overlooking the Tappan Zee, and school-houses where the heads of honest Dutch children were filled with wicked thoughts.

Hanz Toodleburg was short and stout of figure, had a full, round face, a large blunt nose, and a small gray eye. Indeed, there was no mistaking his ancestors, in whose language he spoke whenever the Dominie paid him a visit, which he did quite often, for Hanz had always good cheer in the house; and a bed for a stranger. In short, it was a boast of Hanz that no traveller ever passed his house hungry, if he knew it. And it increased his importance with his neighbors that he raised more bushels to the acre than any of them, and sent better vegetables to the New York market. More than that, he would tell all the big folks in the village, with a nod of his head, that he owed no man a stiver he could not pay before the sun set, and in such a way as to convey a sly hint that it was more than they could do. The neighbors consulted Hanz concerning their worldly affairs, and, indeed, received his opinions as good authority. In fine, Hanz and the Dominie were called in to settle nearly all the disputes arising between the country folks for miles around. And it was said by these simple minded people that they got their rights quicker and less expensively in this way than when they went to law in the village and trusted to the magistrate and the lawyers for justice.

As, however, there always will be idle and gossiping people everywhere to say unkind things of their neighbors, especially when they are more prosperous than themselves, so there were gossips and mischievous people in the settlement who, when engaged over their cups, would hint at suspicious enterprises in which Hanz's ancestors were engaged on the Spanish Main. Indeed, they would hint at times that it was not saying much for his family that his father had sailed with Captain Kidd, which would account for the doubloons and Mexican dollars Hanz could always bring out of a "rainy day." That Hanz had a stock of these coins put safely away there could not be a doubt, for he would bring them out at times and part with them, declaring in each case that they were the last. But how he came by them was a mystery not all the wisdom of the settlement could penetrate. It was conceded that if there was any man in the settlement who knew more than Jacques, the schoolmaster, it was Titus Bright, who kept the little inn near the big oak; and these two worthies would discuss for hours over their toddy the question of how Hanz came by his dollars and doubloons. But they never came to a decision; and generally ended by sending their listeners home with their wits worse perplexed than ever. It was all well enough for old Jacques and the inn-keeper to show their knowledge of history; but the gossips would have it that if Hanz's father had sailed with Captain Kidd he, of course, knew where that bold pirate had buried his treasure, and had imparted the secret to his son. Here was the way Hanz came possessed of the doubloons and dollars. Indeed, it was more than hinted that Hanz had been seen of dark and stormy nights navigating the Tappan Zee, alone in his boat, and no one knew where he went. Another had it that he was sure to part with a doubloon or two shortly after one of these excursions, which told the tale. There were others who said it did not matter a fig if Hanz Toodlebug's doubloons were a part of Kidd's hidden treasure; but it was selfish of him not to disclose the secret, and by so doing give his neighbors a chance to keep as good cows and sheep as he did. Hanz was not the man to notice small scandal, and continued to smoke his pipe and make his friends welcome whenever they looked in. Once or twice he had been heard to say, that if anybody was particular to know how he came by his doubloons and dollars he would tell them. There was a place up in the mountain where he made them.

I will say here, for the benefit of my readers, that the little old house where Hanz Toodleburg lived, and about which there clustered so many pleasant memories, still stands by the roadside, and is an object of considerable curiosity. It is much gone to decay now, and a very different person occupies it. There are persons still living in the village who knew Hanz, and never pass the place without recurring to the many happy hours spent under his roof. That was in the good old days, before Nyack began to put on the airs of a big town. There is the latticed arch leading from the gate to the door; the little veranda, where the vines used to creep and flower in spring; the moss-covered roof, and the big arm chair, made of cedar branches, where Hanz used to sit of a summer evening contemplating the beauties of the Tappan Zee, while drinking his cider and smoking his pipe. It was in this little veranda that business of great importance to the settlers would at times be discussed. The good sloop Heinrich was at that time the only regular New York packet, making the round voyage every week. Her captain, one Jonah Balchen, was much esteemed by the people of Nyack for his skill in navigation; and it was said of him that he knew every rock and shoal in the Tappan Zee, and no man ever lost his life who sailed with him. The arrival of the good sloop Heinrich then was quite an event, and whenever it occurred the neighbors round about would gather into Hanz's little veranda to hear what news she brought from the city, and arrange with Captain Balchen for the next freight. Indeed, these honest old Dutchmen used to laugh at the idea of a man who would think of navigating the Tappan Zee in a boat with a big tea-kettle in her bottom, and making the voyage to New York quicker than the good sloop Heinrich.

I have been thus particular in describing Hanz Toodleburg's little home, since it was the birth-place of Titus Bright Von Toodleburg, who flourished at a more recent date as the head of a very distinguished family in New York, and whose fortunes and misfortunes it is my object to chronicle.

Having spoken only of one side of the family, I will proceed now to enlighten the reader with a short account of the other, "Mine vrow, Angeline," for such was the name by which Hanz referred to his good wife, was a woman of medium size and height, and endowed with remarkable good sense and energy. Heaven had also blessed her with that gentleness of temper so necessary to make a home happy. They had, indeed, been married nearly twenty years, and although nothing had come of it in the way of an offspring, not a cross word had passed between them. It was said to her credit that no housewife this side of the Tappan Zee could beat her at making bread, brewing beer, or keeping her house in good order. The frosts of nearly forty winters had whitened over her brows, yet she had the manner and elasticity of a girl of eighteen, and a face so full of sweetness and gentleness that it seemed as if God had ordained it for man's love. Angeline's dress was usually of plain blue homespun, woven by her own hands, and with her cap and apron of snowy whiteness she presented a picture of neatness and comeliness not seen in every house.

There was a big, square room on the first floor, with a little bed room adjoining, and an old-fashioned bed with white dimity curtains, fringe, and tassels made by Angeline's own hand. Snow white curtains also draped the windows; and there was a tidy and cosy air about the little bed room that told you how good a housewife Angeline was. An old-fashioned hand-loom stood in one corner of the big, square room; and a flax and a spinning-wheel had their places in another. A farm-house was not considered well furnished in those days without these useful implements, nor was a housewife considered accomplished who could not card, spin, and weave. Angeline carded her own wool, spun her own yarn, and weaved the best homespun made in the settlement; and had enough for their own use and some to sell at the store.

In addition to that there was no housewife more expert at the flax-wheel, and her homemade linen was famous from one end to the other of the Tappan Zee. Hanz was, indeed, so skilful in the art of raising, hetcheling, and dressing flax, that all the neighbors wanted to borrow his hetchel. And if needs be he could make reeds and shuttles for the loom, while Angeline always used harnesses of her own make. And so industrious was this good wife that you could rarely pass the house of a night without hearing the hum of the wheel or the clink of the loom.

The good people about Nyack were honest in those days, paid their debts, were happy in their very simplicity, and had no thought of sending to Paris either for their fabrics or their fashions.

Now Angeline's father was a worthy blacksmith, an honest and upright man, who lived hard by, had a house of his own, and owed no man a shilling. This worthy blacksmith had two daughters, Angeline and Margaret, both remarkable for their good looks, and both blessed with loving natures. And it was said by the neighbors that the only flaw in the character of this good man's family was made by pretty Margaret, who went away with and married one Gosler, a travelling mountebank. This man, it is true, asserted that he was a Count in his own country, and that misfortune had brought him to what he was. His manners were, indeed, those of a gentleman; and there were people enough who believed him nothing more than a spy sent by the British to find out what he could.

CHAPTER II.

COMING INTO THE WORLD.

It was mentioned in the last chapter that Hanz Toodleburg had seen twenty years of the happiest of wedded life; and yet that Angeline had not increased his joys with an offspring. Thoughtless people made much ado about this, and there were enough of them in the settlement to get their heads together and say all sorts of unkind things to Hanz concerning this family failing. I verily believe that the time of one-half of the human family is engaged seeking scandal in the misfortunes of the other. And I have always found that you got the ripest scandal in the smallest villages; and Nyack was not an exception. No wonder, then, that Hanz had to bear his share of that slander which one-half the world puts on the other. Not an idle fellow at the inn, where Hanz would look in of an evening, but would have his sly joke. Many a time he had to "stand" cider and ale for the company, and considered he got off cheap at that. And when they drank his health, it was with insinuating winks and nods; one saying:

"What a pity. He ought to have somebody to leave his little farm to."

"Yes," another would interrupt; "if he had a son he'd be sure to leave him the secret of Kidd's treasure."

The gossips of the village were to change their tune soon. Dame rumor had been whispering it around for a month that there was something in the wind at Toodleburg's. And, to put it more plainly, it was added that Hanz was soon to be made a happy man by the appearance of a little Toodleburg. This change, or rather apparent change, in the prospects of the family did not relieve Hanz from the tax for ale and cider levied on him by the idle fellows at the inn. Indeed, he had to stand just twice the number of treats in return for the compliments paid him as a man and a Christian. It was noticed, also, that the Dominie took tea more frequently at Hanz's table; and that Critchel, the little snuffy doctor, who had practised in the settlement for a quarter of a century, and, indeed, assisted in bringing at least one-half of its inhabitants into the world, and of course was considered very safe in such cases, had increased his visits at the house.

Now these honest old burghers had almanacs made with strict regard to truth, and if they prognosticated a storm it was sure to come. They would not consider it safe to navigate the Tappan Zee on a day fixed by the almanac for a storm. On the 5th day of January, 1805, in the almanac that never failed Hanz, there was this: "Look out for a snow storm." This time, however, the snow, if not the storm, was ahead of the almanac. Indeed, it had been falling slowly and gently for two days; and a white sheet of it, at least three inches deep, covered the ground on the morning of the 5th. The weather had changed during the night, and now the air was sharp and cold. Dark, bleak clouds hung along the horizon in the northeast, the distant hills stood out sharp and cold, and a chilling wind whispered and sighed through the leafless trees. Then the wind grew stronger and stronger, the snow fell thicker and faster, making fantastic figures in the air, then dancing and scudding to the force of the gale, and shutting the opposite shore from sight. Nyack lay buried in a storm, and the Tappan Zee was in a tempest. Snow drifted through the streets, up the lanes, over the houses, and put night-caps on the mountain tops. Snow danced into rifts in the roads and across fields, and sent the traveller to the inn for shelter. Lowing cattle sought the barn-yard for shelter, or huddled together under the lee of some hay-stack, covered with snow. Night came, and still the snow fell, and the wind blew in all its fury.

It was on that cold, stormy night that a bright light might have been seen burning in the little house where Hanz Toodleburg lived. The storm had shook its frame from early morning; and now the windows rattled, discordant sounds were heard on the veranda, wind sighed through the crevices, and fine snow rifted in under the door and through the latch-hole, and tossed itself into little drifts on the floor. Nyack was buried in a storm that night. There was an old clock on the mantle-piece, and it kept on ticking, and its ticks could be heard above the storm. And the bright oak fire in the great fireplace threw out shadows that flitted over the great loom, and the wheels, and the festoons of dried apples, and the pumpkins that hung from the beams overhead. And old Deacon, the faithful watch-dog, lay coiled up on the flag hearth-stone.

The old clock had nearly marked the hour of midnight as Hanz came out of the little room in an apparently agitated state of mind. The dog raised his head and moved his tail as Hanz approached the fire and threw some sticks on. "Dere's no postponin' it; and it sthorms so," muttered Hanz, shaking his head. Then he put on his big coat and boots, drew his cap over his ears, and went out into the storm, leaving the big dog on guard. How he struggled through the snow that night, what difficulty he had in waking up his two nearest neighbors, and getting one of them to send his son for Doctor Critchel, and what was said about such things always happening of such a night, I will leave to the imagination of my reader.

It was nearly an hour before Hanz returned, bringing with him two stout, motherly-looking dames. The storm had handled their garments somewhat roughly, and they were well covered with snow. The old dog was pleased to see them, and wagged them a welcome, and made sundry other signs of his affection. And when they had shaken the snow from their garments, and taken seats by the fire, Hanz gave them fresh pipes, which they lighted and proceeded to enjoy while he went to preparing something warm for their stomachs, and doing various other little things regarded as indispensable on such an occasion.

The storm had caught the little house by the shoulders, and was giving it one of its most violent shakes, when the dog suddenly started up, gave a growl, then walked solemnly to the door and listened. A footstep in the old veranda, then the stamping of feet, and a knock at the door came. It was Critchel, the little snuffy doctor, who entered, looking for all the world like an enlarged snow-ball. These were the occasions in which the doctor rose into the most importance, and as his coming had been waited with great anxiety, great efforts were made by those present to assure him of the esteem in which he was held. Even the dog would not go to his accustomed place on the hearth until he had caressed the doctor at least a dozen times. Although held in great respect by the settlers, Critchel was what might be called a shabby-looking little man, for his raiment consisted of a brown coat, which he had worn threadbare, a pair of greasy pantaloons that were in shreds at the bottom, a spotted vest, and a Spitlesfield neckerchief. Indeed, he was as antique in his dress as in his ideas of the science of medicine. He had a round, red face, a short, upturned red nose, and a very bald head, which Hanz always declared held more sense than people were willing to give him credit for. There was no quainter figure than this familiar old doctor as seen mounted on his big-headed and clumsy-footed Canadian pony, his saddle-bags well filled with pills and powders, and ready to bleed or blister at call. He was considered marvelously skilful, too, at drawing teeth and curing the itch, with which the honest Dutch settlers were occasionally afflicted. I must mention, also, that an additional cause of the great respect shown him by the settlers was that he took his pay in such things as they raised on their little farms and could best spare.

CHAPTER III.

THE NEW COMER.

The storm ceased its fury at four o'clock, and a cold, bright, and calm morning succeeded. The hills stood out in sharp, clear outlines, mother earth had put on her cleanest cap, and there was not a ripple on all the Tappan Zee. Hanz Toodleburg was now the happiest man in Nyack, for Heaven had blessed his house and heart during the morning with as plump and healthy a boy as ever was seen. There was a fond mother and a happy father in the little house now; and the sweet innocent babe, their first born, was like flowers strewn along their road of life. It was something to live for, something to hope for, something to brighten their hopes of the future, and to sweeten their love-dream.

In spite of the snow drifts, news of this important event ran from one end to the other of the settlement before the sun was an hour up, and set it all aglow. The roadmaster was early at the door to warn Hanz out to break roads, but excused him when he heard how happy a man he had been made during the night. And when the merry men came along with their oxen, and their sledges, and their drag-logs, ploughing through and tossing the snow aside, and making a way for the traveller, there were cheers given for honest Hanz and the little gentleman who had just come to town. And as they ploughed along through the drifts, they struck up a merry song, which so excited Hanz's emotions that he could not resist the temptation to put on his coat and follow them. And when they reached Titus Bright's inn that ruddy-faced host met them at the door and bade them welcome under his roof, and invited them to drink flip at his expense. Hanz was treated and complimented in steaming mugs, and the health and happiness of mother and son were not forgotten. Even the Dominie was sent for, and made to drink flip and tell a story, which he did with infinite good humor. Then the school-master, who was not to be behind any of them when there was flip in the wind, looked in to pay his compliments to Hanz, for the snow had closed up his little school-house for the day. But, in truth, the pedagogue had a weakness he could not overcome, and when invited to take flip tossed off so many mugs as completely to loose his wits, though his tongue ran so nimbly that he was more than a match for the Dominie, who declined discussing a question of religion with him, but offered to tell a story for every song he would sing. Four mugs of flip and two songs and the school-master went into a deep sleep in his chair, where he remained for the rest of the day.

The question as to who should name the young gentleman at Hanz's house was now discussed. The names of various great men were suggested, such as George Washington and Thomas Jefferson. Hanz shook his head negatively at the mention of these. "It vas not goot to give a poy too pig a name; t-makes um prout ven da grows up," he said. It was finally agreed that the young gentleman should be called Titus Bright, after the little ruddy-faced inn-keeper. And the little man was so pleased with the idea of having his name engrafted on that of the Toodleburg family, that he promised a fat turkey and the best pig of the litter for the christening dinner. More flip was now drank, and the merry party shook hands and parted in the best of temper.

Hanz felt that as Heaven had blessed him and Angeline with this fine boy, and so increased their joys, he must do something generous for his friends. So, on the morning following he sent the Dominie a pig and a peck of fine flour, for which that quaint divine thanked him and prayed Heaven that he might send more. He gave the school-master a big pipe and tobacco enough to last him a month. He also ordered the tailor to make the pedagogue a new suit of homespun, something the poor man had not had for many a day. School-mastering was not a business men got rich at in those days, and poor Wiggins, for such was his name, had a hard time to keep the wolf from his door. Indeed, he thought himself well paid with four dollars a week and his victuals, which he got around among the parents of his scholars. His worldly goods consisted of little else than his birch and pipe, and the shabby clothes on his back. And as the length of his engagements depended on his good behavior, which was none of the best, he was frequently seen tramping from village to village in search of a job.

As for Doctor Critchel, Hanz felt that he owed him a debt of gratitude he could never pay, even were he to give him the farm. It was no use offering the doctor a new suit of clothes, as he was never known to wear such things. As for snuff-boxes, he had at least a dozen. Hanz sent him a goose to roast for his dinner, a fat sheep, and a bag of extra flour, just from the mill.

I may have been too particular in describing how and when this young gentleman came into the world, but my reason for it is that there may be those among my readers who will recognize the great and very distinguished family of Von Toodleburg, which not many years ago amazed New York with its brilliancy, and be anxious to know some of the ups and downs of its early history.

CHAPTER IV.

CHANGED PROSPECTS.

Twelve years have passed since that stormy night when Titus Bright Toodleburg—for the young gentleman as I have said before, was named after the inn-keeper, came into the world. Great changes have taken place since then. Tite, as the neighbors all call him, is now a bright, intelligent boy, and a great favorite in the village. Hanz and Angeline are proud of him, and he promises to be the joy of their declining years. Hanz had always held to the opinion that men with too much learning were dangerous to the peace of a neighborhood, inasmuch as it caused them to neglect their farms and take to pursuits in which the devil was served and honest people made beggars. He had, however, sent Tite to school, and now the young gentleman could read, write, and cypher; and this, he declared, was learning enough to get a man safe through the world if he but followed an honest occupation and saved his money. In addition to so much learning, the young gentleman had early discovered an enterprising spirit, and a remarkable taste for navigation. When only six years old he had his tiny sloops and schooners, rigged by himself, on every duck-pond in the neighborhood. And he could sail them with a skill remarkable in one so young. Indeed, these duck-ponds were a source of great annoyance to Angeline, for whenever one of Tite's crafts met with an accident he would wade to its relief, no matter what the condition or color of the water.

Hanz shook his head, and felt that no good would come of this taste for the sea on the part of Tite. He intended to bequeath him the farm, so that he could spend his life like an honest man in raising good vegetables for the New York market. Following the sea, Hanz urged, was a very dangerous occupation, and where one man made any money by it, more than a dozen lost their lives by storms. But Tite was not to be put off by such arguments. The spirit of adventure was in the boy, and all other objects had to yield to his natural inclinations. And now, at the age of twelve, we find Tite a smart, sprightly cabin-boy, on board the good sloop Heinrich, making the voyage to New York and back once a week, and taking his first lessons in practical seamanship.

Wonderful changes had been developed along the beautiful Hudson during these twelve years. People in the country said New York was getting to be a very big, and a very wicked city. Already her skirmishers, in a line of little houses, were pushed beyond the canal, and were obliterating the cow-paths. The honest old Dutch settlers shrugged their shoulders, and said it was not a good sign to see people get rich so fast. Indeed, they declared that these fast and extravagant New Yorkers, who were building great houses and sending big ships to all parts of the world, would bring ruin on the country.

A ship of five hundred tons had been added to the old London line, and her great size was an object of curiosity. But the man who projected her was regarded by careful merchants as very reckless, and not a safe man to trust.

That which troubled the minds of these peaceable old settlers most was Mr. Fulton and his steamboat. Steam they declared to be a very dangerous thing. And, as for this Mr. Fulton, he should be sent to an insane asylum, before he destroyed all his friends, and lost all his money in this dangerous undertaking. He might navigate the river with a big tea-kettle in the bottom of his boat, but he would be sure to set all the houses along the river on fire. And who was to pay the damages? Steam was, however, a reality, and the little Fire Fly went puffing and splashing up and down the river, alarming and astonishing the people along its banks. She could make the voyage from the upper end of the Tappan Zee to New York in a day, no matter how the wind blew. Hanz Toodleburg called the Fire Fly an invention of the devil, and nobody else. The bright blaze of her furnaces, and the long trail of fire and sparks issuing from her funnel of a dark night, gave a spectre-like appearance to her movements, that rather increased a belief amongst the superstitious that she was really an invention of the evil one, sent for some bad purpose.

A meeting was called at Hanz Toodleburg's house to consider the dangerous look of things along the river. The Dominie and the schoolmaster, and all the wise men in the settlement, were present, and gave their opinions with the greatest gravity. If this Mr. Fulton, it was argued, could, with the aid of the evil one, build these steamboats to go to New York and back in a day, why there was an end to the business of sloops and barges. And if the honest men who owned these vessels were thrown out of business, how were they to get bread for their families? These new inventions, Hanz argued, would be the ruin of no end of honest people.

The schoolmaster, who assumed great wisdom on all such occasions, and who had tossed off several pots of beer during the evening, put the whole matter in a much more encouraging light. He had read something about steam, he said, and knew that it was a very dangerous thing for a man to trifle with. Mr. Fulton had built his steamboat one hundred and nine feet long; and he could get to New York and back in a day, if nothing happened to his boiler, which was all the time in danger of bursting. Then if the boiler bursted, very likely the boat and all in her would go to the bottom. Just let that happen once in the Tappan Zee, and there would be an end to Mr. Fulton and his invention for getting people to New York quick. Just let him set the Tappan Zee afire once, and people would make such a storm that nothing more would be heard of his inventions. When there was such danger of losing one's life travelling in this way, what careful farmer, who had a family depending on him, would think of either going himself or sending his produce to market in such a way? There was no wisdom in the thing. The people would stick to the sloops. That was the only safe way for sensible people to get to market. Let them stick to the sloops, and Mr. Fulton would not build a castle of what he got by his inventions.

The meeting was highly gratified at what the schoolmaster had said, and, indeed, felt so much relieved that Hanz ordered a keg of fresh beer to be tapped. These noisy, splashing steamboats would frighten people, and by that means the good old-fashioned way of getting to market would not be interfered with. It was also a source of great relief to these honest people, that when those extravagant New Yorkers had spent all their money on such wild and dangerous experiments, they would be content to stay at home and mind their own business. Another source of great alarm to these honest people was that several New Yorkers had come to Nyack, and were building large houses, and otherwise setting examples of extravagance to their children, when it was reported that they did not pay their honest debts in town. The people of Hudson, too, were going wild over a project for establishing a South-sea Company, and sending ships to the far off Pacific ocean—where the people were, it had been said, in the habit of eating their friends—to catch whales. Now, as the people of Hudson had no more money than was needed at home, this dangerous way of spending all they had was not to be justified.

Satisfied that they had settled a question of grave importance, and in which the great interests of the country were involved, these honest Dutchmen smoked another pipe and drank another mug of beer, and then went quietly to their homes, feeling sure that the world and all Nyack would be a gainer by what they had done.

CHAPTER V.

TITE TOODLEBURG AND A MODERN REFORMER.

Young Tite Toodleburg has grown up to be a boy of sixteen. A bright, handsome fellow he is, every inch a sailor, and full of the spirit of adventure. There is something more than Dutch blood in Tite, and it begins to show itself. His figure is erect and slender, his hair soft and flaxen, and his blue eyes and fresh, smiling face, almost girlish in its expression, gave to his regular features a softness almost feminine. And yet there was something manly, resolute, and even daring in his actions. There was no such thing as fear in his nature. He had acquired such a knowledge of seamanship that he could handle the good sloop Heinrich quite as skilfully as the skipper, and, indeed, make the voyage to New York as promptly as the greatest navigator on the Tappan Zee. He was expert, too, at taking in and delivering out cargo, could keep the sloop's account, and drive as good a trade as any of them with the merchants in Fly Market. In this way Tite made a host of friends, who began to look forward to the time when he would have a sloop of his own, and be in a way to do friendly acts for them, perhaps to make a fortune for himself.

Tite thought very differently. Navigating the river in a sloop, to be passed by one of Mr. Fulton's steamboats, was not the sort of sea-faring that suited his ambition. He had seen big ships come home, after long voyages, and the majesty of their appearance excited his spirit of adventure. He had also spent his evenings reading the works of celebrated navigators and travellers; and these very naturally increased his curiosity to know more of the world and see the things they had seen. He had also looked out through the Narrows of New York harbor, and his young heart had yearned to be on the broad ocean beyond. If he could only master all the mysteries of Bowditch, be a skilful navigator, and capable of sailing a ship to any part of the world, and see strange things and people—that day might come, he thought to himself. He had listened, too, for hours at a time, to the stories of old sailors who had come on board the sloop while in port. One had been to India, and another to Ceylon; and both told wonderful stories concerning the voyages they had made and the people they had met. Another had seen every port in the North Pacific, had been wrecked on Queen Charlotte's Island, and told wonderful stories of his adventures in rounding Cape Horn. His adventures among the South Sea Islands were of the most romantic kind, and colored so as to incite the ambition of a venturesome young lad like Tite to the highest pitch. There was another old sailor who had sailed the South and North Pacific, had killed his score of whales, and been as many times within an inch of losing his own life.

These stories so fired the young gentleman's imagination that he resolved to try his fortune at a whaling voyage as soon as the people of Hudson sent their first ship out. There was the wide world before him, and perhaps he might find the means of making a fortune in some distant land. But how was he to break this resolution to his kind parents, whom he loved so dearly? What effect would it have on his mother, who doted on him, and for whom he had the truest affection? His mind hung between hope for the future and duty to his parents. Regularly every Saturday afternoon Tite had come home, received his mother's blessing, and put his earnings into her hands for safekeeping. There would be an end of this if he went to the South Sea. Then his parents were both getting old, and would soon need a protector, and if anything serious happened to them during his absence how could he ever forgive himself. Week after week and month after month did Tite ponder these questions in his mind, and still his resolution to see the world grew stronger and stronger.

It was about this time that there settled in Nyack a queer and very inquisitive sort of man of the name of Bigelow Chapman. He was a restless, discontented sort of man, very slender of figure, with sharp, well-defined features, keen gray eye, and wore his dark hair long and unkept. His manner was that of a man discontented with the world, which, he said, needed a great deal of reforming; indeed, that it could be reformed, ought to be reformed, and that he was the man to do it. He had been the founder of Dogtown, Massachusetts, where he had built up a very select community of keen-witted men and women—just to set an example to the world of how people ought to live. Dolly Chapman, his wife, (for what would a reformer be without a wife,) was a ponderous woman, weighing more than two hundred pounds, and a proof that even in matrimony the opposites meet. She was a fussy, ill-bred woman, spoke with a strong nasal twang, and a sincere believer in all the reforms advocated by her husband, though she differed with him on one or two points of religion. And there was Mattie Chapman, a bright, bouncing girl of fifteen, with rosy cheeks and fair hair, ambitious for one of her age, and evidently inclined to make a show in the world. These constituted the Chapman family.

Dogtown, of which I made mention, was a creation of Chapman's. With it he was to demonstrate how the world could be reformed, and how the prejudices were to be driven from other people's minds. Strong-minded people from various towns in Massachusetts came and settled in Dogtown, invested their money, were to do an equal share of work, and receive an equal share of profits, and live together as happily as lambs. But Dogtown did not long continue a paradise. Indeed, it soon became famous for two things: for the name of Bigelow Chapman, and for having more crazy and quarrelsome people in it than could be found in any other town in Massachusetts, which was saying a good deal. The brothers and sisters, for such they called themselves, got to quarrelling among themselves on matters of politics and religion, though charity was a thing they made no account of. In truth, there was more politics than religion in their preaching.

Chapman constituted himself treasurer of the community, and some little private speculations of his led to a belief among the brothers and sisters that his mind was not solely occupied with schemes for reforming the world. To tell the truth, Bigelow Chapman was not so great a fool as his followers. He had intended, when Dogtown got thoroughly under way, to sell out, put the money in his pocket, and employ his genius somewhere else. He, however, undertook the enterprise of building a church on speculation, being persuaded to do so by an outside Christian.

The church was to be a large, handsome building, with a butcher's shop and a grocery, a shoe store and a confectionery in the basement, and a school and a dancing academy up stairs; so that the brothers and sisters could get everything they wanted, religion included, in one locality. But the enterprise failed for want of funds to finish it, and Dogtown went to the dogs, and the Chapman family to Nyack. Report has it that the church was afterwards finished and converted into an insane asylum, where several of the brothers and sisters lived for the rest of their lives.

It was hinted that Chapman had brought some money to Nyack with him, but exactly how much no one knew. The only thing positively known about him at that time was that he had a great number of new ideas, all of which he was in great haste to develope. Indeed, he soon had Nyack in a state of continual agitation. He declared it his first duty to open the eyes of the Dutch settlers to truth and right; then to get them to thinking; and finally to make fortunes for all of them. He begun business, however, by quarrelling with nearly everybody in the village, and asserting that he knew more than all of them.

Twice he had Titus Bright, the inn-keeper, up before the magistrate and fined for selling liquor in opposition to law. He proclaimed it highly immoral to sell liquor at all, and told Bright to his teeth that no honest man would do it. For this he had been twice kicked out of the inn by Bright, who damned him as a meddling varlet, not to be tolerated in a peaceable village. Again he had Bright up before the magistrate, who justified the aggression, but fined the aggressor ten dollars a kick, which Bright considered cheap enough considering what was got for his money. Bright declared it a principle with him to give his customers what they wanted, and let them be the judge of their own necessities. Bigelow Chapman held that mankind was a big beast, to be subdued and governed by laws made for his subjection. It never occurred to him, however, that there might be reason in the opinions of others. Finding, however, that he could not get the better of Bright in any other way, he organized a company and set up an opposition tavern, where a traveller could feel at home and have none of the annoyances of beer. The new inn was to be conducted on strictly temperance principles, and the price of board was to be reduced a dollar a week. But the principle of temperance was carried out so rigidly in the fare that travellers, although treated politely enough, found it difficult to get anything to eat, to say nothing of drink.

While this was going on Mrs. Bigelow Chapman was busying herself getting up an anti-tea-and-coffee-drinking society. She declared that this coffee and tea-drinking was nothing less than an oppression, breaking down people's health and making them poor, while the grocers who sold the stuff were getting rich. It was evident, also, that she was carrying her principles out on the table of the new inn. However commendable these reforms might be in the eyes of a true reformer, they were not exactly the thing to satisfy the wants of hungry travellers. The new inn soon got up an excellent reputation for giving its customers nothing but politeness and clean linen. This not being satisfactory to the travelling public generally, the establishment had to close its doors for want of customers. Chapman was surprised at this. He could not understand why reformers were not better appreciated about Nyack. The stock-holders, however, had lost all their money, and were glad to sell out to Chapman, which they did for a trifle, and that was all he wanted.

People began to inquire what the big building would next be turned into. Mrs. Chapman and her dear husband, as she called him, were always projecting something new. Indeed, she saw two fortunes in the future where Chapman only saw one. The thought invaded her mind that there was a fortune to be made by turning the big house into a great moral progress boarding-school for young ladies, where "all the proprieties" would be strictly attended to. Yes, "the proprieties" would take with steady-minded people. She could attend to the proprieties, and dear Chapman could look after the little money affairs. She did not want to trouble herself with the sordid things of this world; she only wanted to reform it. And to do that you must begin at the bottom. You must teach young people, and especially young ladies, the value of reforms. In that way you enable them to reform their husbands when they get them, and also make them comprehend the value of new ideas. As for old people, she declared it time wasted to try to get new ideas into their heads.

Chapman congratulated his dear wife on this new and grand idea. He agreed with her that a woman was just the thing to straighten up a husband in need of mental and physical reformation. But it would not do to start the enterprise until you could get people to take stock enough to insure a sound basis. He did not care about money himself, still it was necessary to the success of all great enterprises. And seeing that the inn had failed, though based on great moral principles, he was not quite sure that the people would hasten to take stock in the new enterprise.

It was also an objection with Chapman that with such an institution there would be nothing to run opposition to except a few beer-drinking schoolmasters, who got their victuals and fifteen dollars a month for driving a knowledge of the rule of three into the heads of little Dutch children. How different it would be with a church. And then the big inn could be made such an excellent church, at such a small expense. A man owning a church could feel himself strong in both politics and religion, and have all the quarrels he wanted. Chapman was delighted with this new idea of his; and his good wife supposed it was infinitely superior to her own. It was another proof to her that there was no greater man in the world than her dear Chapman. Once get the church going, and with a preacher of the Dogtown school, to preach out and out transcendentalism, and another ism or two, and they could get up an opposition that would be popular with the people. In that way the thing would be sure to go.

Chapman declared this a golden opportunity. He had felt for some time like getting up something that would drive the devil and all the Dutchmen out of Nyack and into the Tappan Zee, and establish an entire new order of things.

It was agreed between Chapman and his good wife that the church should be put on its legs without delay; that the work of reforming Nyack and the rest of the world should begin at once. As funds were necessary to all great enterprises, and Chapman was inclined at all times to husband his own, the good woman got up a regular season of religious tea-parties, exclusively "for ladies." Mrs. Chapman was intent on popularizing the enterprise, and to that end had inserted on her cards of invitation, "exclusively for ladies." There was nothing like tea when you wanted to make a great reform movement popular. Chapman had more than once said that woman, under the inspiration of tea, made a mighty engine in moving the world. Under its influence they gave enlargement and development to progressive ideas. It had been charged that great generals won their most celebrated battles under the influence of strong drink. He had known great generals to win great battles under the inspiration of tea alone. Tea and women were prodigious in their way.

The tea parties were not only got on their legs, but soon became very popular. There were women enough in Nyack to give them, and neither rain nor hail would keep them home of a Thursday evening. The great value of progressive ideas was thoroughly discussed over these cups; and the fact that their husbands were to be brought into a line of subjugation not before anticipated had an inspiring effect. In short, female Nyack began to carry a high head, and to make male Nyack feel that he was no longer master in its own house. Dolly Chapman presided at these tea-parties with that smartness peculiar to women of her class, taking particular pains to explain how much could be done for Nyack and the world—if only the women could get the direction of things into their own hands. A church as the means of carrying out these new and grand ideas was exactly what was wanted. The tea-party women all took up the idea, and the enterprise was made so popular that each resolved herself into a begging committee, and soon had collected the sum of seven hundred dollars, an amount sufficient to put the thing on its legs.

CHAPTER VI.

A LITTLE FAMILY AFFAIR.

While the heads of the Chapman family were engaged in their great work of reform, and Hanz Toodleburg, as the head of the Dutch settlers, was preparing to resist all their efforts, Mattie Chapman and young Tite were engaging in a matter of a very different nature. A little flame of love had begun to burn in their youthful hearts, and was giving out such manifestations of tenderness. I have noticed that when once the little undercurrent of love begins to ebb and flow in young and innocent hearts, it will break over whatever obstacles you put in its way, and rarely stops until it has reached that haven of happiness called matrimony. The parents of these young people seemed to have been cast in opposite moulds, mentally and physically. Their modes of thought, their expectations, and their manner of living differed entirely. Hanz Toodleburg was simple-minded, honest, contented with his lot in the world, smoked his pipe, and lived in peace with his neighbors. And these he esteemed the greatest blessings a man could enjoy. Chapman was restless, designing, ambitious of wealth, and ready always to quarrel with those who did not fall in with his opinions. Indeed, he never seemed happier than when he had a quarrel on hand; and he had the rare tact of turning a quarrel into profit.

It was very different with the young people. In their innocent hearts the fires of love had been kindled, and they were burning brighter and brighter every day. The thought that they should incur opposition from their parents never entered their minds. They would meet together of a Sunday afternoon, and walk by the river side. They would meet and talk over the gate as Tite passed and re-passed Chapman's house. And Mattie was sure to meet him at the gate as he passed on his way to New York. And then there would be an affectionate good-bye, and Mattie would watch him until he had disappeared beyond the hill. The ordinary observer would have seen in Tite's blushes and confused manner, whenever he met Mattie, how the current of his love was setting. And when he returned at the end of the week there was something for Mattie, some little token of his affection; a proof that he had cherished her in his thoughts while absent.

This little love affair did not fail to attract the attention of the Chapman family. Nor was honest Hanz Toodleburg indifferent to what was going on. Indeed, the gossips at the inn had joked Hanz about it, hinting at a future connection of the two families. To all of which Hanz would reply that Tite was only a boy yet, and had a good deal of other kinds of business to do before thinking of what sort of a wife he wanted. "If ta torter ish like ta fader, sho quarrelsome, t'man what gets her for a vife don't lives in t'house mit her," Hanz would always conclude.

Young as Tite was, he began to look on the matter seriously. The whaling voyage was still exciting his ambition, however, and he began to enquire of every one he thought likely to know, when the people of Hudson would send their first ship to the South Sea. Then the thought of leaving Mattie would depress his spirits, and for a time shake his resolution. The trouble with him at first was how he could separate from his parents; now his love for Mattie was added to his obstacles.

Chapman had not failed to notice this little affair of the affections between the young people. He had noticed, also, that it had attracted the attention of his wife. But neither had spoken of it. In short, Chapman was anxious to have his wife refer to it first, to see in what light she viewed it. And Mrs. Chapman was equally anxious to have her dear husband, as she called him, express an opinion on the subject before she gave one. He had once or twice noticed that when the young people were at the gate she would call Mattie and tell her it was time to come in; that she ought not to stay there so long talking to a sailor-boy. Mattie would yield obedience with blushes and an air of reluctance, the meaning of which her mother properly understood.

The truth of the matter was that the affair had engaged Chapman's thoughts for some time; and it suddenly occurred to him that the whole thing might be turned to profit. Toodleburg was a man of some consequence among the people; they had great confidence in his integrity, and implicitly believed him possessed of a secret that would make the fortune of every man in Nyack. He had been evolving that secret in his mind for some time, and if he could in any way get the confidence of Hanz, and obtain the secret, or allow himself to be used in connection with it, he could make money enough to live like a lord in New York. And that was exactly what Mrs. Chapman wanted. The good woman, however, had been so much engaged of late getting the new church on its legs, and negotiating for the services of the Reverend Warren Holbrook, of Dogtown, Massachusetts, who was to spread the doctrines of transcendentalism, and a variety of other isms, before the people, and turn Nyack out of doors, religiously speaking, that she felt that she had not performed her whole duty towards Mattie.

There had been a religious tea-party at Chapman's house, where the affair of the new church had been talked over, and the opening day arranged. Mrs. Chapman was in her best dress, with a profusion of ribbons streaming down her back, and a puffy cap on her head. She had received a letter from the Reverend Warren Holbrook, accepting the offer of three hundred dollars a year and board and washing, and saying, that in addition to transcendentalism, he would advocate the equality of the great human family.

If these poor, benighted Dutch people who lived about Nyack would only be regenerated and made progressive. Mrs. Chapman found great consolation in this letter, and sat down to read it to her dear husband, who had moved up nearer to the lamp and opened the last great-work on the new doctrine.

When she had finished reading it she paused for a moment, and then spoke. "Have you noticed, my dear," she enquired, and again hesitating, "what has been going on between our Mattie—?" Again she hesitated.

Expecting what was coming, Chapman interposed by saying, "Don't be afraid to speak, my darling; I know what you mean."

"I meant," resumed Mrs. Chapman, blushing and looking very serious, "I meant, have you noticed the attention that sailor-boy—(young Toodlebug did you call him?) horrors! what a name—was paying to our Mattie?"

"Burg, my dear, not bug," rejoined Chapman.

"People are beginning to talk about it, and they say such things!" The good woman blushed, and assumed an air of great seriousness. "The young man may be well enough, but then the Toodlebugs are only a common Dutch family."

"Toodleburgs, my dear, not bugs. The name makes a great difference with some people," rejoined Chapman, correctively. "Very natural, my dear, very natural. The most natural thing in the world for young people to make love. And the most natural thing in the world is that people should talk about it. It is according to the principles of true philosophy. You must not be alarmed, my dear, when you see young people make love. Harm rarely comes of it, and it generally ends in a very small affair."

"Yes, my dear," replied the good woman, "and experience has proved to me that it sometimes ends in a very large affair. A little flirtation between young people—"

"Should be encouraged, my darling," interrupted Chapman.

"I was going to say," she continued, "was not objectionable. But when looks come to be serious, the equality of things should be enquired into. Time's a coming when we may be rich, and live in New York, and be somebody, and move with the best of people. I looks forward to it, my dear; and I am sure the enterprises we have on hand will be a success. It will never do to marry our daughter to a sailor-boy, to say nothing of connecting ourselves to a common Dutch family—"

"You talk like a philosopher, my darling; but I have known worse things done, and great results flow from them. That young man promises well, and as for old Hanz, he is a man of more importance than you think. Some of these Dutch people are slow, but solid," rejoined Chapman, shutting up the book. "I have an object in view, and this little, innocent flirtation may help to improve it. At least, it can do no harm."

"It is not good to let anything go on that might lead to harm," resumed the good woman. "Mattie has good looks, and I intend that she shall have a polished education, and shine in society some day. You have always agreed with me, my dear, that it was good to look forward. How could Mattie shine in society with such a husband, and such a name? The very name of Toodlebug would sink us. Yes, my dear, sink us right down—"

"Wrong again, my dear; Tutle-burg. You may put an *e* in it instead of an *r*, if you please. That's where the difference is," interrupted Chapman.

"I don't care, my dear; these polite people would turn up their noses, and get it Too-dle-bug. They are very nice on names. If the young man should get up in the world and keep a carriage, people would say 'there goes Too-dle-bug's carriage—oh! what a name. What low people they must have been.' If they should own a house in the fashionable part of the city. We should both look forward to that, you know. Would'nt it be a horrid name to read on the door? Toodlebug!"

"Tutle-burg, my dear; there's a big difference," interposed Mr. Chapman.

"As you says; but nice people would not pronounce it except with a bug," continued the good woman, looking discomfitted. "You have given so much time to progress and reforming the world, that you don't understand these matters as well as I do. I am sure there would be blushes and smiles enough over such a name. Think of our daughter being Mrs. Toodlebug, (I pronounce it with a b-u-g, you see,) and inviting nice people to her reception. There would be people enough at that reception to make light of the name. Yes, Mr. Chapman, you might as well have her married to a Mr. Straddlebug. It's so very vulgar, my dear."

"As to that," replied Chapman, "the world is a great vulgarity, and only puts on politeness for appearance sake. The young man might have his name changed, or he might add something to it to soften it. How would you like Von Toodleburg, my dear?"

"Never can be softened; never! The Von would do something to lift a family up into respectability. And then, socially speaking, there was such a wide difference between them distinguished Dutch families and them common Dutch families."

"What would you have me do about it, darling?" enquired Chapman, submissively.

"Oppose it, my dear!" replied Mrs. Chapman, bowing, and becoming earnest. "Oppose it. You know how to oppose everything, and surely you can oppose this."

This reply troubled Chapman considerably. He had for once found something he would rather encourage than oppose. But he had a motive for his action, as will be seen hereafter.

CHAPTER VII.

THE TOWN MOVED WITH INDIGNATION.

It was less than a week after the scenes we have described in the foregoing chapter took place, that the good sloop Heinrich arrived, having made her weekly voyage to New York and back. A small, ill-favored man, with a very long red beard, and very long red hair, might have been seen stepping ashore, with a book and an umbrella under his arm, and wending his way up the lane, followed by Tite, carrying a corpulent carpet-bag. There was a combative air about the little man, who stared with a pair of small, fierce eyes, through a pair of glaring spectacles at every one he met. He was dressed in a shabby black suit, that hung loosely on his lean figure. This, with a broad, rolling collar, a pair of russet brogans, and a common straw hat, turned up at one side, completed his wardrobe, and gave an odd appearance to the man. Indeed, the gentleman had no taste for the vanities of the world, and parted his hair in the middle to save trouble. The ordinary observer might easily have mistaken him for a school-master out of employment and in distress. That such a man was to upset the settled opinions of a big town, few persons would have believed. Such, however, was this odd-looking little man's mission, and there was no end of new ideas contained in that little bumpy forehead of his.

The new arrival was the much-expected Reverend Warren Holbrook, from Dogtown last. As I have said before, he looked askance and inquisitively at every one he met as he walked up the lane. He bowed, too, and had a smile for all the females; then he enquired the name and condition of those who lived in each house he came to—how many children they had, and whether they were boys or girls. Now he paused and rested on his umbrella when he had reached a bit of high ground, and gazed over Nyack generally, and then over the Tappan Zee. Here was the new field of the great labors before him. How often he had taken Dogtown by the neck and shaken her up severely. The day might come when he would have to take Nyack by the neck and give her a good shaking up, morally and religiously. Mrs. Chapman had written him to say that Nyack was a bad place, secularly and otherwise.

The whole Chapman family (including the big dog) was out at the door to welcome the stranger; and such a warm greeting as he got. Mrs. Chapman assured him that the best in the house had been prepared for him, and that she had got the town in a state of great anxiety to see him. To tell the truth, this busy, bustling woman had been blowing a noisy trumpet for him in advance, and enlisting a large amount of female sympathy by stating that he was preeminent as an advocate of woman's rights in all things.

Of course the Reverend Warren Holbrook's arrival soon got noised over Nyack, and the female mind was in a state of great agitation. Before bed-time a number of curious and somewhat aged women dropped in to pay their respects to the gentleman, and see for themselves what this man of great natural gifts, who was to reform all Nyack and the world generally, was like.

There was one member of the Chapman family, however, not pleased with the way things were going, and that was Mattie. When the older Chapmans had taken their guest into the house, she embraced the opportunity to have a talk with Tite, and reproached him for what she had seen him do.

"Now, Tite," said she, looking earnestly into his face, "if you have any respect for me, never walk behind a man, carrying his carpet-bag—never! And such a looking man as that! You are as good as he, or anybody else, and if you don't think yourself so, other people wont think so for you. Never think you are not as good as somebody. Don't act as a help for anybody, for if you do you will be set down for nobody all your life."

At first Tite hardly knew what to say in reply. The nature of the rebuke showed the deep interest Mattie felt in him. "If I had taken pay," said Tite, hesitating, "'twould have been different. I carried his carpet-bag, I know, but then I did it as a favor; and, as you saw, declined to take the sixpence he offered me. But I'll do as you say, Mattie, and won't do so again; for I want to please you, you know." The words fell nervously from Tite's lips, and there was a throbbing at the heart he could not suppress.

"My mother," resumed Mattie, in a frank, girlish manner, "brought this man Warren Holbrook into the house at Dogtown, and he got father into such a deal of trouble. He was always quarrelling with somebody. He got up a disturbance in the church. And then the church all went to pieces. Oh, what a church it was! And mother thinks he's such a nice man. I don't. Don't carry his carpet-bag again, Tite. Don't make a menial of yourself for anybody." After saying this she walked part of the way home with Tite, and then they parted with a sweet good-night.

The following day being Sunday, and the Reverend Warren Holbrook having brought several prepared sermons with him, service was held in the new church at the regular morning hour. The women gathered in great numbers, and nearly filled the church; and the odd appearance of the little man, as he took his place in the pulpit, was a subject of general remark.

His sermon, I may here state, was one of the most singular and pyrotechnical ever preached in Nyack. He began by saying that Christ had risen, and was with them in person. He had come to Nyack, he added, to tell the truth and preach to sinners, for he understood the devil had had things his own way for a long time in the town; and he understood also there were sinners enough in Nyack to sink it. The world had reached a stage of wickedness when it needed reforming. It must be reformed, or it would sink under the weight of its wickedness. People were getting rich, and with great riches there always came pride and wickedness. He continued in this strain for nearly an hour, mixing up transcendentalism, rationalism, unitarianism, and a number of other isms, so unartistically as to astonish and confound his audience, and give his hearers something to talk about for a week.

Then he suddenly broke away from his disputed points, as he called them, and took up the subject of woman's wrongs. "My hearers," said he, pausing and pointing upward with the fore-finger of his right hand, "What would the world be without woman? From the very beginning of the world she has been the victim of wrong, great wrong. Man has sinned against her by making her his inferior. God never intended that she should be the inferior of man. He never would have created her with a form so beautiful, and a voice so soft and musical, if he had not intended her for man's superior. And the day will come, and come soon, too, when she will have her rights, and her voice will be heard in the government of the nation. The angel that she is! Woman is a great power. She has made kings and conquerors, and she can unmake them. She has influenced the acts of statesmen, and made children of grave Senators. Yes, my hearers, her power can be made greater than the throne. And yet how few husbands appreciate their wives as they should do." Here the reverend gentleman paused for a few seconds, and cast meaning glances at several of his male hearers, who were evidently not inclined to receive his remarks with favor. Indeed, Mr. Holbrook, while making a high bid for popularity with the female portion of his audience, was throwing an immense fire-brand into the family circle of a number of his hearers.

"My hearers, remember this," resumed this odd little man: "Manage a woman right, and you have a mighty power to carry out the greatest project the world ever saw."

Disjointed and illogical as this sermon was, it was just what Chapman and Mrs. Chapman wanted to put the church of the new ideas firm on its legs. It was popular with the women; and with their favor Holbrook could ride triumphantly over any number of quarrels.

Mrs. Chapman intimated to another admiring female that the little man they had just listened to was very like an oyster—looked better when opened. In short, it was the general opinion of the women that Mr. Holbrook had preached a very sensible sermon; and they were delighted, notwithstanding what their husbands said to the contrary. "We have got a preacher now," said the women, "who will stick up for our rights. You men have had it all your own way long enough." Some of the men, however, were not inclined to let these taunts pass quietly, declaring that they had never listened to such nonsense before. One shook his head, and declared that no good could come of such preaching, since there was no true religion in it. Another snapped his fingers, saying the man was not only a fool, but a mischief-maker. A third said all the trouble in the world had been made by just such meddlesome men. The church of great moral ideas might be a good enough church for some people; but such a preacher as this made more infidels than honest men.

The whole town soon got into a dispute as to whether the Reverend Warren Holbrook was a wise and good man, or simply a mischief-making egotist. The women took the side of Holbrook, and stuck to it, like true women. He preached the right sort of religion, they said, and was a wise and good man, or he could not preach as he did. The men did not believe a word of it, but seeing that their wives were inclined to have it all their own way, and would not hear a word against the new preacher, quietly submitted, as men generally do. That is to say, they surrendered their authority.

Chapman was delighted at the nice little turn his preacher had made in the affairs of the town. Nothing pleased him better than to have a dozen disputes on hand at a time. If only well nursed they could be all made profitable. Woman was the great pillar of Chapman's hopes. He had always regarded her as the great foundation of any church. She could make it popular if she pleased, and she could make it profitable, too. This, in a measure, accounted for the unlimited admiration Mrs. Chapman had for this great progressive clergyman. His great progressive religion was just exactly the thing needed in Nyack. He must next attack the Dominie, and drive him out of his pulpit, for it would not do to have men preaching in an unknown tongue at this enlightened day.

In less than two months from the time this teacher of great progressive ideas landed at Nyack, he had not only got the town by the ears, but so divided his flock that it was now composed almost exclusively of women. The men stayed at home and nursed their wrath. And it was good for them that they did, for the women had things all their own way generally, and Warren Holbrook, ill-favored and formed, was their idol. The pew rents ran up, however, and the contributions of a Sunday increased nearly double. Indeed, the Chapmans felt that they were now on the road to fortune, and Mrs. Chapman's ambition increased accordingly.

All great enterprises, however, are liable to sudden checks, and misfortune too often comes when one least expects it. And so it was with the Reverend Warren Holbrook, the man of the great progressive ideas. He was discovered paying what ladies of strict propriety regard as more than ordinary attentions to a fair young damsel, the daughter of one of the most active members of the church—a woman who had carried her head high, and was so much given to wearing more finery than her neighbors that the few friends she had were always ready to say ill-natured things of her. The young woman was ready enough to embrace matrimony at any moment; but the attentions she received from the reverend gentleman caused great distress among a number of other young women of his church. It was agreed among them that the reverend gentleman was neither fascinating nor handsome, but he had mind, and was smart. Smart was the thing a man most needed in a New England village.

I have said before that the mother of this damsel carried a high head, as well in as out of the church. She seemed also to have more rights than ordinary females, and would give herself a great deal of unnecessary trouble in asserting them, so much so that many of her less strong-handed sisters regarded her with fear. The gentleman's attentions had not progressed far when it was evident to all attentive observers that there must soon be a split in the female division of his church. Indeed, the quarrel in the female division of the church of the great progressive ideas was waged with great fierceness, and had such a number of nice little scandals mixed up in it as to make it quite interesting to people of a contemplative turn of mind.

Every meddlesome old woman in the church must put her finger in the reverend gentleman's love pie, and would speak her mind plainly enough, especially if she had daughters of her own. To use the poor man's own language, he found himself spiked on all sides; and all for love, a thing which has brought no end of mischief on the world. In short, from being an idol he found himself between fires that threatened to consume him, so fiercely did they burn.

The gentleman's position was indeed becoming perilous, when an unforeseen circumstance afforded him the means of relief. There arrived in Nyack late one Saturday night, a man of tall, slender figure, dressed in a suit of plain black, and having the appearance of a young clergyman just from the country. He put up at Titus Bright's inn, gave out that he was from Dogtown, Massachusetts, and after partaking of supper, enquired of the landlord where he could find the Reverend, so to speak, Warren Holbrook. There was something serious in the man's manner, like one who had been grievously wronged. Being told where he could find the object of his search, he paced the room thoughtfully for a few minutes, then muttered to himself, "I must see him to-night. The sooner settled the better. It will not do to wait until morning."

Half an hour later, and the two reverend gentlemen (the stranger and Holbrook) might have been seen seated at a table in a room of Chapman's house. Their conversation had evidently not been of a very pleasant nature, for the stranger, rising to take his departure, said: "You have only to do her justice, and show to the world that you are an honorable man. She is my sister; and unless you keep your promise, solemnly made to her, I will follow you to the end of the earth, and make you the scorned of men. Mark this well: it is the haunted soul of the hypocrite that burns him through life; that makes him a very torment to himself." The stranger returned to the inn, where he paced the room for nearly an hour, and then retired for the night.

The bells rang on the following morning, and the good women of Nyack wended their way to and had nearly filled every pew in the church of great progressive ideas. The choir sung one hymn, and then sung another. But no pastor came. There was something wrong, evidently. Hope and faith were enjoined by a few. Some watched the door, others the pulpit. Whispers succeeded wonder, and murmurs took the place of curiosity. The church was clearly without a pastor; and what was a church to do under such circumstances? At length the whole congregation got into a state of profound agitation. What was the matter? where was the pastor? would'nt somebody speak? These and similar questions were on every tongue. It was suddenly discovered that the Chapmans were also absent.

An indignant female got up and proposed that some one "go for" the Chapmans, and make them explain what it all meant. Another, equally indignant, took a more sensible view of things. "If there's to be no service," said she, "I'm going home to read my Bible in quiet." And she left the church, followed by the rest of the congregation. And as nobody explained, of course every one had his or her own reason for this singular turn in the spiritual affairs of the new church. There was no getting over the fact that the new church had been brought to a stand still. To be plain about the matter, the Reverend Warren Holbrook had put his great progressive ideas into practice during the night by leaving the town, and also by taking with him the young woman to whom he had been paying such marked attentions. The Tappan Zee had never been more troubled in a storm than was the moral sensibilities of Nyack at this news. The very atmosphere was rank with scandal. The men laughed and jeered, and the women shook their heads and talked of nothing else. "After that," said the women, "who can we trust."

"Served you right," replied the men, "for making much of such a fellow. Women never take such men into their confidence without bringing dirty water to their own doors." It was fortunate for Holbrook that he left during the night, for, seeing the temper Nyack was in during that day, there would have been some stones thrown had he remained.

The Chapmans took the matter very cool, however, counted the profits, and put up the church shutters. Such things had happened before, Chapman said. It was a weakness that had marked the history of the world; and it had been a failing with the greatest of intellects. They would yet show to the people of

Nyack what could be done with the right sort of enterprise. The honest old Dutchmen were in high glee over the turn affairs at the new church had taken. They got together in Hanz Toodleburg's veranda, drank their beer, and smoked their pipes, and wished the devil might get the new preacher, "what comes t'down to raise t'tevil mit de peoples, and raises t'tevil mit he self."

The stranger, of whom mention has been made, was more seriously troubled. He heard the news of Holbrook's departure with a sad heart, for he was the kind brother of a young woman to whom the delinquent had made a solemn vow to marry. But that solemn vow he had recently broken in the most heartless manner, and left her hopes blighted and her heart sad. He declared, however, that he would follow Holbrook if he went to the end of the earth, and bring him to justice before God and man.

CHAPTER IX.

TITE TAKES HIS DEPARTURE FOR THE SOUTH SEA.

High above all this hypocrisy, this intrigue, this selfishness and dissimulation, there was something more pure and good. It was love, pure and simple, binding the thoughts and hearts of Mattie Chapman and young Tite. That love which forgets everything else in its truth and purity, had been gently binding their young affections together. And now nothing could separate them.

What sweet joys and touching sorrows are mingled with the wonderful history of love. How surely it marks its objects. It seeks its most precious captive in the strongest and bravest of hearts. Love has dethroned kings, built up empires, set great nations at war, and made statesmen weep with sorrow. Yea, it has made the mightiest to unbend, and brought them bowing before its altar. It holds its capricious empire in every heart, prompts our ambition, guides and governs our actions, makes us heroes or cowards, and carries us hoping through the world.

It was love, then, that was holding its court on the occasion I am about to describe. It was one of those bright and breezy spring mornings, when Nature seems to have decked herself in her brightest colors, giving such a charm to the banks of the Hudson. The young, fresh leaves were out, and looking so green and crisp. The leak and the moss were creeping afresh over the rocks; wild flowers were budding and blossoming, and giving their sweet odors to the wind; birds were singing their touching songs; brooks rippled and murmured their mysterious music; and all Nature was indeed putting forth her beauties in one grand, sweet, soul-stirring harmony.

How I envy the being who, free from the cares of the world, can elevate his soul by holding sweet communion with nature, at spring time. Earth has nothing so pure as the thoughts inspired by such sweet communion with the buds, the blossoms, and the flowers of spring.

It was one of these soft, breezy mornings in early spring, I have said, that Mattie and Tite sat together in a little clump of woods, where the branches formed a sort of bower overhead, and overlooking the Tappan Zee. Every few minutes Tite would get up, advance to a point commanding a view of the river above, and gaze intently in that direction, as if expecting some object of interest.

"She is not in sight yet, Mattie," he said, as he returned after one of these intervals. "But she will be down to-day, I know she will, and then we must part. Think of me when I am away, and I will think of you. Yes, Mattie, I am only a sailor now, but I shall see the world, and that's what I want, because it will make me something better. It will be three years before we meet again; three long, long years. But I will think of you and dream of you through all that time. And I will be so happy when the day of our meeting comes. Be good to my mother and father while I am gone. Be good to them for my sake. You will, won't you, Mattie?"

Mattie's blue eyes filled with tears, the wind tossed her golden curls over her fair neck and shoulders, and there was something so tender and touching in the picture of these young lovers. "I have made you a solemn promise, Tite," she replied, in broken accents. "That promise shall be kept sacred. I shall think of you, and pray for you. Your parents shall be my parents. I will count the days until you return." She paused for a moment and wiped her eyes. "Neither storm nor tempest shall trouble you, Tite, for I will follow you with my prayers that God may carry you safe through all dangers, and bring you safe back to us. But, Tite, take this advice from me. Do all you can for yourself. Rise as high as you can; make all the money you can; and don't forget what we may come to be. People who get money, and take care of it, are sure to rise in the world. People that don't get money never do. But, God bless you, Tite; think of me and I'll think of you." This advice to the young sailor to make all the money he could, and given on the eve of departure, may seem out of place to some of my romantic readers; but it was, perhaps, the best Mattie could have given him. She was a girl of strong affections, and it was only natural that she should have something of the propensity so strong in both her parents. But beyond and above this there was something frank and generous, something of real good in her nature. Young as she was, she saw in Tite's courage and ambition traits of character that promised well for the future. This made her forget that which was so objectionable to her mother—that he was only the son of common Dutch people.

Tite had been looking for the object of his anxiety several minutes, when, turning toward Mattie, he exclaimed: "Here she comes! here she comes!" and they kissed and took an affectionate farewell, each hastening to their homes. The object he had watched for so intently was the ship Pacific, belonging to the Hudson Company's fleet of whale ships, and bound on a voyage to the South Sea, as it was called in those days. There was something grand and imposing about this fine old ship as she moved majestically down the stream, her starboard tacks aboard, the breeze filling her sails so nicely, for she had her royals set. Then her new, white canvas contrasted so strikingly with the green hills that yet shut her hull from view. Who could tell what might befall her in the eventful voyage she was bound on?

A few minutes more and she braced her yards sharp and rounded the point, and stood on her way down the Tappan Zee. Every outline of her hull now came clearer and clearer. There were her heavy quarter-davits, her hoisting gear, and whale-killing gear; her long, sharp boats, lashed so carefully, some to her davits, others athwart her quarter-deck frames; and about all of which there was a mysterious interest. These whale ships were at that day an object of distrust in the minds of the honest Dutchmen along the banks of the Hudson, who never saw them go to sea without shaking their heads and predicting all sorts of disasters, such as would be sure to bring ruin on the men unwise enough to risk their money in such enterprises.

As the ship neared Nyack a group of ten or a dozen persons were seen near the landing, with a boat and two men to take Tite off. There was Hanz, old and grey; and Angeline, her eyes filled with tears, but her face as full of sweetness and tenderness as it was twenty years ago. Tite had been the joy and hope of her life. And now he was going to leave home and sail to the other side of the world, among strange people, and would have to brave dangers of the worst kind.

Who could tell what might befall her in the eventful voyage she was bound on?

There, too, was Doctor Critchel, and the good Dominie, and Titus Bright, the inn-keeper; the first wearing his old brown coat, and looking as snuffy as on the stormy night when he assisted in bringing Tite into the world. They had all come to see Tite off, to say God speed, and to give him some little token of their affection to carry with him on his voyage after whales.

And now that time which so tries a mother's heart had come. "Good bye, mother, good bye, and may God be with you and protect you," said Tite, throwing his arms around his mother's neck, and kissing her wet cheek. "I will come back safe, and never go to sea again." Then he took leave of his father, and each of his friends in turn. In another minute the boat in which he stood waving his handkerchief was pulling swiftly toward the ship. There was not a dry eye in that little group as each figure in it stood gazing out upon the calm waters, and watching the object so dear to the hearts of all in it. And now the boat has reached the ship, men are seen in the gangway, a line was thrown to the men in the boat, the ship luffed a little, and in another moment Tite mounted the ladder and was on deck. The first officer welcomed him, for there was something in his appearance that indicated respectability and true character; and his ship-mates gathered about him, each giving him a warm shake of the hand and a friendly word. Then the good ship moved gallantly down the stream, and Tite appeared on the forecastle, and waved adieus until she disappeared among the green hills of the Palisades.

There was a heart that fluttered, and a hand that waved signals, from a point on the shore recognized by Tite, and responded to, but not seen by the little sorrowing group waiting the return of the boat. It was Mattie's heart that fluttered, and it was her hand that waved the last adieu as the ship passed out of sight. There she stood, a touching picture of truth and love, shedding her tears and waving a last farewell to the object of her heart, and whom she might never see again.

Such are the transmutations of commerce that it would be a curious sight at this day to see a whaleship, under full sail, proceeding up or down the Hudson river. It was no uncommon sight then. The enterprising people of Hudson shared the whale-fishery business with New Bedford and Nantucket; their fleet of ships were fitted out in the very best manner, and some of the most famous whaling captains sailed from that port.

CHAPTER X.

MR. AND MRS. CHAPMAN DISAGREE FOR THE FIRST TIME.

A bright light burned in Chapman's parlor that night, and the ponderous Mrs. Chapman sat nursing her dignity in a great new rocking-chair. Her little pale-faced husband, with keen eyes, and his hair somewhat longer than usual, sat beside the lamp on the round table pouring over a book. There was an air of improvement about the parlor, an evidence, indeed, that the Chapmans had renounced their Dogtown habits, and were bent on getting up in the world. New carpets, new mirrors, new furniture, and window-curtains such as had not been seen in Nyack before, had been got from New York. You must make your style of living, Mrs. Chapman said, keep pace with the progress of the family. And it would not do to let those new, rich, and stylish people who were coming up from New York get ahead of you in the way of elegance.

Mrs. Chapman no longer condescended to prepare the sausage meat and pumpkin pies; in a word, to do the work of her own kitchen. She could afford, she said, to keep two "helps," a cook and a chambermaid, to take it easy and put on the lady, and to give evening parties that quite outdid in the way of nice little suppers anything their neighbors could give. There was, however, a number of people in Nyack who shook their heads at the pretensions of the Chapmans; said they were putting on too many airs, and made no response to Mrs. Chapman's invitations. Others, when a little scandal was necessary to keep up the interest of an evening, would insinuate that they had "originally" been very common and vulgar people. But now, like most New England people of that class, they were not only trying to force their opinions down other and honester people's throats, but had a way of meddling with business that did'nt concern them, and making themselves disagreeable generally. When Holbrook disappeared in disgrace, there were persons malicious enough to say that the Chapmans had better mend their own morals before they went to patching other people's up.

Mrs. Chapman could dress of an evening in silk, wear kid gloves that came from France, and had plenty of real French lace on her caps. Few persons in Nyack at that day could do such things and pass for honest people.

"My dear," said Mrs. Chapman, addressing herself to her small, but intellectually great, Mr. Chapman; "my dear." She paused for a moment, as her face assumed an air of seriousness. "We must turn our backs entirely on Dogtown. Dogtown won't do to elevate the family on. We never can rise in the world with Dogtown on our shoulders. And if we would live down that scandal brought on us by Holbrook, (an indiscretion, I think you called it,) we must keep our heads up." She paused, shook her head in pity, and raised her fat, waxy hands. "I can't sleep of nights, thinking of it. Lays a body's feelings out terribly. But he was so wonderfully clever." Her face brightened up as she said this. "Wonderfully clever," she interpolated. "It was his mental greatness I always subsided to and admired. Clever people have their weaknesses as well as people what are not as clever. I sometimes thought you had yours, my dear—"

"My dear!" interrupted Chapman, with an air of surprise, "what do you mean? Hav'nt I been a finished husband, and a loving father?"

"You are just as good, my dear, as husbands can be made." Mrs. Chapman said this condescendingly, and with an air of admiration truly grand. "But then, you know," she said, more mildly, "there was that handsome widow you used to be so polite to, my dear. You know I detected her waving a handkerchief once. Then you said it was one you left at the house; and so I never thought of it again."

"I never let the past trouble me, my dear, never. A man of forethought, of progressive ideas, looks always ahead, and by his acts proves that he is up square with the spirit of the age. I have a new conception. Yes, my dear, a new conception. Nothing figurative about it, my dear. I have a new and grand conception, which I have been evolving in my mind for some time, and now I am getting it into a scheme which I am sure will be profitable."

"My dear husband," said Mrs. Chapman, in a strain of intense excitement, "do let us know what it is."

"Of great importance to us both," he replied, with great seriousness, as he brushed his long black hair back over his parchment-like forehead.

"I'll be bound it refers to what took place to-day between our Mattie and that young sailor. I saw it all; and you saw it all, too, my dear, and you never said a word. We never can agree on that matter, my dear, never. On everything else we can. You can't mistake what two young people mean when they go to waving handkerchiefs, and picking wild flowers in the woods. This little love matter must be stopped before it gets into a big one. Yes, it must, my dear. So fine a young woman as our daughter condescending to marry a sailor! As I said before, my dear, you know I have had experience in these matters—"

"In other matters, you know, Mrs. Chapman, I have always yielded to you—"

"And I have always yielded to you," resumed the anxious woman, "and never considered it a condescension. But in this I must have my own way." And Mrs. Chapman got up and walked to a window overlooking the Tappan Zee. The night was bright and starlight, and shadows were flitting and dancing over the smooth waters. The picture of the ship, with Tite waving Mattie an adieu from the forecastle, haunted her mind.

"If that ship goes to the bottom of the sea, not a tear shall I shed—not a tear!" resumed the speaker, in an agitated tone. "And I have as tender a heart as anybody. But we must elevate the family. That's laudable, you know. Nice people are very particular about these things. And you know how much there is in names. Think of elevating the family by taking a man by the name of Toodlebug into it! Think of our going to live in New York with such a name. Everybody would say Toodlebug! Toodlebug! and nobody would come to our daughter's parties." The good woman ran on in this way for several minutes, compelling her dear Chapman to keep the peace. At length she settled back into her rocking chair, and there was a pause.

"My dear," said Chapman, meekly, "I have always held that a man could commit no greater folly than that of quarrelling with a woman on a question of family pride. In such a contest the man is sure to get the worst of it. I say this understandingly, my dear." And Chapman shut up his book, and looked up into his wife's face, as if to watch the changes of her countenance.

"We may agree on that matter yet, my dear. A man is never so low by birth (I mean in this country, at least,) but that he may rise to the highest office of honor and trust—"

"Not with such a name as Toodlebug—never!" Mrs. Chapman interrupted, curtly.

"That's a mistake, my dear. Names never distinguished people. A man's merit and money are the things that do it. This is a free country. A woman may have as many quarrels as she pleases, and have her own way in things generally. Nothing personal, my dear.

"But to go back to what I was pondering over when you interrupted me. A family never gets through the world easy without a solid basis; and I was thinking how to give a solid basis to our little family. Marrying is all well enough in its way; but the woman who marries a man without a solid basis, either in money or character, marries into misery. That's my philosophy—"

"Exactly!" interrupted Mrs. Chapman, with a stately nod of the head, and rubbing her fat hands. "Now you talk as I like to hear you. There's no getting up in the world without money."

"I intended to make that point in my logic, and was coming to it, my dear. You see, we have got the building and everything in it, all our own. And we have got two or three thousand dollars, all put away for a wet day. Property all honorably made. Heaven knows I would not have a dollar that was not. That, my dear, is a good beginning for a good basis. We must keep adding to it; keep the tide flowing in the channel of success. I was thinking, my dear, of inventing a new religion."

"My dear!" exclaimed Mrs. Chapman, with an air of astonishment, "what an inventive head you have got. But you have said so often that there was too much religion in the world, and not enough of true goodness."

"Of the old kind, I meant, my dear;" resumed the little man. "What I mean is to invent a religion that is new and novel, has something broad and attractive in it, and that people of a curious turn of mind would pay for enjoying. That's the kind of religion that pays, you see. And if we could put the church on its feet again with something of that kind. It's the propensity people have to go galloping after new things in religion that we must study and turn to our advantage if we would be prosperous." The little man fretted his fingers nervously through his unkept hair, and his face assumed an air of great seriousness.

"How, my dear," enquired Mrs. Chapman, "could you put the church on its feet with such a load of scandal on its back? Could'nt you invent something else that would be novel and profitable?"

"There's where my new conception was coming in. That's the point I was considering when you interrupted me with Mattie's love affair," Chapman replied, looking more serious than ever.

"It struck me that we might do something profitable by getting up a company for the discovery of Kidd's treasure. 'The Great Kidd Discovery Company' would be a good name, my dear. You must always give a company a good name. Then you must manage it with tact and prudence. A prodigious enterprise, my dear. These simple-minded and honest Dutch people would fall into it like a flock of sheep. They honestly believe Kidd was a bold pirate, who amassed a great fortune by plundering towns on the Spanish Main. That, having more gold and silver than he could invest to advantage, he buried it on the bank of the river, a few leagues above this place, where he entered into an agreement with the devil to stand guard over it until he returned. They believe, also, that Hanz Toodleburg, whose father knew Kidd well, and perhaps had something to do with his adventures, is the only man now living who possesses the secret of where that treasure is buried."

CHAPTER XI.

MRS. CHAPMAN CULTIVATES NEW ACQUAINTANCES.

It was spring-time of the year 1824. A new era in the history of the nation's wealth and progress seemed to have fairly begun. Strong and vigorous intellects ruled in the councils of the nation and inspired confidence in the people. Science was breathing new life into our enterprise, and leading us rapidly into new fields and richer prospects. It was also brushing away the prejudices that had narrowed our thoughts and confined our action to things of a past age. Steam was an adjustable power now, a reality; still there were sensible men who shook their heads in doubt; and the men who declared it would soon revolutionize the commerce of the world were set down as not safe to do business with.

Steamboats of improved model and of increased size seemed to spring up every day, and might be seen passing up and down the Hudson night and morning. Now a company of reckless New Yorkers proposed to build a steamboat two hundred feet long, and with an engine of one hundred and fifty horse power, to navigate the Hudson to Albany at the rate of thirteen miles an hour. This great experiment, regarded so hazardous at that time, sent the honest and peace-loving Dutchmen along the banks of the river into such a state of alarm that they called meetings, and in the most solemn manner declared that no man's life would be safe while sailing at such a dangerous rate of speed. And they further declared that all these new-fashioned methods of putting an end to the lives of honest people must be stopped. In fine, they predicted nothing but distress and ruin on all who had anything to do with them.

It was at one of these meetings, held in Nyack about this time, and presided over by the school-master, that a number of these honest and peace-loving old settlers resolved, after much grave deliberation, that a man who paid his debts and was contented with what he had was the only true Christian. And it was further resolved, that the world was getting to be very wicked and very full of foolish people, who were in such a hurry to get to the devil before their time that they had devised these steamboats to carry them. And seeing that it was neither wisdom nor prudence for honest people to travel on such craft, they would also not send their vegetables to market on them.

This resolution was kept good for a number of years, the honest people who made it firmly believing that all good and prudent persons would follow their example, and in that way drive the steamboats from the river. Alarming as these things were, there were others which fairly frightened these honest people out of all their courage. The gossips had gathered in force at Titus Bright's inn one night, to enjoy a pipe and a mug of his new ale. There was the school-master, and Doctor Critchel, and Hanz Toodleburg, and other choice spirits, who knew all about the affairs of the nation. When they had discussed all manner of subjects, Titus drew from his pocket a newspaper and read, to the astonishment and evident alarm of his guests, that a man in England had invented a machine to do away with horses. The doctor set down his ale and adjusted his spectacles, and gazed at the speaker with an air of surprise and astonishment, while Hanz and the school-master suddenly ceased smoking.

"Now don't get alarmed, my friends," said Titus, watching with evident delight the increasing alarm of his guests. "It is all here, and true. He has invented a steam-horse, with an iron stomach and wheels; and the animal can, with good management, be made to run over a road at the rate of twenty miles an hour. Yes," added Titus, with a look of great seriousness, "people are already risking their lives by riding in this way."

The doctor heaved a sigh, and, half raising his pipe, gave it as his opinion that a man who would invent such dangerous machines must be in league with the devil. This profound opinion was endorsed by both Hanz and the school-master. The latter, in short, suggested that such men were generally vagabonds, whom it were well to throw into the Tappan Zee, with stones around their necks.

"If the world was going to the devil in this way, what was the use of living in it," inquired the school-master, finishing his ale, and passing his mug for a fresh draught.

"Sure enough, sure enough!" a number of voices ejaculated simultaneously.

"Truly, the dragons are to be let loose upon us," resumed Bright, passing the schoolmaster his mug of ale. "An' here's now in New York, that's got to be so wicked honest folks can't live in it, a lot o' crazy men talking about building one of these here steamboats big enough to cross the Atlantic."

"Der won't be much heerd of de mans nir de vomans vat goes in um," interrupted Hanz.

"Peoples is not sho crazy as t'too any un de sort. 'Tis all hombug;" joined the doctor.

"So I say, doctor!" interposed the school-master.

"Here it is, gentlemen," resumed Bright; "all down in the newspaper. No getting over that." Thus was this important subject discussed until a late hour, the gossips going to their homes with serious faces and heavy hearts.

It is a very well established fact that the question of building steamships large enough and strong enough to cross the ocean was discussed by a number of

New York merchants who were ready to embark capital in the project, several years before the keels of the Royal William, the Savannah, the Sirius, or the Great Western were laid. But we must leave this subject for the present, and return to our friends, the Chapmans.

These people professed to be plain and practical, brought up according to the creed of New England. They also affected to despise the small vanities of the world. The effect of prosperity, however, on their natures was singularly instructive, since it entirely changed their manners. No sooner did fortune favor them than Mrs. Chapman began to display an ambition for vulgar show, such as well-bred people never indulge in. She never failed to remind her friends that she was brought up in Boston, where everything was very refined. She regarded it as a compliment to herself that she had an intellectual husband. He had a big head, if he was small, and could carry any number of books in it. That was what Boston people liked. Her thoughts seemed continually navigating between religion and the fashions. She had no deep affection or love for any one, not even for her daughter Mattie, whom she viewed in the light of a rather valuable ornament, in the disposal of which she must make the best bargain she could, not so much for the girl's sake as her own. She could toss her head as disdainfully as any of your fine dames; and she could discourse as glibly about genteel society as a successful milliner just set up for a lady. She had plain Mrs. Jones for a neighbor, and would drop that honest woman a nod now and then, out of mere politeness. But she never condescended to associate on terms of equality with the Jones family. Mrs. Jones's husband was a common, unintellectual sort of person, who retailed groceries for a living.

A singular and mysterious change had now taken place. Chapman no longer got up quarrels with his neighbors. Indeed, he had a good word to say whenever he met Titus Bright. He could shake hands with Doctor Critchel, and agree with the Dominie on matters of religion. In fine, if he was everybody's enemy before, he was now everybody's friend. He admired the Dutch for their honesty and true-heartedness. This singular change gave the gossips of the town something to talk about for a week. The Chapmans and the Toodleburgs were now the very best of friends. Chapman could be seen of an evening sitting in Hanz's little ivy-covered porch, enjoying a pot of ale. And Hanz had been seen smoking his pipe in Chapman's garden. All this meant something, the gossips said, and something of great importance. Where two such men got their heads together, and pipes and ale were called in, there was sure to be something deep going on. Hanz Toodleburg, they said, never smoked his pipe with a man like Chapman but that there was something in the wind. Then Mrs. Chapman and her gushing, blue-eyed daughter had condescended to visit at Toodleburg's, and could make themselves quite agreeable at Angeline's tea-table. And then Angeline, good, kind Angeline, with her face still bright with gentleness and love, was always so happy When Mattie called. Then there was something so simple, so frank and straightforward in Mattie's nature. Angeline could not help loving her. And the affection she cherished for Tite, who was the idol of her thoughts, strengthened the ties of their love.

"We have not forgot you, you see," said Mrs. Chapman, as she bowed herself into Toodleburg's little house one evening. "We expected company at home to-night, but says I to my dear husband, 'you know, my dear husband,' (here Mrs. Chapman bowed to her dear husband, who had followed her,) 'we have been promising so long to visit Mr. and Mrs. Toodleburg.'"

Angeline bowed and invited her visitors to be seated, while Hanz gave Chapman a hearty shake of the hand, and an assurance that no man was more welcome under his roof. "Always glad to see mine friends," said Hanz. "You shall take seats, and be shust so much at home as you is in your own house." And he drew one big chair up for Chapman, and another for Mrs. Chapman. "Peoples always makes themselves at home in mine house."

"You must excuse our humble little place," Angeline said; "we are plain, every-day people." And she made Mrs. Chapman a low courtesy, as that stout, bustling woman, apparently overcome with the heat, settled her solid circumference into a chair.

"Dear a me," rejoined Mrs. Chapman, "what happy people you ought to be. Everything so comfortable round you, you know, and all your own. What a blessing to have things all your own." Here Mrs. Chapman raised her bonnet carefully and used it as a fan.

"Yes, we are quite unpretending people," Angeline repeated. "What we have got is our own. We are getting old now, and if we die owing nobody a shilling we shall die in peace." And her sweet face lighted up with a smile, the true reflex of that goodness her heart was so full of.

"It's so warm—I'm about melted," rejoined Mrs. Chapman, not appearing to notice what Angeline had said. "And this is my new bonnet, you see. Bonnets cost so much money now. People are getting so fashionable, and to be anybody you must keep up appearances." She held her bonnet up admiringly. "And my dear, good husband there—he's such a good husband—says I'm a very expensive wife. Always buys me what I want, though." Here she raised her waxy, fat hand, and dropped a bow of approval to the little husband, who was quietly surveying the scene from Hanz's big chair. "My husband is so intellectual, and does so much for other people. He's always doing for other people. But he's a treasure to me, for all that—"

"My dear, my dear," interrupted Chapman; "what a kind way you have of paying compliments. Mrs. Toodleburg will not understand you, my dear. What more than any one else have I done for other people?"

"You have been a perfect Christian, my dear, so you have," resumed Mrs. Chapman, giving her head a toss and pressing the fore-finger of her right hand on the arm of the chair. "Why, Mrs. Toodlebug—pardon me; I never did pronounce names correct." She turned condescendingly to Angeline. "You must know that my dear husband created a whole town once. Then he built a great and flourishing church, founded on advanced moral ideas. And he intended to have sold it for the good of others, and would have sold it, but for an unforeseen circumstance."

"A very unforeseen circumstance, my dear," rejoined Chapman, shaking his head admonishingly. "You see, I have got one of the very best wives in the world. She has a philosophy of her own, and we agree in everything."

"Shust like me and mine vife," said Hanz. "We agrees in everything. Lived dese forty nor more years togeder, mitout a quarrel." Hanz had been sitting where a pale shadow of the dim light played over his broad, kindly face, and, with his long, white hair curling down his neck, gave a clearer outline to the picture.

"Never had even a little quarrel?" resumed Mrs. Chapman, inquiringly. "I have heard married people say it was so nice to have a little quarrel now and then. But my dear husband is such a good husband, Mrs. Toodleburg. Just like yours." Here she turned toward and dropped Angeline a bow. "I never want to live to see the day when I shall have to marry a second husband." Here she turned and dropped a bow to her dear Chapman. "I should be always praising you, my dear. And unless my dear second husband was a saint there would be trouble in the house, you know. My dear, let us drop this subject. It is not pleasant to look to far into the future." Here she turned to Angeline, who had proceeded to get some strawberries and cream for her guests.

"You are so nice and comfortable here," she resumed; "it takes one back to the good old times, when everything was true and simple." Mrs. Chapman gave quicker motion to her tongue. "You have your loom, and your spinning-wheel, and homespun made by your own hands. How delightful."

"My dear, my dear," interrupted Chapman; "what a homily on the beauties of economy you are reading our friends—"

"Don't interrupt me, my dear," resumed Mrs. Chapman, and she again turned to Angeline. "Do you know, Mrs. Toodlebug, that I have always felt that we ought to be the best of friends?"

"You are very kind," said Angeline, "very kind. We are very plain people."

"That's why I like you all the better," Mrs. Chapman resumed, with an air of condescension. "My husband and your husband must also be the best of friends. They can make a fortune by it, you know. You see, my husband proposes to make your husband's fortune. He is the greatest man to make other people's fortunes. Yes, he is. My husband's head is full of great progressive ideas. And he has made the fortunes of so many men." Here Mrs. Chapman lowered her voice to a whisper, and drew her chair a little nearer to Angeline. "There is another little matter that should make us firm friends. I would not mention it, you know; but I feel that it is no secret." Here she dropped one of her most significant bows. "I have taken such a liking to your son. Such a promising young man, he is. That voyage will make a man of him; who knows but he may come home with a large fortune. I have known stranger things than that. I have been encouraging a little love affair between him and my daughter Mattie. You have seen my Mattie? She is clever, wonderfully smart, handsome, too; and if she gets the right kind of a husband, will shine in society."

"My poor boy, my poor boy!" exclaimed Angeline, her eyes filling with tears at the mention of his name. "How, how, how I should like to see him tonight. There is where he used to sit, (here her voice yielded to her emotions,) and here is the chair we always kept for him. Perhaps we shall never see him again. He was so good and so kind to us. I hope God will be good to him, and will watch over him, and carry him safe through dangers, and bring him back to us. Oh, I know God will be good to him. We are both old now, and have nothing to live for but him." Again she gave way to her grief, and as the tears flowed buried her face in her hands.

"My dear, good friend," rejoined Mrs. Chapman, rising from her chair, and placing her hand consolingly on Angeline's shoulder; "there is nothing in the world to weep for. Nothing in the world. I would be proud of a son who had courage and ambition enough to go on one of these voyages. It is proof, my good woman, that he has something in him. And if he should bring home a fortune, you know. Oh, he'd have so many friends. Don't weep, my good woman, don't weep. He'll be such a joy to you when he comes home. And I will encourage Mattie to think of nobody else."

CHAPTER XII.

A STRANGE GENTLEMAN.

Angeline had just recovered from her grief, and was setting strawberries and cream before her visitors, when a loud knock was heard at the door, which Hanz proceeded to open; when a tall, well-dressed man, with dark, well kept hair, piercing black eyes, features of great regularity, and having the manners of a gentleman, entered and introduced himself as Mr. Luke Topman, just from New York. "I am a stranger to you all here," he said, in a deep, clear voice, "and I owe you an apology for calling at this seemingly late hour. I said I was a stranger," he repeated, "but the business I am on may make us acquaintances." The stranger stood for a moment, with his eyes fixed on Chapman. Still no recognition passed, and their manner was that of strangers who had never met before.

The figures here grouped together were of the most opposite kind, and presented a picture at once striking and effective. A table stood in the centre of the little room, and on it burned a candle, casting a pale and shadowy light over and giving clearer outline to each figure. There was the old loom, with its harnesses, its reed, and its shuttles; the flax-wheel and the distaff, forming a quaint setting, but representing a past age and the primitive habits of the people who used them.

There was Hanz and Angeline on one side. Time was writing its record in deep lines on their faces, and whitening their gray hairs. Frank, simple-minded, honest, and contented, they had enough to carry them through life comfortably; and why should they, Hanz said, trouble themselves about anything more? They represented an age and a people perfectly happy with what it had pleased God to give them. On the other side there was Chapman and Mrs. Chapman, exact types of the people they represented. Ambitious of making a show in the world, grasping, restless, selfish, intriguing, seeking always for means to advance themselves, studying the future for their own advancement, and ready to use even religion as an assistant to gaining their objects. Such was the contrast presented in the picture before us.

Again apologizing for calling at what seemed a late hour, the stranger proceeded. "I am in great haste, madam. I came all the way from New York to-day. Crossed the ferry only an hour ago, and am somewhat fatigued. My business is of great importance, and with Mr. Toodleburg. I was directed here, and am glad to find him so comfortably situated."

"Very well, very well," rejoined Hanz, his face lighted up with a smile, and his white hair flowing; "dat's me, mine friend. You be's welcome to my little home. Yees, mine friend, you shall be so welcome as I can make you." Hanz shook him heartily by the hand, and invited him to sit down. "You be's had no shupper, eh?" he resumed. "Der's no man what comes nor goes hungry to my house."

The stranger bowed and said, "Thank you—you are very kind; but I supped on the other side of the sea, and have no need for any more."

"Mine gracious!" exclaimed Hanz. "You comes all de way from New York to she me. You eats anoder shupper, shure."

The stranger persisted that he would eat no more that night. The appearance of the man at so late an hour excited serious apprehensions in the mind of Angeline lest he should bring news of some disaster to the good ship Pacific.

Then turning to Mrs. Chapman, he said, "I hope, madam, I have not intruded on your privacy here to-night?"

That lady, having dropped him one of her best bows, assured him there was nothing private so far as she was concerned. "We are friends and neighbors of these good people," she replied with a forced smile and an air of condescension. "We like to be neighborly, and just dropped in to make a friendly call. That's all, sir."

"I am very glad to meet Mr. Toodleburg. Very glad to find him such an excellent person," the stranger repeated, turning to Hanz, and again taking him by the hand. "Topman, I said my name was; Luke Topman, senior partner of the enterprising house of Topman and Gusher, doing a large miscellaneous business in Pearl, near Wall street. You are, doubtless, well acquainted with the reputation of the firm." Here Mr. Topman compressed his lips, brushed his fingers through his hair, and addressed himself to Chapman, who up to this time had maintained an air of indifference to what was going on.

"Perfectly well," replied Chapman, with an air of surprise. "Highly respectable and equally responsible house, that. Why, sir, it is somewhat curious that we should meet here. A relative of mine did business with that house a long time. Highly satisfactory—highly."

"We endeavor to make everything satisfactory with our customers," resumed Mr. Topman. "Happy to have met a gentleman so familiar with the reputation of our house. Pray, may I enquire to the name?"

"Chapman—Bigelow Chapman. My wife, Mr. Topman; my enlarged and better half. Mr. Topman, my dear, of the firm of Topman and Gusher. Doing a large miscellaneous business, and highly respectable."

"What a strange meeting this is. You used to know each other? How curious!" interposed Mrs. Chapman, rising from her seat and dropping Mr. Topman one of her most stately bows.

"By reputation. Perhaps I should have said general reputation, my dear," returned Chapman. During all this time Hanz was kept in ignorance of the object of the stranger's visit. Yet the whole scene was such as could not fail to excite his curiosity to the very highest pitch.

"And now," said the stranger, "as the night is warm, and ladies never care to hear anything about business, I propose, Mr. Toodleburg, that we retire to the porch. You can enjoy your pipe, there; and, if you will permit me, I will enjoy a cigar. Our friend, here—he will permit me to call him so—will join us."

The three now proceeded to the porch; where, when they had become seated, the stranger discovered the object of his visit. "I have been informed on good authority," said Mr. Topman, "that you possess the secret of where Kidd's treasure is buried—"

"Vel, vel, vel!" exclaimed Hanz, raising his hands in astonishment; "if dat ish'nt so pig a lie as ever vas told. No, mine friend, I knows nothin' apout dis Mr. Kidd, nor his money. Dis one big lie de peoples pout here gits up, as has nothin' petter to do."

"It's somewhat singular," said Chapman, fixing his keen black eyes on the stranger, "it was that that brought me here to-night. Mr. Toodleburg may be innocent of all knowledge of Mr. Kidd, as he says. But the people sincerely believe that he does, and that he possesses the secret of where his treasure is buried. The belief is just as good as the reality, and may be made equally profitable."

"Exactly," interposed Mr. Topman, "exactly! Just what I was going to suggest." Here Mr. Topman put his thumbs in the arms of his waistcoat, and drummed on the front with his fingers. "If these honest people believe Mr. Toodleburg knows where the money is buried, why, sir, there's your solid basis for a grand joint stock company, dividends twenty per cent., payable quarterly. That's what takes. God bless me, Mr. Toodleburg, here's a fortune in your fingers. Capable heads, sir, and capable hands. There's all, sir, that is required to give the thing popularity and insure its success." Mr. Topman paused for a moment, threw himself back in his chair, and cast a patronizing glance at Hanz. "Progressive idea, sir. Grand Kidd Discovery Company. Capital one hundred thousand dollars, all paid in. The man fortunate enough to get twenty shares is sure to make a fortune."

"Den if he pe so grand, why you don't make all de fortune, and keep him yourshelf?" said Hanz, rubbing his head and dropping his pipe.

"Having the secret," resumed Mr. Topman, blandly, "of course you are indispensable to the success of the enterprise. Think of it, sleep over it, and I am sure, sir, you will wake up in the morning resolved to place yourself in the hands of Topman and Gusher." Mr. Topman made another pause, and threw his hands over his head. "No matter whether you have the secret or not. Stick to it that you have; and refer your men to Topman and Gusher."

Again Hanz shook his head, and smoked his pipe thoughtfully. The whole thing was new and strange to him. Never in his life before had anything taken him by such surprise. He had enough to carry him through the world comfortably, and something to give his poor neighbors when they stood in need. Why should he trouble his head about Mr. Kidd. He did not know where a dollar of his money was buried.

"Mine friends," said Hanz, "I likes you poth. And I thanks you, and ish much opliged to you for dis offer to makes my fortune. But, what I do mit sho much moneys, eh? My neighbors all say 'Hanz Toodleburg steals him,' Maybe I gits prout mit him. Den everypody says Hanz Toodleburg gits apove his pisness. Mit a fortune perhaps t'tivel gits into mine head. Der ish nopody now put me und mine Angeline—"

"There's your son, Mr. Toodleburg," interposed Chapman, who until now had remained almost passive. "You ought to regard him above everything else, you ought. I feel a deep interest in that young man, you know. If you could have a fortune for him when he comes home—well, that would be the making of him."

"Shure enough, dere ish mine poor poy, Tite. He ish such a goot poy. It most preaks his muder's heart to have him go dis long voyages," said Hanz, taking the pipe from his lips, as his eyes filled with tears. "If I only could have a fortune und de little farm for mine poor Tite when he gits home."

"Give us your hand, sir," said Mr. Topman. "You talk now like a man, and a father. I'm a father, sir, and know how to feel for you. Had a son at sea four years. Gave him a fortune when he came home. A most enterprising and highly respected merchant now. Has ships at sea, rides in his carriage, and a balance in his bank." The thought of providing a future for Tite was more than Hanz could resist, and his unsuspecting nature yielded to the temptation.

"And now," said Mr. Topman, rising from his chair, "if Mr. Toodleburg will sign these papers—they merely set forth that he possesses and will confide to the house of Topman and Gusher, their heirs or assigns, the secret of where Kidd's treasure is buried, and that he shall have a tenth interest in all the profits. A sure gain and no risk, you know."

The three gentlemen now returned to the little room. Topman handed Chapman the paper, and requested that he would read it, which that gentleman affected to do.

"Perfectly straightforward and correct," said Chapman; "perfectly! I am sure you are very kind to these people, and I wish the great Kidd Discovery Company every success."

Angeline brought the little old ink-bottle, and Hanz, with feelings of hesitation, it must be confessed, signed the papers, when the visitors retired for the night.

CHAPTER XIII.

CAPTAIN BOTTOM, THE WHALE-KILLER.

On the morning of the 24th of June, the good ship Pacific was sailing gallantly down the coast of Brazil, all her canvass spread to a light breeze, her port tacks aboard, and heading for Bahia.

The air was hot with the breath of tropic winds, and the horizon to the west and south was festooned with fierce red clouds. The sun was just setting, and spreading the broad ocean with a crimson light, giving a weird and curious outline to every feature of the ship. There was something grand, even enchanting and sublime, in the picture here spread out, presenting as it did the highest example of God's goodness and reality.

The scene changed suddenly, as the sun disappeared. The fierce, red clouds melted into softness and tenderness. A pale, yellow light spread along the heavens and over the sea; and the ship that a few minutes before had looked like a white-winged phantom floating over a sea of fire, now assumed the appearance of a maiden decked in her bridal robes.

A man of short, stout figure, a sort of compromise between an alderman and a dwarf, with very short legs, a broad red face, wide mouth, crispy grey hair that stood nearly erect on his head, a red, punky nose, and keen, grey eyes, paced watchfully up and down the quarter-deck. He was dressed in white pantaloons and jacket, both fitting tight to his skin, and wore a Panama hat, with a long black ribbon streaming behind.

He would pause at the hand-rail every few minutes, scan eagerly along the sky from north to south, as if studying the strange and sudden changes that were going on in the heavens. Then he would exchange a few words with the officer of the watch, and resume his walk. Eight bells had just struck, the wind began to freshen and veer to the southwest, and the sky became overcast and filled with white, fleecy clouds.

An order was given to take in studding-sails and get the ship "snug" for the night, and quickly obeyed. Order and regularity prevailed on board the good ship Pacific; and the promptness and cheerfulness with which both officers and men performed their duties showed that they had a more than ordinary interest in the ship and her voyage. Fashion had not then made slaves and idlers of our young men of wealthy parents, and it was, indeed, thought no disgrace for a gentleman of position to send his sons on one of these voyages, to do duty before the mast. It taught them how to face danger and endure hardships. It developed their manliness, and made them more self-reliant. It gave them a knowledge of the world they could not get elsewhere, and laid a good foundation for a fixed and lasting character. Indeed, some of our richest and most enterprising merchants have dated their prosperity from one of these voyages.

The short, bluff-looking man pacing the quarter-deck was Captain Price Bottom; and a more honest-hearted old salt never sailed the sea. His great skill in killing whales had made him famous among whalemen throughout the Pacific. He had made three successful voyages, bringing home cargoes that had enriched his owners, put money in his own pocket, and secured him a reputation he esteemed of more value than a fortune. In truth, he regarded whales just as a terrier does rats, and found his highest enjoyment in killing them. And yet nothing pleased him better than when a whale showed pluck, as he called it, and made a square, fierce fight for his life. A man had a chance then to show his skill and power over the brute, he said. He held, too, that man's highest object in life was to know how to kill a whale skilfully; and he heartily despised the whale "as would submit quietly to the harpoon, and die like a lubber." He also affected great contempt for the landsman who had lived like a gentleman, and never killed a whale in his life.

"There's no lunar to-night," said Captain Bottom, pausing at the quarter-deck rail, and addressing himself to the officer of the watch. "There's a goin' to be dirt, sir, there is; and them royals and topgallant-sails is got to cum in. Would'nt surprise me if we had to double-reef topsails afore mornin'. Tell you what it is, Mr. Higgins, there's that ar north star with a towel over her face again. Sink me if there'll be any lunar took to-night." The captain shook his head, gave his Panama a tip, and walking aft, stood beside the binnacle watching the compasses for several minutes. Then returning to where the officer of the watch stood, he resumed:

"Never made a bad landfall in my life, Mr. Higgins. Never shall be said of Captain Price Bottom that he lost his reckonin'. It's judgment; yes, Mr. Higgins, it's good judgment and sound sense what makes a good sailor. A man may cram his skull till it hurts with Bowditch, but if he hain't sense he'll never be a sailor. Same in killin' whales. If a man hain't got sense, the whale is sure to get the advantage of him." Again he paused, as if courting a reply; but Mr. Higgins merely bowed assent to everything the captain said, every few minutes keeping an eye aloft at the sails.

"Man what gets his navigation aboard ship knows his business. Got mine there; yes, sir! Did'nt know a Bowditch from a Bible when I went aboard ship. Can do my amplitude and variations now without looking at a nautical almanac. Can, sir, by Jove!"

The ship bounded gallantly over the sea, leaving in her wake a long silvery train of phosphoric light. Drawing no response from Mr. Higgins, the captain raised his night-glass and scanned along the heavens to the west. "We'll get somethin' out o' that quarter, butt end foremost," said the captain, lowering his glass.

Mr. Higgins was first officer of the ship, a position secured to him, not because he had worked his way up to it, but through the influence of a rich father, who was a large owner in the ship and her venture. He was a tall, well-formed, fine-looking young man, with delicate and well-cut features, and black hair. He was also a fine scholar and a perfect master of the theory of navigation, and a voyage or two to Europe had given him a slight knowledge of the practical part of it. Yet he was more an ornamental than a practical sailor; and it was this that made Captain Bottom, the whale-killer, hold him in no very high respect. Indeed, he had several times said, in the presence of Mr. Higgins, that it was all very well for a young gentleman to be a scholar; but a sailor what had his head full of books never made a fortune for his owners.

"Eight and forty hours more, Mr. Higgins! Yes, sir, eight and forty hours more—keepin' her as she's going—and we have the land off Bahia." Captain Bottom gave his head a significant shake as he spoke. "Using judgment, you see; not books, Mr. Higgins. Captain Price Bottom has sailed seventeen years, and never was deceived by that chart. Don't make charts now as they used to make 'em, Mr. Higgins," he concluded, shrugging his shoulders.

The wind now came over the sea roaring like a fierce lion, indicating the rapid approach of the gale.

"If we make land off Bahia in forty-eight hours, then I'm mistaken," rejoined the first officer, satirically. "There's something coming that will give us enough to do before morning."

The words had hardly escaped his lips when the full force of the gale struck the ship, roaring and shrieking through her shrouds, and nearly throwing her on her beam ends. The sea was soon lashed into a tempest, and made a clean sweep over her decks. The canvas was carried clean from the bolt-ropes, the sheets were let go, and the lighter sails clewed up, and an attempt made to get the ship's head to the wind and lay her to. But the mizzen-sails were all gone, and she fell off, and refused to obey her helm. The lashings had given way, and the larboard, waist, and quarter boats were all swept from the davits, the frames sprung, and every timber in the good ship's hull worked, and strained, and complained, like a frail thing that must soon go to pieces. Every order, however, was obeyed promptly and cheerfully, for both officers and crew felt that their lives, as well as the saving of the ship, depended on the way in which each man performed his duty.

Just before the gale came up five young men, including Tite, might have been seen grouped together in the waist of the ship, pondering over a chart.

Several books and nautical instruments were lying around. They were all, except Tite, young men of wealthy parents, who had joined the ship to enjoy the excitements of a whaling voyage. These young men, with Tite, had formed a school of instruction, and every evening got together in the same place to improve their knowledge in practical navigation. One of them, a young man who had endeared himself to all on board by his courage and the gentleness of his manners, was third mate, and took a leading part in instructing the others. It would, indeed, have been difficult to find two young men whose characters bore a stronger resemblance than his and Tite's. Between them there grew up the strongest friendship.

The ship was now laboring in the trough of the sea, when a loud crash was heard aloft. The fore, main, and mizzen top-gallant masts had gone in rapid succession, and the swaying mass of wreck was threatening the destruction of the ship. Death now stared every one in the face. There was no hope of saving the ship and the lives of those on board, except in the strength and courage of those willing to go aloft and clear away the wreck. But who was there to do this perilous work?

Amidst the confusion caused by the excited elements there was the sturdy little captain, calm and cool, and giving his orders with that clearness and decision which had always characterized him. Men were called for to go aloft and cut away the swaying wreck, and save the ship. The first to obey this summons was young Tite Toodleburg, whose example was followed by the young man I have described as third mate, and one of his companions. They mounted the fore, main, and mizzen rigging, and working with all their strength and skill soon had the swaying wreck cut away, and the ship relieved of her strain. But in descending, the third mate, who had so gallantly performed his duty, lost his hold, and the ship giving a terrible lurch, he was plunged into the sea, and seen no more.

The ship now gradually righted, and with the aid of a storm-sail in her mizzen rigging, for her top-sail had been torn into shreds, her head was got to the wind.

In that latitude gales of this kind are of short duration, generally; and in half an hour from the time it struck the ship there was a calm, smooth sea, and all hands were engaged repairing damages.

On the following morning the ship was proceeding on her course, with a light breeze from the north and a clear sky. Captain Bottom was there on the quarter-deck, directing affairs, and in a talkative mood.

"She's a good ship, sir, this old Pacific is, Mr. Higgins;" said he, again addressing that officer. "Never knew her get off her feet before." He always spoke of the ship as if she were a thing of life. "Bless her staunch old soul!

Made her timbers talk, eh? Wants a man as has got confidence in the craft what's under him. Then if she goes down, why he feels like being a hero and keeping her company.

"But it makes me feel bad, Mr. Higgins, that we have lost our third mate, poor fellow! He was a good sailor, and a brave young man, and had such good friends at home, who thought so much of him." And as he said this tears glistened in his eyes, and ran down his cheeks. "I'm sorry for that young man, I am, so I am, Mr. Higgins," said the old sailor, wiping the tears from his bronzed cheeks. "I do hope his soul will sail in peace in a better world." Again he shook his head sorrowfully, and then paused for a minute as if to regain control of his feelings. "God forgive me," he resumed, "for making a woman of myself. Don't do it often, Mr. Higgins."

"Shows that you have a kind heart, sir, and can shed a tear when it is touched. I appreciate you for it. There is something manly in the tear of a brave sailor," returned the officer, coldly, but politely. "We shall get a good observation to-day, and if the men work hearty all the spare spars and sails will be up by nightfall." Mr. Higgins's mind was evidently on his duty, and not being inclined to enjoy the captain's conversation, he took every opportunity to change the subject.

"Give us your hand, Mr. Higgins," said he, rather unannoyed than otherwise by what that officer had said. "But look you here!" He lowered his voice as he took the officer's hand, "There'll be no whales to kill where that poor fellow has gone. Not a whale. I promised his poor old father—a good old red coat killer he was, too, in the Revolution—that this here son of his should kill the first whale. Yes, I did, Mr. Higgins. And that's what mortifies me. He's dead, you see, poor fellow. T'was'nt my fault that I did'nt keep my promise. There'll be no whales to kill where he's gone, poor fellow!" Again he shook his head feelingly, then raising his hat, wiped the sweat from his bronzed brow.

He now sent for Tite, who came upon the quarter-deck nervously, and saluted his superior. "Well, my hearty," said Captain Bottom, "here's my hand. You're a sailor, every inch on you. And a brave man, too, if Captain Bottom does say it." Tite was not a little surprised at this familiarity on the part of his captain, for he had before coming on board been led to believe that the most severe discipline ruled on board a whale ship.

"There's the true sailor in you, my hearty," continued the captain, again shaking Tite warmly by the hand. "You saved the ship, my hearty. There'd a bin no more of the good old Pacific—God bless her! nor none of us standin' here, but for you, my hearty."

"I only done my duty, sir," rejoined Tite, modestly, as the color came into his face. "I hope, captain, to merit your praise to the end of the voyage." The young sailor made a bow, and was about returning to his duty.

"Avast, a bit," interrupted the captain. "Your name's Toodlebug, is'nt it, my hearty?"

"Yes, sir," replied Tite. "Titus Bright Toodleburg; usually called Tite. Hope, sir, to improve myself in navigation and seamanship under your command. I shall always feel proud, sir, that I sailed with you. Some one may trust me with a ship some day."

"That's the talk, my hearty; keep a sharp look ahead," rejoined the captain, his face lighting up with a smile. "Cram Bowditch into yer head, and keep a sharp look ahead. Have ye so ye can bring the sun down to dinner and put the north star in yer pocket afore ye get round Cape Horn. You'll be a sailor yet, my hearty." Again Captain Bottom shook Tite by the hand warmly.

"Git yer head full of navigation; and with good judgment to help ye out, ye can look an owner in the eye without winking, and tell him ye want a ship. And if that recommendation don't do, tell him you have killed whales with Captain Bottom, a man what never let a whale git the better of him. And if he has never heard of Captain Price Bottom, of the good old ship Pacific, then he never should own a ship, and don't sail for him. That's my advice, my hearty. So keep a sharp look out ahead." Here he tapped Tite on the shoulder, exultingly.

"It's very kind of you," returned Tite, modestly, "to take this interest in me, a stranger to you. I shall do my best to merit your confidence and respect."

"A stranger, eh? Not a bit of it!" resumed the captain, quickly. "Look ye here, my hearty. Your good old father and me was old friends. That was years ago, you know. Meeting you brings an old love affair of thirty years right back to my heart again. Yes, my hearty, that old feelin's just as good as new this minute. God bless yer father; and God bless yer mother, too! Here's a hand what'll always give a warm welcome to the son of old Hanz Toodlebug—"

"Then you knew my father? I hope, sir, I may never do anything to lessen your respect for him."

"Know'd him?" resumed the captain. "Yes, sir, and yer mother, too. And when Captain Price Bottom says he know'd a man, he means it. Your father and me was rivals!" Here he touched Tite on the elbow, and winked significantly. "That is—well, it's rather a delicate subject—he courted yer mother, and so did I! There, sir, there's just what it is. She was as trim a young craft then as ever spread sails, and as full of goodness and good looks." Captain Bottom again paused for a moment, shook his head despondingly, and placed his hand on his heart. "A number of young bloods like me trimmed their sails, but did'nt overhaul her. Many a heart-flutter she caused me in them days. And just when I thought, says I to myself, 'I'm to wind'rd,' and had got ready to make fast to her—" Here he paused for a moment, and then lowering his voice, continued: "Well, what does she go and do? Blow me, my hearty, if she did'nt go off and marry your father. That's what dismasted me. Never bore him nor her any ill-will. 'God bless ye both,' says I; 'may ye be happy and have a large family!' And it does me good to know that they was prosperous. Your father had a home to take a woman to, and that is what a woman should look to. Price Bottom was poor then, and without a shillin' in his pocket. It was disappointment that made me take to the sea, though. Went from the fo'castle t'where you see me now—Captain Price Bottom, sir, of the good ship Pacific. It's a man's own exertion that lifts him up in the world. There's my poor old woman at home to-night—God bless her and the two little ones! thinking of me, and praying for me, and wondering where we are. Laid her up a nice little fortune; wolf can't bark at her door. That's a gratification, my hearty. Made three successful voyages, you see. This, our fourth one, is to be the last. Keep a sharp look ahead, and there's a future for you, too. Ah, there'll be a heap of happiness a'tween me and my old woman when this voyage is ended. A true wife at home, and a lovin' husband at sea—ah, my hearty, them's jewels!"

Tite listened with surprise to the story of this strange and eccentric man. He had never heard either of his parents mention his name. He, however, regarded it as very fortunate that he should be on board a ship commanded by a captain who held his humble parents in such high regard. The jolly old sailor finished his story by enjoining Tite to keep what he had said a matter of confidence. He also made him third mate, to fill the place of the young man who fell from the fore-mast into the sea during the gale.

"You shall take a hand at killing the first whale; shall command the larboard boat. And you shall never want a friend while Captain Price Bottom treads this quarter-deck," he concluded.

Tite bowed, and thanked his benefactor again. He then proceeded to his duty, as the ship headed for Bahia, with a fair wind.

CHAPTER XIV.

THE COMING WINTER, AND A MERRY-MAKING.

November was come now. The day I write of was damp and cheerless. Grey, vapory clouds swept over the Tappan Zee, and a sad, sighing wind tossed it into crests. A drizzling rain fell over Nyack, and the little town looked as if it had just taken a bath and gone to sleep for the night. The hills wore a cold and bleak look, the foliage had lost its bright, golden tints, and now looked faded and colorless. The leaves, too, were falling, and the naked trees seemed weeping and cold. Sheep browsed on the hill-sides, or nibbled coldly under the branches of sheltering trees. In the wet, dripping barn-yard cattle were seen huddled together under a lee, now seeking warmth in the fresh shocks, now proclaiming their troubles in subdued lowing.

The very landscape seemed weeping and melancholy. Even the summer birds, whose songs give such a charm to the woods, were gone. And there was the loon upon the lake gabbling his welcome to the approaching winter. The rain, too, had filled the brooks, and their waters were gurgling down deep, shadowy dells, mingling their touching music with the sad, sighing wind. There were pleasant memories entwined in that departing summer; and it now seemed as if all nature was joining in a requiem to its fading beauties.

The settlers had gathered their winter fruit, and the cider-presses had finished their work for the season. Squashes were hung up in the cellar, the corn was shucked and in the bins, and heaps of ripe, lusty pumpkins stood in the fields. In the houses fresh flitches of bacon hung by the fireside, while festoons of dried apples decorated the beams overhead. There, too, were the young nut-gatherers, coming home of an evening with their well-filled satchels. There was to be peace and plenty at the settlers' fireside this winter, for an all-wise Providence had so ordained it in an abundant harvest.

It was a custom with Hanz Toodleburg, as it was also with many other of the settlers, to entertain his friends and neighbors with a merry-making when the harvest was gathered. Hanz had invited his neighbors on the evening of the day I have described, and notwithstanding the cold and cheerless character of the night, the little house was full ere it was dark. The bright, happy faces of the women, and the jolly, ringing laugh of the men, all dressed in their neat new homespun, presented a pleasant picture of rustic life. Each man came armed with a long pipe, while his good vrow had some little present for Angeline. Hanz had a warm, hearty shake of the hand for each of his guests. Indeed, he welcomed each of the good vrows with a kiss and an admonition to be happy while they were under his roof. And these good vrows put their hands to the wheel, and assisted Angeline in preparing the feast. Indeed, she soon had her table spread with as good and well-cooked fare as could be found in the county.

There was the cold boar's head, decorated with flowers; the fattest turkey, roasted before the great fire; boiled beef, bathed in odorous krout, and declared delicacies by every sturdy Dutchman; a spiced ham, decorated with vegetables. Then there were apple and pumpkin pies just baked, cuddled apples, and jam, and fresh cranberry sauce. And these were backed up with new cider and home-brewed ale, and coffee. Such was the supper Hanz had prepared for his friends, and which he invited them to eat and be happy.

The good-natured Dominie was there, and so was Doctor Critchel and the school-master. Nor was Titus Bright, the inn-keeper, forgotten. They were equally important characters in the settlement, and no honest Dutchman, who had any regard for his reputation for hospitality, would think of giving a merry-making without them. The good Dominie was fond of puddings and pies, and preached that the three highest objects a man had to live for were peace, contentment, and a good dinner. The Dutch regarded this as good enough religion for them—better, perhaps, than that preached by the man of the church of progressive ideas. The school-master could sing a good song, and, although an idle, shiftless fellow, got more invitations to supper than any other man in the settlement. As for the inn-keeper, he was a merry little man, who made everybody laugh, and was held in high esteem by all the good vrows around Nyack.

Now that the supper was ready, there was a general exchange of vrows, for it was not considered etiquette to sit at table with your own wife during one of these feasts. Then the Dominie invoked God's blessing on the bounties He had spread before them, thanked Him for the bountiful harvest, and for the love He had shown these happy people. He then proceeded to carve the boar's head, while every man and woman present went to enjoying the feast.

When supper was over and the table cleared away the men took to their pipes and discussed their crops, and the women discoursed of carding, and spinning, and housewifery in general. Then there was a dance around the apple-basket, and a dance in which every man kissed every other man's vrow, and in which the Dominie joined, and was as jolly as any of his flock. And they danced to the music of a fiddle, played by Lame George, who lived up in the mountain. Then the Dominie told a number of amusing stories, and the school-master sang them several of his best songs, and cider and ale was drank.

And while the pleasantry was at its highest, a loud knock was heard at the door. The revelry ceased for a moment. There was the postmaster's boy, bearing a letter with several curious stamps on it. Hanz was overjoyed. He shook the boy's hand, and then scanned over the letter. "God pless mine poor poy, Titus!" he exclaimed. "He wrotes dat ledder. Yes, he does; mine poor poy Titus does;" and he struck his hands on his knees, and laughed with joy. "He ton't forgets his old fadder. He be's a goot poy, mine Titus." And he shook hands with the Dominie and the inn-keeper. Indeed, he seemed so completely unmanned that he was powerless to open the letter. Then he took a candle in his right hand, and again scanned and scanned the superscription. "Sumthin' goot in dat ledder. Mine poor poy Titus writes him!" he ejaculated, in a subdued tone.

Then tears gushed into her eyes and moistened her pale cheeks..

During all this time, for it seemed long to Angeline, she became pale with anxiety. Then tears gushed into her eyes and moistened her pale cheeks. But they were tears of joy, not sorrow—the wealth of that pure, honest heart now beating so violently in anticipation of the good tidings. When Hanz had somewhat controlled his feelings he sat down in the big chair, and with Angeline looking anxiously over his shoulder and holding the candle, opened and began reading the letter "Yesh, t'is mine poor poy Titus as writes him," he said, pausing for a moment. "Hish name shust as he wrotes him when a poy." The rest of the company looked on and listened in silence. Then he resumed the reading. "Vell, dere wash a pig sthorm, and t' ship most goes down to t' pottom. Den she does'nt go to t' pottom. No, she no goes to t' pottom. Den mine poy, he shaves t' ship." Hanz went over the letter in this incoherent manner, and then handed it to the Dominie to read for the entertainment of the company. The letter was dated at Bahia, where the ship had put in for fresh supplies, as was the custom with whalers. He gave a glowing account of the voyage, and the storm, and the persons he found on board. The good Dominie was several times interrupted by some one of the company invoking a blessing on Tite's head. And when it was announced that he had been made third mate of the ship, an expression of joy broke on every lip. The school-master shook Hanz warmly by the hand, and the innkeeper declared it would not surprise him if Tite came home captain of the ship.

"High, high!" exclaimed the Dominie, re-adjusting his spectacles; "here's news. An old acquaintance has turned up." Then turning to Critchel, he touched that odd old gentleman on the elbow, saying: "You remember the old grave-digger of thirty years ago, oh, Critchel?"

"Well, very well," replied Critchel; "he was a clever old man, and did his business well. He used to say I brought people into the world, and he sent them out."

"Bless me!" resumed the Dominie; "if here is'nt his son come to life again. The poor fellow! we all knew him well. Tite says here that he has found a good friend in the captain, an old acquaintance of his mother. And who do you think it is?"

Not one in the company could answer, although Angeline blushed, and looked confused. "Price Bottom, son of that clever old man, the gravedigger," concluded the Dominie.

"How strange," said the inn-keeper. "Old Bottom had many a glass of ale at my house, and never troubled anybody, except to dig their graves."

"He was very poor," rejoined Critchel, in a subdued voice, "and died leaving my bill unpaid. But he was an honest man, and paid when he had it."

"The son was a queer young man," resumed the Dominie. "Nobody seemed to care anything about him. And when he left the settlement it was thought he had got into the city and became a worthless. But here he is, made a man of himself and has not forgot his old friends."

This was good news to Angeline and Hanz. Still the name of Price Bottom, the grave-digger's son, revived old if not pleasant memories. The odd old captain had not forgotten his first love. The flame of that love always burns, but never dies out. Disappointment may cross it, may for a time veil its charm, but never can quench it. How strange, Angeline thought, that her darling boy, the consolation of her heart, should have met this once discarded lover, and under such circumstances. And that he should be such a friend and protector to her boy only showed how good a heart he had.

The good news gave an additional charm to the evening's entertainment. One after another shook Hanz and Angeline by the hand, and congratulated them on the happy prospect. Indeed, they seemed the happiest people on earth.

Mugs of fresh cider were filled and drank to the health of Captain Price Bottom, of the good ship Pacific—the poor fellow who had only a grave-digger for a father, and left the settlement friendless and without a shilling.

And now these sturdy settlers again took to their pipes, and having smoked in silence for at least five minutes, embraced and kissed their hosts, and parted for the night.

CHAPTER XV.

MRS. CHAPMAN AND THE UPPER CIRCLES.

Let us go back, gentle reader, into the village of Nyack on that same damp, stormy night, and into the house of Bigelow Chapman, the reformer. A very different picture was presented there. The reformer was up stairs, studying plans for the future. His spacious parlor was furnished with a profusion of furniture, of the most approved style, and such as was not common in the country at that day. They have got a new piano, too; and a nice young gentleman in reduced circumstances, a foreigner, is expected up from New York to give their daughter lessons on it. This little affair of the piano and the foreigner has set the whole town to talking, and people are putting on grave faces, and inquiring how they can afford it. But it seems they do afford it, and also to have the best of carpets on their parlor floor. And they have shown a taste for art in several engravings hung on the walls.

The Chapmans expected company from the city that night. A bright coal fire and a globe lamp on the centre-table are shedding a soft, mellow light, and adding an air of comfort and cheerfulness to everything in the room.

Mattie was sitting alone in the parlor reading a letter by the light on the centre-table. Her dress was a plain black silk, made high at the neck, and with an open stomacher, disclosing an aggravating bit of white lace. There was always something neat and becoming in Mattie's dress, and the white ruffles that now encircled her neck and wrists added the charm of simplicity to her appearance. Her hair, too, was almost golden, and hung in long, careless curls down her shoulders.

There was something of deep interest to her in that letter, for she read and re-read it, as her soft, blue eyes, so full of love and tenderness, almost filled with tears. Then she kissed it, and kissed it, and pressed it to her bosom. "Oh, how I wish he was here to-night, that I could tell him how much I love him;" she said, resting her head on her hand thoughtfully. "I would tell him all my thoughts and feelings, just as he has told me his. He is so true to me, and it never shall be said that I am not true to him, poor fellow!" she mused, and putting the letter to her lips again she kissed and kissed it. "They never can get me to love any one else, never!" she resumed, when the door opened and Mrs. Chapman entered, arrayed in her best millinery, and her front hair screwed into the tightest of curls. The good woman had evidently resolved to put on her very best appearance.

"These disappointments are very annoying, my daughter, very," she spoke, advancing and fretting her hand nervously. "If our company does not come then—well, all our dressing will be for nothing. I wanted you so much to see

Mr. Gusher, my daughter. He's such a nice young gentleman, so clever and agreeable—and has such a distinguished look, my daughter." Mrs. Chapman expanded herself, while emphasizing the word distinguished. She then filled the great arm-chair with her weighty person. "To get prepared for company, and city company at that, and then have company not come!" she resumed, casting a glance at Mattie, to see if she could discern in her countenance what impression she had made. But Mattie remained silent and thoughtful.

"It's not Mr. Gusher's fault, though. We must charge it all to the storm, I suppose. Then I did want you to see Mr. Gusher so much, my daughter. He is such a nice young man—and has such prospects. And prospects is what a young woman should look to when gentlemen come seriously inclined to matrimony—"

"Mother," said Mattie, interrupting, "I have got such a nice letter. It has made me so happy. I know you would like to read it. You always like to read my letters, you know." And Mattie looked playfully in her mother's face, and handed her the letter. "You will be delighted to hear from him. He says so many kind, good things."

Mrs. Chapman took the letter and scanned over it hastily. "And so it has come to this, has it?" she said, looking admonishingly at Mattie. "A letter from that sailor-boy, the son of them common Dutch people. Your father shall see this. Our daughter has stooped so low as to pledge herself to such a common man!"

"I love you, mother," said Mattie, "and I don't want to be disobedient; but I love him, and I know he loves me. Yes, mother, I love Tite just as much as if he was a rich man's son. I dreamed last night that he came home a rich man, and brought me so many nice things; and that we were married, and were so happy." And she threw her arms around her mother's neck and kissed her so affectionately. "Who knows, mother, but that he may come home rich? But even if he comes home poor, I know he will be good and true to me," she concluded.

"How very sentimental you are, my daughter," rejoined Mrs. Chapman, the little curls about her brow seeming to get tighter as her broad face grew redder. "Sentimental people never prosper, though—never knew one yet that did. Was silly and sentimental once myself. That was before I married your father."

"Oh," rejoined Mattie, playfully, "I am real glad that you remember those things, mother. Was father rich when you were married?"

Mrs. Chapman shook her head, and looked confused for a moment. "He was not rich, my daughter. But then he was so clever—and had such intellectual prospects. Brought up as you have been, my daughter, and with such accomplishments, and such prospects!—to throw yourself away on a sentiment. Just think of it! What would my mother have said if I had gone off and married a man just for sentiment's sake? I brought you up in strict regard to all the proprieties, and now you insist that you won't be a lady."

"Don't fret so, mother," said Mattie, again putting her arms around her mother's neck, and kissing her. "I will be a real good, obedient girl, and do anything you bid me. But then—" Here Mattie paused for a moment, and looked roguishly up into her mother's face.

"But then—what?"

"Well, I don't think we shall agree about Mr. Gusher. The truth is, mother—I don't know why—but then I don't think I ever can love him. But then, you know, mother, I have not seen him yet; and you would'nt have me love a man before I saw him?"

"Perhaps not, my daughter; but I would have you look up, remember your quality, and consider what you may be. If you condescend to look down on that sailor-boy, there's no hope of the family ever moving in the upper circles. But he'll never come back. That ship'll go to the bottom as sure as the world. Something tells me she will go down, and I know she will."

At this Mattie's eyes filled with tears, and she buried her face in her hands and gave vent to her emotions in sobs. "Mother, mother," she rejoined, after a short pause, "how cruel of you to say so, even if you thought so. He was so manly, and so kind to me."

At this Mrs. Chapman rose from her chair with an air of injured dignity, and walked in silence up and down the room for several minutes. Then she heaved a sigh, extended her hand, and resumed: "Your tears, my daughter, are what tear down my pride. No use, I see; my advice is all thrown away—all thrown away! Oh, what a thing it is to have a daughter, and yet not have a daughter. I mean to have a daughter that will have her own way." Again Mrs. Chapman resumed her chair, and became thoughtful and silent.

"You know I love to please you, mother, for you are such a good mother to me in everything else," rejoined Mattie, kneeling beside her mother, placing her arms on her knees, and looking up lovingly in her face. "You know I like to please you, mother," she repeated; "and I won't marry anybody until Tite comes home. But then you must not say anything more to me about Mr. Gusher."

"That's poor consolation—very poor consolation, my daughter," replied Mrs. Chapman, rebukingly. "Exactly what I did'nt want you to promise. Then you have promised yourself to the young man? I'd never have got your father if I'd made such a promise to such a young man. I have always looked forward to the time when we should have a fine house on the Battery, and move in the higher circles."

Chapman now entered the room, which put an end to the conversation between Mattie and her mother. Chapman smiled for once, and was evidently in a pleasant mood. After rubbing his hands and taking a seat by the fire, and looking first at Mattie and then at her mother, he said: "I have good news to tell you. The storm has prevented Gusher from getting here to-night. But the Kidd Discovery Company matter is settled, and will be a great success. No need of inventing a new religion now. Hanz has got his head full of the project. Has made all his Dutch neighbors believe there is a fortune in it for them all. We go on an expedition up the river to-morrow night, in search of the d——l's sounding-rock. That's the place where Kidd buried his treasure, you see. These honest old Dutchmen firmly believe that Kidd had an understanding with the devil when he buried it there. Just show them how to start an enterprise and make money, and they are as ready to make it as anybody."

CHAPTER XVI.

A NIGHT EXPEDITION.

The wind and the cold had moderated, and a heavy grey mist hung over the Tappan Zee on the following night. Hollow, echoing sounds came over and through the mist clouds, and re-echoed up the mountain. The scene was one common at that season of the year; still there was something strange and mysterious in the very atmosphere that composed it. Gloom hung over everything, and touched a melancholy chord in one's feelings. Curious figures, dim and indistinct, seemed to move and dance up and down, and thread their way through the curtain of mist, like phantoms in winding sheets. They were but delusions, betraying the eye. But there is a reality now; a steamer is seen cutting her way through the deep gloom, and throwing a long trail of light high up over the grey mist and reflecting curiously in the heavens.

Two stalworth men were seen walking down the road that night about eight o'clock, dressed in a style common to boatmen. One carried a pair of oars over his shoulder; the other had a well-filled haversack slung across his, and a crowbar in his right hand. They halted on reaching Bright's inn, and having stacked the oars and the bar against the little porch, entered, and were greeted by a number of friends already refreshing themselves at the counter. The appearance of these men—for they were known to be the best boatmen on the Tappan Zee—greatly surprised Bright and the gossips who were enjoying his ale around a little table. One and then another invited them to drink, but they refused, saying they had merely dropped in to light their pipes and look for the men who were to join them. Various questions were now put to them concerning their mission and its object. But the boatmen affected a mysterious air; and all that could be got from them was that when they returned it would be with money enough to buy all Nyack. They seemed somewhat disappointed at not meeting some one, whose name they would not disclose, at the inn.

Bright now mixed warm punches and set them before the boatmen, saying that on such a night they were just what were needed to prop a man's courage up. The men, however, steadily refused all invitations to drink, and when they had lighted their pipes, and bid the host and his customers good night, left the inn and proceeded to a landing at the bank of the river, where a boat with two men in it was waiting them.

The manners of the boatmen had so excited the curiosity of the inn-keeper and his guests, that no sooner had they left the inn than Bright and several others put on their hats and followed, resolved to see for themselves what was going on. Imagine, then, what must have been their surprise to find the men in the boat Bigelow Chapman and Hanz Toodleburg—both with heavy overcoats on. The boatmen were welcomed by the men in the boat, whose voices were plainly heard, and after exchanging a few words they threw in their oars carelessly and followed themselves. In another minute the little craft was heading up the stream, and disappeared in the thick mist.

"I have it all!" said Bright, turning to his companions with an assuring nod of the head, and lowering his voice. "Toodleburg—Chapman—a Dutchman and a Yankee—pick-axes, crowbars, and big ropes. Put them all together; add going off at night to it—dark and misty night at that—and there's something we'll all hear from in the wind. If Hanz and that quarrelsome Yankee have got their heads together, then the devil will get cheated out of Kidd's money. Sarves him right, too. Now them two is after Kidd's money. Always knew old Hanz could tell where it was."

The inn-keeper and his friends now returned to the inn and discussed the matter over warm punch until nearly midnight, or until their wits became so confused that the four men in the boat increased to forty. In short, Nyack waked up on the following morning to find herself filled with the wildest reports concerning this midnight expedition and its object.

The little boat moved on steadily up the stream, her sturdy oarsmen pulling at a measured stroke through the bewildering fog. In this way the boat was kept on up the river until past midnight, a glimpse of the land being caught here and there, an assurance to Hanz that they were not far out at sea. Indeed, Hanz began to get somewhat uneasy, and to wish himself back with Angeline in the little house. As this expedition, however, was to establish a solid basis for the great Kidd Discovery Company, out of which a fortune for Tite was to come, he was willing to run the risk of being lost in the fog for a night or two.

Towards morning the men became uneasy and hungry, and began cursing Kidd and all connected with him, and enquired of Chapman if he knew where he was going. Indeed, one of them declared it his belief that they had been brought on a fool's errand. Chapman, however, assured them that he knew exactly where Kidd had buried his treasure—that it was on a point not many miles below the Highlands, and under a big rock called the d———l's sounding stone. That if they kept on they would reach the place before daybreak. Hanz assured the men that every word Chapman said concerning Kidd was true, and this inspired their confidence, for they honestly believed his father to be an intimate friend of the pirate, and of course ought to know all about his money.

The boatmen now rested their oars and proceeded to refresh themselves. And while they were doing this, and wondering what this night expedition really meant, Hanz smoked his pipe and nursed his courage. In his heart, however, he wished himself out of the affair and in a more honest occupation. As for Chapman, he told a number of stories tended to excite the cupidity of the boatmen. After resting an hour or two the party proceeded about five miles further up the river, and landed just at daybreak on a point jutting into the west side of the river, and just above which there was a dilapidated little cabin, inhabited by a laboring man and his wife.

It would not do to disturb these poor people at so early an hour, Chapman said, nor to tell them what sort of a mission we were on. Thereupon Hanz and he proceeded up the bank of the river, to make, as he said, a discovery. So the boatmen were left to take care of themselves. The boatmen waited for nearly two hours, still neither Chapman nor Hanz returned. Where they had gone was fast becoming a mystery. The men at length became alarmed and disappointed, and proceeded towards the little house to enquire the name of the place, and see what they could do to get breakfast. Before they reached the house, however, the door opened and two half-naked, tow-headed urchins came toddling out, and as soon as they saw the strangers scampered back in a state of great alarm. A lusty dame, ragged and shoeless, and with her hair hanging loose about her neck, now came to the door, with a broom in one hand and a frying-pan in the other.

"Where on arth are you two come from?" enquired the woman, in a surly tone, as she raised her broom. "Another lot o' fools com'd to look for Mr. Kidd's money," she continued, without waiting for a reply. "Seems as if all the folks atween this and Yonkers had got crazy about Mr. Kidd, and was a comin' up here to dig for his money."

The men confessed that she was right in regard to their mission, and begged that she would get them some breakfast, for which they would pay her liberally.

"Yes!" rejoined the woman, angrily, "I know'd what you'd cum fur. Thar ain't nothin' in this house to get breakfast on—nothin' fur my poor old man and the two little children. Work's hard to get up here. And them fools what comes up here to dig for Mr. Kidd's money eat up what little we had, and did'nt pay fur it, nither. Go home, like honest men, and get some honester work than comin' up here thinkin' you kin find Mr. Kidd's money. Don't believe in Mr. Kidd—I don't!" The woman kept swinging her broom as she spoke. Then the two children ventured back and peered from behind her skirts at the strangers. "Don't believe he had any money, anyhow. If he had he was a mighty fool to come up here and bury it. People round here would 'a stole every dollar on it long ago. There's a Yankee and a Dutchman diggin' a big hole a piece above here—expectin' to find Mr. Kidd's money."

Such was the reception these boatmen met with at the hands of Mrs. Brophy, whose husband, a short, thick-shouldered, bullet-headed son of the Emerald

Isle, with a short, black pipe in his wide mouth, and in his shirt and trousers, came to the door and seated himself on the sill.

"Is it Misther Kidd's money ye's is afther?" he enquired, querulously, putting his elbows on his knees and resting his head in his hands. "Much luck may ye's have finding it. Divel a cint meself iver saw uv Misther Kidd's money, an' we've liv'd here this two years an' more. It's mighty little uv any other man's money—not enough, troth, to get bread for the childher—have we seen."

The boatmen enquired of Mr. Brophy if he could tell them where the devil's sounding-stone was. There was indeed a superstition amongst these poor people that Kidd had buried his money under a rock he gave that name to; and that there was an agreement with his satanic majesty, who was to stand guard over it, and allow only those who had the talisman to lay hands on it. This talisman, it was also believed, would open the devil's conscience, and cause him to lift the stone and unlock the great iron chest containing the gold and silver. Loud noises, it was said, were heard under the stone, which was the voice of the devil rebuking the follies of the men who came in search of this treasure. These poor people also believed that Kidd had murdered a woman in cold blood, and buried her under the same stone; that she would come to life when it was lifted; and that her ghost haunted the spot every night, and not less than a score of Dutchmen had seen it. The more religious of them declared that the ghost would hold communion only with a certain priest, who came once a year, at midnight, to invoke in an unknown tongue a blessing on her troubled spirit.

"The divel's soundin'-stone is it ye's wants?" ejaculated Mr. Brophy. "Shure, it's beyant—a mile, about—perhaps two—perhaps not so many—perhaps more. Much good may it do ye's when ye's finds it. An', an', an', the ghost standin' there ivery night." Mr. Brophy resumed his pipe, and after two or three whiffs resumed: "Ye's may dig holes till yer childhers wears rags, as mine does, an' not a mouthfull uv bread in the house, an' not a cint of Misther Kidd's money ye'd git. An' the ghost standin' there, too!"

Being satisfied that these poor people had nothing to give them to eat, the boatmen presented the woman with two dollars and what liquor there was in their flask, telling her to spend the money in bread for the children. This little act of kindness so softened the poor woman's feelings that she invoked numerous blessings on their heads; adding at the same time that it was more money than she had seen for a month, though persons in search of Kidd's gold and silver had beset her house.

The men now returned to their boat, and breakfasted on what they had in their haversack. And when it was nearly noon, and they were beginning to get alarmed, Chapman returned, apparently in the best of spirits, and accompanied them to a comfortable farm-house, about a mile up the bank. Here they found Hanz, very contentedly smoking his pipe, in the company of two others, who at first affected to be strangers. It soon became apparent, however, that these men had met Hanz and Chapman here by appointment. And it was also apparent that they were engaged in the same business of searching for Kidd's treasure. One was an ill-favored, talkative little man, who wore spectacles and the shabbiest of clothing, and seemed to pride himself in a bushy red beard and hair. In short, he was about as dilapidated a specimen of rejected humanity as Nature in one of her wildest freaks could have produced. Indeed, I may as well inform the reader that this person was Warren Holbrook, who, since his departure from Nyack, had been enlightening the people of this neighborhood by preaching the gospel of the "great advanced ideas," and in that way picking up enough to keep the wolf from the door, though it would not put clothes on his back.

Holbrook declared that the world had not used him well generally; but he never thought of looking into himself for the cause. He was willing, however, to relinquish the gospel of the advanced ideas for a business that would put money in his pocket and clothes on his back. Here he was, then, engaged in the business of getting up the great Kidd Discovery Company, by which every man who invested in it was to make a fortune.

The other was a slender, well-formed young man, perhaps twenty-five or six years old, of dark olive complexion, and black, oily hair that curled all over his head. His large black eyes were full of softness and were well set under beautifully arched-brows. There was, indeed, a moorish cast about his features, which were prominent and well lined; and when he spoke, which he did with a foreign accentation, he disclosed a row of white, polished teeth, every one set with perfect regularity. His hands, too, were soft and delicate, and on each of his little fingers he wore a large seal ring. He wore, also, a heavy gold neck-chain, and his dress was of plain black, made in the latest style and in great good taste. Romantic young girls just out in society might have been excused for selecting just such a man as a model lover.

The young man I have described above so neatly dressed, was Philo Gusher, of the great accommodating house of Topman and Gusher, extensively engaged in making discoveries and fortunes for all persons kind enough to honor them with their investments.

The boatmen found these men in a room at the farm-house, seated around a table on which stood a bucket half filled with what appeared to be ugly black sand. Just as they entered Mr. Gusher rose from his seat and exclaimed:

"Greatest discovery what was ever made. There is nothing like it in history. I tell you it is a great thing, gen-tle-men!" Here he raised his right hand, and then lowering it ran his fingers into the dark sand, and drew out a number of discolored Mexican and Spanish dollars. "Wis zat—what is in zat bucket, gen-tle-mens—and ze ouse of Topman and Gusher (me) is on a solid basis, as you shall see." Here he rang a dozen or two of the discolored dollars on the table, adding, "Zis Kidd Discovery Company is one zing so great as you ever did see, gen-tle-men."

"And we are indebted to this good, honest old man for all of it—I should say," rejoined Chapman, checking himself, "for selling us the secret." Hanz had been smoking his pipe quietly, and seeming to take but little interest in what was going on. Chapman now slapped him on the shoulder violently, and shook his hand. "We are indebted to you for this great and successful enterprise, eh? See the fortune now, don't you?"

"Perhaps I toes, und maybe I ton't," replied Hanz, relieving his mouth of the pipe. "I shees t' shand, und I shees t' tirty tollars—how I know where he comes from, eh?" Hanz began to have his suspicion aroused, and to feel that he had got into queer company. "T' tollar might get back to t' tivel when you gets him, if I vas only back mit mine Angeline!" said he, shaking his head doubtingly.

"It is very generous of our friend here," interposed Holbrook, running his fingers through his tufty red hair, and looking askance through his spectacles at Hanz, "to affect that he cares nothing about our discovery. Very kind of him. But we found the treasure exactly where he said it was buried."

Hanz shook his head, and looked with an air of surprise at the speaker. "If I tells you where dat gold und dat tirty shilver be's buried, und you goes dar und finds him, ten I be's asleep, und ton't know what I tells you."

"Te gen-tle-man," interposed Gusher, going off into a rhapsody of delight, "is very modest. It is very good of him to be so modest. But he, I am sure, will accept ze thanks of Topman and Gusher. Tis Kidd, gen-tle-men—he must be one jolly, generous fellow. I loves tis gen-tle-man Kidd. He bury his dollars here in bushel baskets full. We find him, eh?" Here he again ran his hand into the sand, and drawing out several more discolored dollars threw them on the table. "Te great big Kidd Discovery Company is one great fixed fact—one grand success, gen-tle-men. When ze customer come wiz his money, we shall say here is ze zing what makes you one grand fortune; invest your money and put your trust in Topman and Gusher."

Here, indeed, was the capital stock on which the enterprising firm of Topman and Gusher had started a great and flourishing joint-stock company. The boatmen listened to what they had heard with surprise and astonishment. They, in short, firmly believed that what they had seen in the bucket was treasure taken from the place in which it had been buried by Kidd.

CHAPTER XVII.

MR. GUSHER IS INTRODUCED TO MATTIE.

The Reverend Warren Holbrook was left in the farm-house to further develop the discovery, and lift the great enterprise into popularity among the confiding people in that portion of the country. The rest of the party, including Gusher, returned to the boat near sundown and set off for Nyack, the sturdy oarsmen singing a merry song. There in the bottom of the boat was the bucket containing the black sand and discolored dollars—the capital stock of the great Kidd Discovery Company—which Chapman and Gusher affected to guard with particular care.

They reached Nyack the next day about noon, looking fatigued and careworn, for they had enjoyed but little sleep since leaving. During their absence all sorts of wild rumors had been circulated concerning the object of the expedition. Imagination had made some of its highest flights, and even found a relative of Kidd, who was to join the expedition a few miles up the river, and who possessed the power to make the devil surrender sounding-rock—in case he proved obstinate and refused to acknowledge Hanz's authority. Titus Bright's inn was the place where all the wisdom of the settlement concentrated of a night. And it was here that all the various features of the great expedition were discussed over ale and cider. Sundry honest Dutchmen shook their heads suspiciously, and declared no good would come of it if Chapman got his finger in. Others said it was all clear enough now where Hanz Toodleburg got his dollars and his doubloons. It was no wonder that he was so much better off than his neighbors. Another declared that he had more than once told Hanz he would never get to heaven, and that secret on his mind.

When the boat reached the landing a number of persons were gathered there, all anxious to know what success had attended the expedition, and what discoveries had been made concerning Kidd's money. News that the expedition had returned soon spread over Nyack, and the town was greatly agitated. The arrival of Gusher, a gentleman of such distinguished personal appearance, tended still further to increase the agitation, and to give wing to wilder rumors. Hanz was received with salutations of welcome, for every one seemed glad to see him back. But where this foreign-looking gentleman came from, and what was his history, were questions they confounded their wits over without finding a satisfactory solution.

Considerable ado was now made in getting the bucket and its contents on shore, which was done with as much care and ceremony as if every grain of black sand it contained had been gold. And when a number of the coins had been exhibited to the bystanders, and the genuineness of the metal they were made of shown to be beyond doubt, the boatmen ran a pole through the handle and carried it on their shoulders up the road, creating such a sensation in turn that they were followed by a curious and astonished crowd, which seemed to increase at every step.

The effect was exactly what Chapman wanted. He had the precious treasure carried to his house and deposited, while Hanz and the boatmen proceeded to their homes, stopping at Bright's inn on the way, where they gave a marvellous account of their expedition and what they had discovered.

The portly figure of Mrs. Chapman, arrayed in her best millinery, stood in the door ready to welcome her dear husband and Mr. Gusher, who had proceeded in advance of the crowd.

"Allow me to welcome you to my house—such as it is, Mr. Gusher," said she, making a low courtesy, and then extending her fat, waxy hand. Mr. Gusher bowed in return, and received the hand formally.

"Madam, I am so very happy to have ze pleazure to zee you in your own house," replied Mr. Gusher, raising his hand to his heart, then lifting his hat and making another formal bow.

"I am sure you will forego all ceremony, Mr. Gusher, and make yourself at home. We are plain, unpretending people, and like to receive our friends in a plain, unpretending manner," resumed Mrs. Chapman, escorting her guest into the parlor, and begging him to be seated. "It seems so very long since we met in New York, Mr. Gusher. I never shall forget that visit, made so pleasant by your kindness. I have spoken of you so often, Mr. Gusher, to my daughter, that we both feel as if we were well acquainted with you—"

"Madam," interrupted Mr. Gusher, again putting his hand to his heart and making a formal bow, "you do me so many compliments as I don't deserve. I have anticipated ze pleazure and ze honor so much to zee your daughter. I am zure I shall be delight wiz her. If I shall speak Englis so well as you, then I shall be so happy. Then I makes myself agreeable to your daughter, I am so sure." Mr. Gusher was indeed quite embarrassed at the number of compliments Mrs. Chapman seemed inclined to bestow on him.

"Nyack is so dull and stupid—so very dull, Mr. Gusher. We only endure it, you know. And there are so few nice people in it—so very few we care about associating with," resumed this fat, fussy woman, giving her head a toss and extending her hands. "A few, a very few nice people have come up from the city—we find them very agreeable society, quite a relief. We intend to set up a residence in the city. How delightful to look forward to the day. We can then live in a style more agreeable to our taste."

"Oh! madam," rejoined Mr. Gusher, "I am sure you must be very happy. Your house is so very elegant. I should be so happy in zis house. (Pardon, madam, I cannot speak Englis so well.) And zen, wiz your beautiful daughter." Mr. Gusher placed his hand to his heart again, bowed his head gracefully, and assumed a sentimental air. "Oh, I shall be so happy to have my home like zis. And your beautiful daughter—she would sing to me, and she would play me sweet music, and read to me some poetry. You shall zee I am so proud of ze poetry—"

"How very kind of you," interrupted Mrs. Chapman, bowing condescendingly; "how very kind of you, to pay my daughter this high compliment. And, then, coming from so distinguished a foreigner. Indeed, Mr. Gusher, I have had a mother's responsibility in educating my daughter up to the highest requisitions of society. Then she's only a young, thoughtless girl yet, you know. Indeed, Mr. Gusher, if it was not that she is so intellectual—I say this out of respect to her father, whose intellectual qualities she inherits—I should feel alarmed about her. Indeed I should. She is so much admired. And there is nothing spoils a young, ardent girl so much as admiration."

Chapman now entered the room and suggested that Mr. Gusher, their guest, must be very much fatigued after so arduous an expedition. Mr. Gusher was thereupon shown to his room, and left to his own contemplations. In truth, he was glad enough to escape in this way from a continuation of this fussy woman's compliments. He had, however, created in his mind a beautiful picture of Mattie, with oval face, fair complexion, soft blue eyes, flowing golden hair, and a form that Diana might have envied, and a voice so sweet in song. As to her parents, they knew nothing of him, (perhaps it was well they did not); and he knew nothing of them. There was a mystery overhanging the means by which he had been brought in contact with these peculiar people. But the more he revolved the beautiful picture of Mattie over in his mind the more his anxiety to see her increased.

Mr. Gusher rested for two hours, and then re-appeared in the parlor, so exquisitely dressed and made up. Every hair on his head seemed to have been curled so exactly. The gentleman had evidently taken great pains to get himself up in a style that should be faultless. I may mention, also, that Mr. Gusher regarded himself as a very valuable ornament in the atmosphere of fashionable society—just such a nice young man as an ambitious woman just setting up in society would require at least a dozen of to make her first reception a success.

Mrs. Chapman and Mattie were already in the parlor, waiting to receive Mr. Gusher, "My dear sir!" exclaimed Mrs. Chapman; "you are looking so much improved. I hope you are rested? And now, sir, allow me to present you to my daughter—Miss Mattie, my only daughter. This is Mr. Gusher, my daughter. You have heard me speak of Mr. Gusher so often." Mattie blushed and looked confused, then courtesied in a cold and formal manner.

"I am so glad to make you my compliments," said Mr. Gusher, making one of his best bows, and moving backward with a shuffling motion, "I am so glad to make you my friend," he continued, bowing and placing his right hand on his heart. Mattie's beauty was quite up to the picture Mr. Gusher had drawn of it in his imagination. But her manner was so cold and formal that it not only disappointed but annoyed him. Instead of an ardent, impressible, romantic and even demonstrative girl, bubbling over with warmth and vivacity, here she was, as cold and formal as a charity school matron of forty summers.

"I hope, sir, that you will find your visit to Nyack pleasant," she replied, tossing her long, golden curls bewitchingly over her fair, full shoulders with her right hand, then motioning Mr. Gusher to be seated "Nyack is a very dull place, though. I am sure you will not find much in it to interest you. My mother tells me you are to make but a very short stay. I don't wonder you are anxious to get back, sir—"

Mrs. Chapman was at this time in a state of great alarm lest Mattie should say something not strictly within the rules of propriety. She shook her head and cast a significant glance at Mattie, then raised the fore-finger of her right hand to her lips, admonishingly.

"My daughter has not heard of the great enterprise yourself and my dear husband are engaged in—"

"I am so glad to make you my compliments!" said Mr. Gusher, making one of his best bows..

"Why, yes, mother, I have," interrupted Mattie; "did'nt Mr. Toodleburg and father go up the river to buy up all the vegetables for the New York market?"

"Oh, horrors! horrors! Why, my daughter, what put such a strange thought in your head? Think of it. Your intellectual father going into the vegetable business—and with a common old Dutchman! Oh, horrors, my daughter! What could have put such a thought in your head?" The fat, fussy woman affected to be overcome, and raised her hands in the very agony of distress.

"My daughter, Mr. Gusher, has a way of talking so at times. A little satirical, you know—inherits it from her father."

"My mother has spoken of you frequently, Mr. Gusher. I almost felt acquainted with you before you arrived. You do business in the city, she says. The weather is so very bad, I am sure you will not enjoy such a dull place as this," said Mattie, turning to Mr. Gusher and resuming the conversation, cold and emotionless.

"No, no, miss," rejoined Mr. Gusher, smiling; "I am zure I shall be so happy wiz you. Wiz you to zay so many good zings to me, my heart shall be in ze paradise." Here Mr. Gusher made a bow, and pressed his hand to his heart. "Wiz you for ze bird of zat paradise, oh, I shall be so happy."

"Then you and father are going into business, Mr. Gusher? I do hope you will be successful. If you can only get father to stick to business," resumed

Mattie. "He is smart at inventing new religions, and other things. Mother, (here she turned to her mother, who was in a state of great alarm,) how many new religions has father invented? I know how many churches he has built—"

"My daughter, my daughter!" exclaimed the impatient and perplexed woman. "Such things as churches don't interest Mr. Gusher. Mr. Gusher moves in distinguished society, and goes to a fashionable church."

"Oh, yes, madam, I go to ze very fazionable church. I go to zee ze ladies, and to enjoy ze sentiment of ze music. Zen I shall enjoy myself wiz your daughter more as well in your house. I shall do zat. Your daughter, she shall zing to me, and she shall play to me, and she shall read to me some poetry. I am so much love ze poetry."

"Truly, Mr. Gusher, I should make but very poor work in entertaining you by singing or playing," replied Mattie; "and as for poetry, I never had any taste for it. Father made me read Pilgrim's Progress until it has got to be a favorite book with me. Did you ever read it, Mr. Gusher? It is very interesting."

"Nevare, nevare!" returned Mr. Gusher, shaking his head and extending his hands. "I nevare read ze book of ze Progress Pilgrim. I read ze book what describe to me ze paradise of ze heart—love." How very aggravating, thought Mr. Gusher. Instead of a girl with a whole volume of poetry in her soft blue eyes, here was one whose very nature seemed devoid of sentiment. Still there was something in this cold and reserve manner, this indifference to Mr. Gusher's attractions, that tended to excite his ambition, for he was excessively vain.

"Your dear mother say I go to ze fazionable church. Yes, I go to ze fazionable church. I zee so many nice ladies, so many beautiful ladies, all my friends; and za make me so many compliments. Oh, yes, Miss Chapman, I have so many beautiful young ladies for my friend in ze church."

"I don't see how it can be otherwise, Mr. Gusher," returned Mattie, bestowing a look of admiration on him. "I am sure you would have a great many admirers if you lived in Nyack. But, then, you would not think of living in such a dull place."

"You do me so much honor, miss," rejoined Mr. Gusher, rising and making a bow. "I hope it shall be my honor to count Miss Chapman—what shall I say?—well, I will say as one of my so good friends."

"Indeed, Mr. Gusher, I have no such ambition. You have so many beautiful friends now. You would not, I am sure, condescend to include a simple country girl like me among them. I assure you, Mr. Gusher, I am not ambitious."

"You will have discovered by this time," said Mrs. Chapman, rising and making a low courtesy, "that my daughter delights in being eccentric. Oh, sir, she says a great many things she never means. She has got ambition enough. She would'nt be a Chapman if she had'nt."

Dinner was now announced. "I shall be so happy to escort you," said Mr. Gusher, nearly doubling himself in a bow, and extending his arm.

Mattie hesitated for a moment, blushed, and seemed confused. "Please, Mr. Gusher," she said, bowing and extending her right hand, "escort my dear mother." Here was an awkward situation. Mr. Gusher's knowledge of etiquette was for once put on trial by a plain, simple-hearted country girl. But his offer was intended only as a compliment, and surely, he thought, the girl would accept it in that light.

Turning nervously to Mrs. Chapman he extended his arm, saying: "Pardon, madam, pardon. You will understand?"

"Oh, certainly, Mr. Gusher," returned the ponderous woman. "You are so very kind—so very kind, Mr. Gusher."

Never before had Mr. Gusher escorted a woman of such ponderous circumference. Mattie followed, her roguish smiles indicating that she enjoyed what she considered a joke played at Mr. Gusher's expense. The picture presented by the meeting of such extremes was indeed a ludicrous one.

I will not weary the reader with a description of or explain a family dinner such as that generally spread by the Chapmans, nor with the many apologies made by Mrs. Chapman that they had not something better to set before so distinguished a guest as Mr. Philo Gusher. Chapman was already seated at the table, busy with a huge fork and carving-knife.

"We don't stand on ceremony here," said he. "Our visitors are always welcome, and expected to make themselves at home. (Pointing with the carving-knife to opposite sides of the table.) Take seats, take seats, now," he concluded.

Mrs. Chapman made a motion to seat Mattie on Mr. Gusher's left, an honor she did not seem to appreciate, for she insisted on taking a seat opposite—her proper place.

When dinner was over Mr. Gusher escorted Mattie back into the parlor. "You shall understand me better, miz, I am sure you shall, as we get better acquainted. And now you shall zing to me, and play me some music," said he, opening the piano and arranging the stool and music. "You will zee I shall make myself agreeable," he repeated two or three times, then extending his hand. But instead of accepting it Mattie returned a cold, formal bow, and proceeded to the piano unaided.

"The truth is, Mr. Gusher," said Mattie, running her fingers up and down the keys, and looking up archly in Mr. Gusher's face, "I am only taking lessons, and can't play or sing so as to interest you."

"Excuse, miz. You want I pay you ze compliment. Well, I shall do zat when I hear ze music."

The fair girl now tossed her golden curls back over her shoulders, and began singing one of the most solemn and melancholy of pieces, to her own accompaniment. Her voice was indeed full of sweetness, and she could sing with some skill and effect; but she was just at this time more inclined to play on Mr. Gusher's feelings than to do justice to her musical talent.

"There's something sweet and touching in this melancholy music, I like it, Mr. Gusher," she said, pausing and looking up in his face tantalizingly; "don't you?"

Mr. Gusher shook his head disapprovingly, and shrugged his shoulders. "No, no, miz; I nevare like ze funeral music. I go to ze funeral of my friend wiz music like zat."

"I am very sorry to hear you say so, Mr. Gusher. I play it whenever mother will let me. And I enjoy it so much. Reminds me of a dear young friend now far away."

"Now, miz, I makes my discovery," returned Mr. Gusher, turning over a leaf of the music, and looking enquiringly into Mattie's face. "Zat young friend, so far away, wiz his memory so near ze heart. Well, I shall think no more of zat. You shall zee I shall make my compliments, and shall cut out zat one young friend what is so far away. You shall zing me some grand music, so full of ze love, and ze poetry, so as my heart shall lift up wiz joy." Here Mr. Gusher flourished his hands and executed several waltzing steps, as an expression of how his feelings were excited by music.

Mattie turned suddenly around to witness this peculiar exhibition, when Tite's letter fell from her bosom to the floor.

"Ze revelation! Ze re-ve-la—what shall I say? If I only speak ze Englis so good as you, now!" exclaimed Gusher, affecting a loud laugh. And stooping down quickly, he attempted to seize the missive. Mattie was too quick for him. Regaining possession of it she restored it carefully to her bosom, an expression of joy and triumph lighting up her countenance.

Disappointment now took possession of Mr. Gusher's feelings. His manner indicated what his heart felt. Never before had his expectations and his ambition been so lowered, or his vanity so exposed. He had expected to find a beautiful, simple-minded country girl, ready with hand and heart to become a willing captive to his charms. And yet he had failed to make the slightest impression on her. Nor was that all. Her heart and her thoughts were evidently engaged in another direction. What, he enquired of himself, could her mother have meant by the encouragement she gave him to visit her home and see her daughter? His curiosity to find out who it was that held such possession of this beautiful girl's affections was now excited to the highest pitch.

CHAPTER XVIII.

ROUNDING CAPE HORN.

Mr. Gusher, with his pride wounded, and a heavy heart, took leave of the Chapmans early on the following morning, and crossed the ferry on his way back to New York. The black bucket containing the capital stock of the great Kidd Discovery Company, in which his fancy pictured a dozen or more fortunes, and which he bore with him, afforded no relief for his disappointment. It might be the means of his owning a fine house, riding in his own carriage, and being considered a rich man by society. But, after all, riches only embodied the hard features of dollars and cents. Who could find romance in the pursuit of dollars and cents? he thought. You could carry fame into the grave with you. Dollars and cents might buy you a fine coffin, and bring rich friends to your funeral; but they left you at the tomb door.

Had Mr. Gusher gone back to New York in the belief that he had made an impression on the affections of that pretty, simple-hearted country girl, Mattie Chapman, what a happy man he would have been. He resolved, however, not to be vanquished in this way—not to give it up—but to continue his attentions, and if possible gain a victory over her affections.

And now, gentle reader, you must accompany me to a very different part of the globe, and see what is going on there.

The ship Pacific had been refitted and put in sailing order at Bahia, and was now on her course for the Straits of Magellan. On reaching the latitude of the straits strong adverse winds set in, and gale succeeded gale until the sea became lashed into a tempest. The weather, too, was biting cold, and the crew suffered intensely. Not a gleam of sun had been seen for three weeks, and the ship's progress had to be worked by dead reckoning.

Morning after morning the sturdy old captain would come on deck, thrust his hands deep into the pockets of his pea-jacket, and look intently over the wild watery scene. Then he would shake his head despondingly. "Never caught it this way afore," he would say, addressing the officer of the watch. "Never caught it this way afore. Somebody's brought bad luck aboard, or we should'nt have such weather as this." Then he would disappear into the cabin and ponder over his chart, trying to work out the ship's position. But a strong current and the high wind, both setting in one direction, had carried him far beyond his reckoning, and into the vicinity of the Faulkland Islands.

All the light spars had been sent down, and for fifteen days the ship had labored in the sea under close-reefed topsails and jib, trying to make weather, but without gaining a mile.

On the sixteenth day the weather cleared up a little and the sun came out, and an observation was got, which showed that the ship had been carried into the vicinity before described. For once the sturdy old whale-killer had got drifted away from his course. But he declared it was all owing to the sea getting tipsy, the compasses getting tipsy, the chronometers getting tipsy, and the sun keeping himself rolled up in a blanket. You could'nt, he said, get a ship to look the wind in the eye when all the elements were tipsy. He was a lucky mariner who could get round Cape Horn without being tossed off his feet for a month—everything seemed to stagger so.

The wind now changed suddenly and blew as fiercely from the opposite direction, and the cold increased. The ship was at once got on her course for the straits, her reefs were shook out, and she bowled over the sea at the rate of nine knots. Still the sky continued black and cloudy, and the horizon misty and dim. The sea ran high, and broke and surged, filling the air with a cold, cutting spray, while the ship labored and strained in every timber.

Have you, my gentle reader, ever seen the broad ocean in an angry mood on a cold, pitiless winter day, when the horizon was hung with cold, penetrating mist, when all overhead was black with fleeting clouds, when the seas broke in their fury and threatened to destroy the frail bark under your feet, and when rain, hail, and snow alternately swept through the atmosphere, like showers of keen-pointed arrows—have you, I say, ever contemplated this sublime and impressive scene without acknowledging within yourself how omnipotent was God, and how feeble and insignificant a thing was man?

There is, perhaps, no other place in the world where Nature so combines all her elements to give an emphatic expression to the power and reality of the Divinity, as in the vicinity of this famous old Cape.

The bold, rugged headlands of Patagonia were sighted on the morning of the 4th of December. The wind had subsided a little, but a strong current was setting through the straits, and short, sharp seas, such as are experienced in the Bay of Fundy, indicated the ship's position as clearly as if a good observation had been got. Snow and ice nearly covered the ship, and the men continued to suffer from the cold. There was a feeling of encouragement now that the ship would round the Cape without any further trouble. But before noon a violent snow storm set in, and the bold, bleak hills of Patagonia disappeared from sight. The wind, too, veered ahead again and increased, and the ship had to be headed for the coast of Terra del Fuego, on the other tack.

Early on the following morning the look-out's attention was attracted by large spots of white light—now opening, now shutting—high up in the heavens ahead. It was Tite's watch on deck, and the look-out pointed him to the curious phenomena, which had not before attracted his attention. At the same time a painful and piercing chill seemed to pervade the atmosphere, and to seriously affect the feelings of the men on deck.

Tite watched these curious phenomena for several minutes, without comprehending what they meant. He thereupon called the captain, who came quickly on deck. As soon as his eye caught the gleam of light, he walked aft to the binnacle, and stood watching the compasses for a minute or two.

"There's trouble ahead," he said. "Call Mr. Higgins, and all hands—call them quickly. We are close upon an iceberg."

The first officer and all hands were quickly on deck, ready to obey orders. Every eye on board was now watching in the direction of the light.

"It's an iceberg, and a big one, too, Mr. Higgins. If she strikes it, there's an end of us!" said Captain Bottom, addressing the first officer, who seemed indifferent to the danger that threatened the ship. A rustling noise, as of strong tide-rips breaking ahead, was heard, the sound increasing every minute. The braces were now manned, the order to "go about" given, and the helm put down. But the ship had hardly begun to gather headway on the other tack, when she refused to obey her helm. It seemed, indeed, as if she was under the influence of a powerful attraction, drawing her to destruction.

Another minute and she struck with a deep, crashing sound, that made every timber in her frame vibrate, so great was the shock. A gleam of grey light now began to spread over the fearful scene. It was daylight, that friend which so often comes to the mariner's relief. The ship had struck broad on, and the berg seemed to have grasped her in its arms of death and refused to let her go. Each succeeding sea lifted the helpless ship, and then tossed her with increasing violence against the jagged ice-cliff. And as her yards raked the boulders, huge blocks fell with crushing force on her deck. Stanchions were started, the bulwarks crushed away from the knight-heads to the quarter-deck, on the port side, and the deck stove in several places. It seemed as if there was but a minute between those on board and death. Still the staunch old ship forged ahead, lifting and surging with every sea, and seeming to struggle to free herself from the grasp of the berg. All hope of saving the ship seemed gone now. Both officers and men waited in suspense, expecting, every lurch the ship made, to see her go to pieces.

It was one of those moments when presence of mind and seamanship seem of no avail to save a ship. On sounding the pumps it was found that the ship's hull was still tight, and that she had made but little water. Still she forged ahead, and great blocks of ice continued to fall on her deck.

When all eyes were turned towards the captain, and each waited with breathless anxiety, in the hope that he would give some order that would at least be a relief to their feelings, even though it were folly to execute it, Tite mounted the fore-rigging to the top-mast trees, the surging ship threatening to dash him against the ice wall every minute. In that fearful position he remained for several minutes, scanning over the scene ahead, and hoping for some gleam of hope.

There was still a hope of saving the ship. He waved a signal of encouragement to those below, and quickly descended to the deck. About half or three-quarters of a mile ahead there was a point indicating the termination of the berg. If the ship could be kept forging ahead she might possibly round the point and clear the berg in safety.

Tite communicated to the captain what he had seen, and his belief that the ship could be saved. All hands now went to work cheerfully, clearing the deck forward of the ice that had accumulated there. Then the fore-top-sail was clewed up, the spanker set, the yards braced up sharp, and the ship continued forging ahead with increased motion. Every yard of distance gained was measured with a watchful eye, and increased the confidence of those on board.

"We shall save her yet, captain," said Tite, a smile of satisfaction playing over his face. "We won't give up the good old ship!"

"God bless you, my hearty, God bless you!" returned the old captain, grasping Tite's hand warmly. "It's you shall have the credit of it if she weathers the point. Yes, sir, you. Killin' a whale is killin' a whale. Gives a sailor fair play in a square fight. But this being run down by an iceberg, and ship and all hands crushed to powder, gives a sailor no chance to show what there is in him. When a man gets killed according to his liking, why, then he's satisfied. But there's no way you could get satisfaction in being killed by an iceberg. It was'nt my own life I was thinking about, Mr. Toodlebug. Not a bit of it." Here he again grasped Tite firmly by the hand, and lowered his voice to a whisper. "It was my good old woman, sir, and the two little ones. Heaven bless them and keep them from harm!"

The ship still made fearful surges, and the ice grated and cut her planking; but she neared the point gradually, and this brought a feeling of relief to all on board. Open water beyond, and the bold, sharp lines of the point, made it almost certain that the berg terminated there. The point was reached at last. The ship seemed to give a leap ahead, and, as if by mutual consent, payed off and parted from the icy grasp of the monster. Cheer after cheer went up as the old ship, in her distressed condition, swung away and was out of danger.

The ship was now headed for Puntas Arenas, where many years ago the Spaniards founded a penal settlement. Intermarrying has, however, reduced the people to mere dwarfs in stature; and they have so retrograded in civilization that they are the greatest thieves and the worst savages to be found along the coast.

CHAPTER XIX.

MAKING A FORTUNE

Kidd Company stock was a feature in Wall street. The firm of Topman and Gusher, having luminated the great Kidd Discovery Company, had got it fairly on its feet in that mart of the money-changers. The firm was considered highly respectable now, and had counting-rooms in Pearl street, near Wall, second floor, furnished in a style of elegance it would be difficult to surpass, even at this day. If you would fortify the standing of a great and enterprising firm, Topman said, in his polite way, you must do it with elegant and elaborate furniture in your counting-room. Show is the thing two-thirds of the people in the world are attracted and deluded by.

The newspapers, too, were telling curious stories as to how Kidd's treasure was discovered, and also making statements of a very unreliable nature, setting forth that already several million dollars had been recovered, and that any man engaged in it would surely make a fortune for his heirs, no matter how numerous. The more unreasonable these statements were, the more readily did people invest in the stock. Not a solid man in Wall street had heard of the firm of Topman and Gusher eight months ago. The great beacon lights of the street now condescended to bow and shake hands with Topman, to take more than a glance at the firm's name when it was brought to their notice on certain bits of paper which the enterprising firm, for mere convenience sake, gave now and then as "equivalents". In short, Mr. Topman was a man of such impressive manners that he quite captivated Wall street, and to have those solid-pocketed old gentlemen speak encouragingly of the house, was, he considered, gaining a great financial victory. In addition to this Topman lived in a fine house, sumptuously furnished, on the west side of Bowling Green, had a servant in livery to open the door, and rode in his own carriage.

Mrs. Topman was a showy, dashing woman of thirty-five, or thereabouts, tall and slender, and somewhat graceful of figure, and might have passed for a beauty at twenty. But there was a faded look about her now, and she had a weakness for loud talking and overdressing. She was evidently a woman of doubtful blood, and "no family," as society would say in these days. Indeed, first-rate society, such as Bowling Green boasted of in those days, considered itself very select, and dealt out its favors to new-comers with a cautious reserve.

As little or nothing was known of Mrs. Topman's antecedents, first-rate society cut her—did'nt even condescend to drop her a sidewalk recognition. But, as pushing one's self into society was quite as much practised then as now, and as Mrs. Topman was a pushing, vigorous woman, she resolved that if she could not carry the outworks and compel a surrender on the part of first-rate society, she would at least have a circle of her own. And she had just as good a right, she said, to call her circle of society first-rate, as her neighbors who kept their doors shut had to "consider" themselves such. It was only an assumption at best. So the aspiring lady received what she called select company on a Tuesday, and entertained generally on Thursday evenings. But her neighbors tossed their heads, and said they were only third-rate people who went there.

Gusher, however, flourished in what might at this day be considered elegant hotel society. He was such a nice young man, dressed in such good taste, and had such unexceptionable manners. And there was such a distinguished air about Gusher, that Bowling Green was half inclined to look on him with favor. Mr. Gusher was a stock beau as well as a stock boarder at the City Hotel, where he was an object of admiration with all the languishing young ladies of the house. Indeed, the landlord of the City Hotel regarded Mr. Gusher as a valuable parlor ornament for the entertainment of his female guests of an evening, for he was an exquisite dancer, could sing, and make such gracious bows. Now and then a sensible girl had been heard to say she thought him a little soft; but her companions usually set that down to envy. Then it got whispered about that he was an unfortunate foreigner of a very distinguished family, and had been exiled from his native Spain for engaging in a revolution. Such were the prospects of this distinguished firm, socially and financially.

Nyack, too, had been kept in a state of agitation all winter over the discovery of Kidd's treasure, and wonderful stories were circulated of the fabulous amounts that were recovered every day.

Spring had come again, and the hills around Nyack looked so fresh, and green, and beautiful. Chapman had got Kidd stock into high favor with all the honest old Dutchmen in the county. And it was curious to see how these heretofore cautious people parted with their money for what Chapman called a "profitable equivalent."

Mrs. Chapman seemed to have increased in circumference and loftiness. She could get new and expensive dresses, and silk ones at that, every time she went to New York, and she went quite often now. And none of her neighbors could wear such fine lace on their caps. It was surprising to see how this fat, fussy woman could toss her head and talk of common people now. It was very annoying, she said, to have to live in a little country town like Nyack, and mix with everybody. Then her dear little intellectually great Chapman was such a jewel of a husband, and was so clever at inventing the means of making a fortune for other people.

The brain of Nyack was terribly disordered over the fortunes that were to be made in a month for all who invested in Kidd Discovery stock. Even the good Dominie, led away by the temptation, had invested all his savings, and had his pockets full of Chapman's "equivalents," from which he looked for a fortune in a very short time. Finally the innocent settlers began to regard Chapman as a great genius, who had invented this new way of making their fortunes out of sheer goodness. "I want to tell you, my good friends," he would say to them, patronizingly, "you will appreciate me better as we become better acquainted. Invest your money, and there's a fortune for you all." And they took his word, and invested their money, and, many of them, everything they had.

We must go back into the city now. It was a morning in early May. Knots of men were standing on the corners of Wall and Pearl streets, each discussing in animated tones some question of finance or trade. Men with hurried steps and curious faces passed to and fro, threading their way through the pressing throng, as if the nation was in peril and they were on a mission to save it. And yet it was only an expression of that eagerness which our people display in their haste to despatch some object in the ordinary business routine of the day.

It was on this morning that a woman of small and compact figure, dressed in plain green silk, a red India shawl, and a large, odd-shaped straw bonnet, called a "poke" in those days, on her head, and trimmed inside with a profusion of artificial flowers, the whole giving her an air of extreme quaintness, was seen looking up doubtingly at the door opening to the stairs at the top of which Topman and Gusher had their counting-rooms. She had the appearance of a woman in good circumstances, just from the country, where her style of dress might have been in fashion at that day. Her age, perhaps, was in the vicinity of forty, for her hair was changing to grey, and hung in neat braids down the sides of her face, which was round and ruddy, and still gleamed with the freshness of youth. Her shawl-pin was a heavy gold anchor and chain, and her wrists were clasped with heavy gold bracelets, bearing a shield, on which was inscribed a sailor with his quadrant poised, in the act of taking the sun. I ought also to add that she carried a big umbrella in her left hand, and a small leathern satchel in her right.

This quaint little woman's manner was exceedingly nervous and hesitating. Twice or thrice she advanced up the passage to the foot of the stairs, hesitated, returned to the door, and looked up at the number, as if still uncertain about some project on trial in her mind.

Men were passing in and out, and up and down the stairs hurriedly, as if some important business required all their attention. The little woman took no heed of any of them, and indeed seemed confused in her own thoughts.

Drawing a newspaper from her leathern bag she read in a whisper, at the same time tracing the lines with her finger, "Great Kidd Discovery Company. Capital $150,000. All paid in. President, Luke Topman. Corresponding Secretary, Philo Gusher. No. —— Pearl street." The little woman nodded her head, and looked up with an air of satisfaction. "I'm right. This is the place," she muttered to herself. Then putting the paper carefully into her pocket, and hugging the big umbrella close to her side, she advanced with a more resolute step up the passage, and was soon at the top of the stairs.

Again the little woman paused, for the number of names over doors seemed to confuse her. Just across the passage in front of her, however, she read over a half-glass door, and in large gilt letters, "Topman and Gusher, General Commission Business." And just below, and across the panes of ground glass, were the significant and attractive words: "Kidd Discovery Company. Capital $150,000. Luke Topman, President. Philo Gusher, Corresponding Secretary."

The little woman advanced and knocked timidly at the door, which was opened by a nicely-clad and polite youth, whose business seemed to be to admit customers. The little woman bowed and returned the young man's salutation.

"A lady visitor, Mr. Gusher!" said the young man, motioning the lady to enter. "That is Mr. Gusher, madam; junior partner of the firm."

A polished mahogany railing separated the vulgar customer from the highly dignified looking clerks inside. Indeed, there was an air of elegance about the establishment that somewhat surprised the little woman at first, and caused her some embarrassment.

"Ah, madam; pardon! pardon!" said Mr. Gusher, rising from his desk at the announcement and advancing to the railing. "I shall do myself ze pleazure, and ze honor of receiving such commands as you shall confide to ze firm," he continued, smiling and bowing gracefully.

"A little investment," returned the visitor, nervously. "I have a little money, left by my husband, who is at sea. I have no immediate use for it; but want to put it where it will be entirely safe. Entirely safe, above all things; a good dividend will not be objectionable. I am sure, sir, you understand that—"

"Ah, madam, you shall zee. Pardon! you will enter and take one seat." Mr. Gusher now condescended to open the gate, as he called it, bring the little woman inside, and bid her be seated. "Ze Kidd Discovery Company, madam, is one grand enterprise. You shall zee. And ze profit shall be so great you will not know where to put him. For ze safety of ze investment, (pardon, madam,) you shall accept ze honor of zis firm. O, madam, I cannot speak ze Englis so well. If my partner is here you shall zee he will satisfy you as ze reputation and ze honor of zis firm will be so great. You shall invest your money, and you shall zee zat ze honor and ze reputation of zis firm shall makes him safe." Mr. Gusher made a low bow, and pressed his hand to his heart in confirmation of what he had said.

A number of suspicious-looking men now entered the office and advanced to the railing, all affecting great eagerness to purchase and pay their money for Kidd Discovery stock. "You shall zee, mad-am," said Mr. Gusher, extending his right hand and shrugging his shoulders, "how much ze demand for ze stock in zat grand enterprise is. Ze rush for him is so great ze price will be double very soon—as you shall zee."

"Don't know how my husband would like it if he was here," replied the little woman, who had been nervously twitching and working her fingers, now opening the satchel, then shutting it. "Leaves me money enough to keep me comfortable when he goes away. Good provider, my husband is. Commands a ship, he does. Says 'look ahead, my darling,' when he goes away. 'Take good care of the coppers, darlin', don't let rogues and thieves get them; and remember that one-half the world is hard at work slanderin' t'other. Keep an eye t' wind'rd, darlin'. We've sailed along smoothly enough through life together, but there may be a dismal storm ahead. Life storms are dangerous. Here's a kiss, good little woman—good bye.' Then he goes away, and I sees no more of him for three years. That's a long time, sir. But he is so fond of the children, and such a dear, good husband to me."

"Mad-am," said Gusher, again bowing and pressing his hand to his heart, "wiz so good a lady for his wife, I am sure he shall be so happy and so proud." Detecting the small vein of eccentricity in the little woman's character, Mr. Gusher was evidently inclined to encourage it, hoping that it would still further develop her generosity.

"You are sure my investment will be perfectly safe?" enquired the little woman, looking up anxiously in Mr. Gusher's face.

"Oh, madam!" rejoined Mr. Gusher. "Oh, mad-am! Perfectly, as you shall zee. Ze honor of ze firm is pledged to zat."

The little woman now drew two thousand dollars from her satchel, and after counting it on her knee, passed it to Mr. Gusher. "I will invest this," she said, again looking up anxiously at Mr. Gusher, and then fumbling over the contents of her satchel, as if it still contained something she was in doubt how to dispose of. "I will take your word," she resumed, as if some sudden change had come over her mind. "Life's short, and speculation uncertain. I am from Yonkers. You have heard of Yonkers, sir? Yonkers on the Hudson. People of Yonkers are boiling over with excitement about the great discovery. Thank you for your kindness, sir. I hope the shares will go up. If

I should double my money, as you say I will, how father would laugh when he comes home. I call my good husband father, you know." The little woman ran on in this strange and confused manner until Gusher began to think she was never going to stop.

"Invested my money—independent—don't want nobody to know it. Will invest another thousand dollars if it turns out right. Yonkers people expect to get rich soon by Kidd shares. Nobody'll know it, you know. Don't want nobody to know it, you know. Come down here to invest so nobody would know it, you know—"

"I am so glad," interrupted Mr. Gusher, receiving the money, "you put your confidence in ze house. You shall zee zat ze honor of ze firm shall be your protection." As he proceeded to arrange the little equivalents with the picture of the big spread eagle at the top and the coffer dam at the bottom, the little woman fixed her gaze on the counting-room furniture, which seemed to attract her attention to an uncommon degree. Elaborately-finished and highly-polished mahogany desks were arranged around the room, the floor was covered with a soft carpet, and there were carved oak chairs, upholstered in green plush. The walls were hung with engravings and paintings representing favorite ships and steamboats, and a huge safe stood wide open, displaying shelves and drawers filed with books and papers. It was, indeed, a part of the firm's philosophy that what you lacked in substance you must make up in show.

There, too, was a door leading into Topman's private office, furnished with exquisite good taste. Topman was the great financial monument of the firm. Gusher did the elegant and ornamental.

George Peabody, the great philanthropist, made his fortune and his fame in a little dark, dingy office in Warnford Court, London. The pretensions of the great firm of Topman and Gusher were not to be confined by any such examples of economy.

A very clerical-looking man, with a round, smooth face, a somewhat portly figure, a high forehead, and a very bald, bright head, fringed with grey hair, and nicely trimmed grey side whiskers, stood at a desk, turning and re-turning the leaves of a big ledger. He was dressed in a neat black suit, and wore a white neckerchief. There was ledger No. 1, and ledger No. 2, and ledger No. 3, all so elegantly bound, and expressive of the business relations of the great firm of Topman and Gusher. It looked very much, however, as if the portly gentleman was only a part of the ornamental department of the great firm, for, having turned and re-turned the pages of No. 1, he would take up No. 2, and continue the occupation. It is true, he would pause now and then, and exchange a smile and a bow with some one of the customers waiting for stock.

There was also a slender, mild-mannered, and precisely-dressed young man, standing at another desk, and looking through a pair of gold-framed spectacles into a ledger. This was Mr. Foblins, registry clerk to the great firm. Mr. Foblins had a brigade of figures in column, and seemed continually busy putting them through a course of tactics known only to the firm. Mr. Foblins had his customers in column, with the number of shares and the amount invested, in front and rear ranks.

The word "Cashier" was painted over a third desk. And here a rollicking, talkative little man, with a round fat face, and a round bald head—a sort of fat boy that had been overtaken on the road of life by maturity—and who seemed to have a joke and a pleasant word for everybody, and was in the best of humor with himself, stood counting and re-counting, and passing out and receiving in money. This was Mr. Books, the merry little man of the establishment. Books entertained an excellent opinion of himself, and was in high favor with the customers, for he was witty, musical, and talkative. More than that, he was a stately little man, and well informed in all the great political movements of the day, and would entertain customers on the condition of the nation while counting their money. It was evident that Mr. Books was not in sympathy with the great enterprise his employers were developing, for he was continually saying witty but malicious things about Gusher, and would even point significantly with his thumb over his right shoulder. When a more than ordinarily verdant customer would come with his money, Mr. Books would shrug his shoulders, drum with his fingers on the desk, and hum a tune to the words—

"Fortunes made, and fortunes lost;Fools seek the phantom here at last," &c., &c.

Books had several times intimated an intention to set up a great enterprising banking and miscellaneous firm of his own. Indeed, his popularity with the patrons of the house was doing Mr. Books no good, especially as it entailed the necessity of his taking so great a number of drinks during the day that he would offer to bet the reputation of the firm that he was the tallest man in the establishment, and a politer man than Gusher. So good an opinion had Mr. Books of himself when under these little delusions, occasioned accidentally, as he would say, that it became a serious question with him whether his proud position was due to Topman and Gusher or his own great merits. In fine, it had more than once occurred to him that the firm was indebted to his personal popularity for its great reputation.

Mr. Gusher consulted Mr. Books, and entrusted him with the little woman's money. Then he proceeded to Mr. Foblin's desk, that gentleman turning over the pages of his big ledger preparatory to making an entry.

"What name did you say? I have the amount," enquired that gentleman, looking up earnestly over his spectacles.

"If you please, madam," said he, approaching the little woman with a bow, "you shall have no objection to give me your name. It is necessary as we shall keep ze book so correct."

The little woman hesitated for a moment, fingered the handle of her satchel nervously, then looked up inquiringly in Mr. Gusher's face. Then touching him timidly on the right arm with the fore-finger of her left hand she whispered, "Nautical, nautical, my nautical name?" Then her lips motioned and her finger pressed on Mr. Gusher's arm. Mr. Gusher looked at the little woman with an air of surprise and astonishment.

"Nau-tick-el? I do not understand zat, madam."

"Elizabeth Judson Bottom. That's my name," resumed the woman, raising her voice, and seeming to speak with a feeling of relief. "Bottom is my husband's name." Here she lowered her voice again. "Nautical. Commands a ship. Is away off in the South Sea, my husband is. There's nobody got a better husband than I have." The little woman said this with an emphasis and a smile of satisfaction lighting up her face. "You may have heard of my husband, sir? He is well known among nautical people. My husband sails the celebrated ship Pacific, and has made three successful voyages. You hav'nt had much to do with ships if you hav'nt heard of my husband. There, there, that looks just like the ship he sails in." The little woman pointed to the picture of a ship under full sail hanging on the wall.

"Madam, I am sure I shall know your husband," said Mr. Gusher, returning with the paper representing the number of shares the little woman had paid her money for. "I shall be so happy to zee him when he shall come home." Mr. Gusher handed her the paper, saying: "Now, madam, you shall take good care of zis. Your money, it shall be perfectly safe."

While this interesting little episode was being performed up stairs, an open carriage, showily caparisoned and drawn by a stylish pair of well-groomed bays, drew up at the door. A desperate effort had evidently been made to get the coachman into some sort of livery, for he wore a tall black hat, with a broad velvet band, and a buckle in front as big as an ordinary sized horse shoe. His coat, too, was of green cloth, covered all over with large brass buttons, and he seemed proud of his white gloves and tight-fitting breeches, which he kept looking down at every few minutes.

This was Mrs. Topman's new "turnout," which she had recently set up in opposition to one indulged in by a circumspect and very aristocratic neighbor. Topman alighted from the carriage, received and returned the bows of several persons on the sidewalk, and soon came hurrying into the counting-room, where he was received with great respect by the combined dignity of the firm.

"Madam," said Mr. Gusher, again addressing the little woman, "allow me to have ze pleazure as I shall present to you zis gentleman." Here Mr. Gusher introduced Topman, his partner, and gave him a short account of the business she was on.

"Why, my dear, good lady!" said Topman, grasping her hand with a freedom indicating that they had been old friends. "Your husband and me—why, we were old friends. If there is any man in the world I respect and admire, that man is Captain Price Bottom. If there is any man living I would rather make a fortune for than do anything else, that man is Captain Price Bottom. Yes, madam, not many years ago I used to swear by Captain Price Bottom; and if Captain Price Bottom was here to-day, I will venture to assert, on the word of a gentleman, there is no man who would sooner swear by your humble servant—"

"I am so real glad! My husband made friends wherever he went," interrupted the little woman.

"Glad! glad!" resumed Topman, "so am I. God bless him, wherever he goes! Go back, madam, and get all your neighbors interested in this great enterprise. Tell them the managers are old friends of your husband. Get them to bring in their money, madam, and secure a fortune!" Mr. Topman now showed the little woman the discolored dollars, a matter of great importance, which Mr. Gusher had omitted.

"Our motto is, madam, 'Never invest your money until you have seen your basis.' If you see your basis, and it is satisfactory, then come down with your money and await your fortune. You see the basis, now put your faith in the firm!" concluded Mr. Topman, politely bowing the little woman out. She took her departure for home, fully satisfied that she had a good friend in Mr. Topman, and that she had made a permanent investment.

CHAPTER XXI.

COMING EVENTS CAST THEIR SHADOWS.

The Great Discovery Company had run its race of prosperity. A few months passed, and the prospects of those connected with it began to change. Chapman went about Nyack shaking his head despondingly, and saying that he had been deceived by Hanz Toodleburg, who had deceived them all with his story about Kidd's treasure, and would be the cause of their losing a large amount of money.

"I never would have been caught in such a trap, but I believed Hanz Toodleburg to be an honest man, a very honest man, and I put faith in his word. But I have been deceived. Well, it is not the first time my confidence has been abused in this way," Chapman would say, holding up his hands, while his face assumed an expression of injured innocence.

Hanz, on the other hand, protested his innocence. Never in all his life, he said, had he taken a dollar of money not his own, and honestly made. He was persuaded to do what he had done by the gentlemen whom he supposed engaged in an honest enterprise. In truth, he had never suspected them of a design to get honest people's money in a dishonest way.

"If I toos t' shentlemens a favors, und ta makes t' money, und I makes no money, und t' peoples don't get no money pack, what I cot t' do mit him?" Hanz would say, when accused by the settlers of aiding designing men to get their hard earnings. But all he could say and protest did not relieve him of the suspicion that he was a participant in getting up the enterprise. In short, there was the old story of his knowledge of where Kidd's treasure was buried lending color of truth to the statements made to his injury by Chapman.

The innocent Dutch settlers would gather at Bright's inn of an evening, smoke their pipes, mutter their discontent at the way things had turned, compare their "equivalents," and relate how much saving it had cost them to get the money thrown away on them. If it had not been for Hanz Toodleburg, they said, not a man of them would have believed a word of the story about Mr. Kidd and his money. Indeed, they would insist on laying all their sorrows at Hanz's door.

Chapman had also circulated a report, which had gained belief among the settlers, that the trouble was caused by the devil refusing to surrender the key of the big iron chest; that he had been heard under sounding-rock, making terrible noises, and threatening to destroy every man working in the shaft. Then it was said that the ghost had reappeared and so frightened the men that they had refused to work. Another story was set afloat that the bottom had fallen out of the pit, and the iron chest containing the treasure had sunk beyond recovery. The simple fact was that the cunning fellows never expected to find a dollar.

These strange stories agitated Nyack for several weeks, and under their influence Chapman so managed to divide opinion that Hanz had to bear the greater share of blame for bringing distress on the poor people. One and then another of his neighbors would chide him, and say it was all his fault that they had lost their money and had nothing to show for it but these worthless bits of paper.

To add to Hanz's troubles, Chapman entered his house one day, and openly reproached him for bringing distress on his friends. "You know you have done wrong, old man," said he, assuming the air of an injured man. "You would not have deceived me—no man would—but that I took you for a Christian. And when I take a man for a Christian I put faith in him. That's why I put faith in you. I believed you honest, you see."

Chapman's familiar and even rude manner surprised and confounded Hanz. In vain he protested his innocence, and offered to call the Dominie and Doctor Critchel to testify that he had never in his life wronged any man out of a shilling.

"You sold us something you had not got," continued Chapman, in an angry tone, "and in that you committed a fraud. Honest men don't do such things—never! Mr. Toodlebug. I thought you were a friend; but you have deceived me—have deceived us all!"

The plot was now beginning to develop itself, and Hanz for the first time began to see what a singular chain of adverse circumstances Chapman had drawn around him. Never before in his life had a man openly charged him with doing wrong. Angeline was even more troubled than Hanz, and listened with fear and trembling to the words as they fell from Chapman's lips. What could have worked this change in a person who had so recently expressed such friendship for them? Her pure, unsuspecting soul would not permit her to entertain the belief that her husband could do wrong. She attempted to speak and enquire what this strange and unaccountable scene meant; but her eyes filled with tears, her face became as pale as marble, and her resolution failed her. Her little, happy home had been rudely invaded, and a grasping, avaricious enemy had shown himself where she expected to find a friend.

"I don't want to distress you, Mr. Toodlebug, I don't," said Chapman, keeping his keen eyes fixed on Hanz. "I don't want to distress you, I don't. But you must show that you are an honest man. Honesty is the best policy. I've always found it so, at least. You must make this thing all right, if it takes all you have to do it." When he had said this he put on his hat and rudely took his departure.

"Angeline, mine Angeline," said Hanz, "if dish bat man should make me loose mine goot name, den mine life it pees very misherable. What I toes I toes t' oplige t' gentleman. How I toes wish mine Tite, mine poor poy Tite, vas here." He sat thoughtfully in his chair for several minutes, then sought consolation for his wounded feelings in a pipe.

Chapman had not been long gone when Mattie came rolicking into the house, as if to form a bright and sunny contrast with the scene that had just ended. She carried a little basket in her hand, was dressed in a flowing white skirt and sack, wore a broad sun hat encircled with a blue ribbon, and her golden hair was decorated with wild flowers. There was something so fascinating in that merry, laughing voice, something so pure, innocent, and girlish in that simple dress and that sweet, smiling face, that it seemed as if Heaven had ordained her to represent truth and goodness. Setting the basket down on the table she ran to Angeline, embraced and kissed her, not perceiving that trouble had depressed that good woman's spirits.

"And you, too, good Father Hanz," she said, turning to him, and saluting him in her free, frank manner; "you shall have a kiss, too." And she took his hand and imprinted a kiss on his cheek.

She suddenly discovered that something was the matter, paused, and looked at Angeline with an air of surprise. Her first thought was that they had received bad news from Tite, which they were trying to conceal from her. Almost unconsciously her gentle nature began to beat in sympathy with Angeline's, and a tear stole slowly down her cheek. "You have heard from Tite; is he sick? have you heard bad news?" she inquired, in rapid succession, as she watched every change in Angeline's features.

Angeline shook her head, and looked up sweetly but sorrowfully in Mattie's face. "Nothing, nothing, my good child," she replied, kissing Mattie's hand. But there was the tear of sorrow writing its tale on her cheek. "God will bless and protect our Tite," she resumed; "but we have heard nothing from him since the letter you saw."

"I am so glad," rejoined Mattie, her face lighting up with a sweet smile. "I think about him every day, and I know he thinks about me. So, now, mother Angeline, you must cheer up. You will, won't you? It won't do to be sad when Tite is away." And, after patting Angeline on the shoulder and kissing her cheek, "you shall see, now," she resumed, bringing forward the basket, "what nice presents I have brought for you, Mother Angeline. Made these all with my own hands."

Here the happy, smiling girl drew from her basket a number of frills and wristlets, a worsted-worked candle mat, and a cambric handkerchief, in one corner of which she had ingeniously worked Angeline's name. "They are all for you, Mother Angeline, all for you," she said, tossing them one after another into her lap. "You are so good. Keep them all until Tite comes home. Then you can show them to him as a proof of what a true and good girl I have been."

Hanz viewed this act of kindness on the part of Mattie with an air of surprise and astonishment. It was in such beautiful contrast to her father's rudeness and severity that he was at a loss how to account for it.

"Vel, vel!" exclaimed Hanz, raising his hands, "you pees sho goot a gal as I ever did she. Yes, mine shild, I never shees no petter gals as you pees." And he rose from his chair, and approaching Mattie, patted her on the shoulder encouragingly. "You pees such a goot girl," he repeated, "and you will pe mine goot friend, eh?"

"Certainly I will. Why should I be anything else?" replied Mattie, looking up smilingly in his face.

Hanz shook his head. "It pees sho now as nopody can shay who pees his friend, and who pees not his friend. I pees sho glad you pees mine friend."

"I should like to know, Father Hanz, what troubles you?" resumed Mattie, whose quick eye read in his face the trouble that was making his heart sad. "Tell me what troubles you, Father Hanz, and I will be a friend to you, no matter who it is."

"Mine shilds," replied the old man, drooping his head, "dar vas un man, he shay as he pees mine goot friend. Dat friend he pees mine enemy. He prings shorrow into mine house. Unt he prings dat shorrow when mine poor Tite he pees sho far away as I ton't know where he is."

Tears again filled the old man's eyes as he spoke, and he paused, shook his head, and buried his face in his hands. There was something in the old man's unwillingness to disclose who it was that had caused him this trouble that excited Mattie's suspicions.

"You must tell me, Father Hanz," said she, encircling his neck with her right arm and patting him on the cheek encouragingly and affectionately with her left hand, "who has caused you all this trouble."

Hanz looked up earnestly and enquiringly into her face. Still there was a doubt in that look it was impossible to mistake.

"You ton't know, eh? you ton't know, eh? Maype as he is petter as you ton't know, mine shild. T' man what prings shorrow into mine house; t' man what shays I pees one tief t' mine neighpors—dat man he pees no friend of mine." Again the old man paused, and looked up inquiringly into Mattie's sweet face, as if anxious to trace the secret of her thoughts. And as he did so the breeze tossed the grey hairs over his forehead, as if to cover up the wrinkles age had written on it.

"Mine taughter, mine taughter," he resumed, grasping Mattie's hand firmly, "I'se gettin' old now. Tare von't pe no more of old Hanz Toodleburg shoon. You never know'd nothin' pad of old Hanz Toodleburg—does you, mine taughter?"

"Never, never! Why, Father Hanz, nobody has been saying anything against you," replied Mattie, smiling.

"Dar has, too," resumed Hanz. "What I lives for now is mine goot name, and mine poor Tite. I pees a friend to everypody what needs a friend, and now what I needs mineshelf is one goot friend. You she, mine taughter, if mine little farm he pees gone, and if mine sheep, and mine cows, and mine everything pees gone, den der is nothin' for mine Tite when he comes home."

The old man paused for a moment. It was impossible for him to keep the secret of his trouble from Mattie any longer. He opened his heart to her and disclosed the fact that it was her own father who had brought sorrow into his home. Yes, it was her father who had led him like a child into trouble, and then thrown around his acts such a chain of suspicious circumstances that you could scarcely find a man in the village, where but a short time ago Hanz was so great a favorite, who did not believe him guilty of inventing the Kidd Discovery Company, and bringing ruin and distress on his neighbors. There was the paper Hanz had signed, setting forth that he possessed the secret of where Kidd's treasure was buried, and bearing the proof that he had sold it for a consideration. Chapman understood the value of this, and went about the village showing it as a proof that there was at least one man innocent, and that man was himself. There, too, was the old story that had clung to him through life—that he knew all about Kidd, his father having sailed with him on the Spanish Main. And there was the expedition up the river, in which he had played so prominent a part.

Chapman well understood the effect these things would have on the minds of the ignorant and superstitious, and he turned them against Hanz with such skill as to completely get the better of him. In short, he would assert his innocence with so much plausibility that the simple-minded settlers began to believe him the saint he set himself up for, and Hanz the sinner who had got all their money.

Mattie heard this strange declaration made by Hanz against her father with feelings of sorrow and surprise. She hung down her head and remained silent for some time, for her mind was bewildered with strange and exciting thoughts. Then, looking up, she said:

"Cheer up, don't be sad, Father Hanz. You will always find a friend in me. My father shall also be your friend. We are going to leave Nyack, but I will come and see you, and be your friend. Don't think bad of my father, and he shall yet be your friend." And she kissed Angeline and Hanz and bid them good bye.

Mattie had never for a moment entertained the thought that her father would knowingly wrong these old people. Her heart was too pure, her nature too trusting, to entertain a suspicion of wrong. She had seen him engaged in transactions she did not understand; she had seen him associate with men she did not like, but she never enquired what his motive for so doing was. How he became acquainted with, and what his business with Topman and Gusher was, had been a mystery to her. The object was clear enough to her now. The conversation she had overheard one night between her father and Topman, relative to a meeting at Hanz's house, and getting him to sign a paper purporting to sell them a secret, was all explained. This conversation put a powerful weapon in her hand, and if used skilfully she could save her father from trouble and also protect old Hanz. Indeed, her mind ran back over a train of curious circumstances, which now became clearer and clearer, and when linked together discovered the object they were intended to effect. There was no mistaking the motive. Still, like a true and loving daughter, she saw her father only in the light of innocence and truth. The more she contemplated the matter the more sincerely did she believe him an instrument in the hands of Topman and Gusher, of whose designs she had heard others speak.

CHAPTER XXII.

THE CHAPMANS MOVE INTO THE CITY

Chapman had developed Nyack pretty thoroughly, had made money enough to feel independent, and attributed it all to his own virtues. He had got up no end of quarrels, invented new religions, established a hotel on principles of high moral economy, advocated broad and advanced ideas in everything, and kept the settlement in a state of excitement generally. Chapman was indeed a great human accident. There was no confining him to any one thing, either in religion, politics, or finance. He had a morality of his own, which he said belonged to the world's advanced ideas, and it was not his fault if there were so few persons enlightened enough to understand and appreciate it in its true sense.

Chapman was indeed not one of those men who carry blessings into a community with them, but rather one of those who seem to delight in planting curses wherever they go, and leaving their victims to reap the bitter fruit in poverty and ruin. Himself a mental deformity, none of his enterprises had been of any real benefit to the community, while his last and most reprehensible one had resulted in emptying the pockets of the old Dutch settlers, and leaving them bits of worthless paper to remember him by.

And yet this man could talk of himself like a very saint. He had the power, too, of making many of those who had suffered by his acts believe him honest. Indeed, while one portion of the community was cursing him for a knave, another was defending him as a really useful man—an opinion Mrs. Chapman was always ready to endorse. In short, Chapman had supporters in Nyack who would have sent him to Congress out of sheer love for his talents, which they were sure would have found a happy field for their development. Mrs. Chapman always sought to conciliate these friends, and would invite them to tea. On these little occasions, after discussing the merits of cider-vinegar and homemade pumpkin pies, and the care respectable people should exercise over the company they kept, for there was pure New England "grit" in the lady, she would recur to her dear husband.

"All Nyack will confess how intellectually great he is," she would say; "and show me the person who has done more to elevate the moral respectability of Nyack. Nyack was such a dull, sleepy place when—when we first honored it with our company. See what it now is. My dear husband worked up these low Dutch people so; yes, and he improved their morals. And I flatter myself I have elevated its society—a little."

Chapman had now thoroughly developed Nyack, financially and religiously. He had saved up a nice little fortune, enough with care and good management to keep him comfortable and give Mrs. Chapman a wider field for the exercise of her love of display. There was now little chance of making any more money out of Nyack, either by getting up quarrels between neighbors or inventing new religions. So the Chapmans resolved to go into the city and set up for very respectable people. As nobody wanted the big house for a church Chapman rented it to Titus Bright for an inn, and as nothing was said about moral restrictions, that worthy friend of the thirsty and weary traveller kept it in the good old-fashioned way of giving customers what they wanted and asking no questions. He would much rather, Chapman said, have seen it put to a less profane use, but as Bright was a responsible tenant, and could pay more rent than any one else, the morality had to sink in the necessity.

A few months passed and the Chapmans were set up in New York, in a spacious and well-furnished house on the east side of Bowling Green. Chapman was soon busy looking after the affairs of the great firm of Topman and Gusher, which I need scarcely tell the reader was a creation of his. Mrs. Chapman soon had enough to do at pushing her way into society. But the more she pushed the more did little social obstructions seem to rise up and defeat her efforts. She would associate with first-rate society, she said, or none; and Mattie should be introduced and shine in the "upper circles."

Bowling Green stood on its dignity in those days. There were very nice and very old families living there then, and they kept themselves rolled up in their wealth and comfort, and looked coldly down on all new and pretentious people. West Bowling Green, too, put on airs of superiority over East Bowling Green, which it affected to designate with the term "rather vulgar." They were quiet, well brought up people on the West side, people who had made a family name and were proud of it, whose superior enterprise and genius had raised them above ordinary people, and who had acquired wealth by honorable means.

There was, indeed, a charm about these families, made more attractive by the simplicity and gentleness of their manners, for they were refined, and entertained their friends generously. In short, West Bowling Green and a portion of the Battery had at that day a social empire of its own, which had a flavor of rich old wine about it, and was as distinct as distinguished in all its surroundings. It rode in its own carriage, had orderly and well-dressed coachmen, wore an air of great circumspection, dined at five o'clock, and lived like a well-bred gentleman.

East Bowling Green had begun to lose cast, and, indeed, was under a cloud socially. Its society was made up of new, fast, and somewhat showy people, whose antecedents it was difficult to get at, (at least West Bowling Green said so,) and who, for want of a family reputation, put on the airs of a vulgarian.

These people spent their money freely, and seemed to have enough of it, but they aspired to make a show rather than secure real enjoyment. They associated with third-rate people, and vied with each other in giving parties and balls to which all the young swells in town were invited. In fine, East Bowling Green had a cheap, retail flavor about it which all its show and extravagance failed either to conceal or atone for.

Mrs. Chapman had resided three months in Bowling Green, and yet first-class society had kept its doors closed—did not even condescend a smile. This was very mortifying to a lady whose pretentions were quite equal to her dimensions. A few second and third-rate people had made a formal call, or left a card. But it was merely as a matter of ceremony. Mr. Pinks, the elegant old beau of the Green, who was looked up to by first-rate society everywhere, and considered himself born to stand guard over it and protect it from vulgar contact, and who was accepted as authority in all matters of etiquette, and had standing invitations to dinner with all the best families, had called to pay his respects and congratulate the lady. But Pinks considered this strictly a matter of duty—to make an observation.

When Beau Pinks reported the result of his call to the Warburton family, who were first-rate people, and the Warburton family spread it through West Bowling Green, there was great amusement in the neighborhood.

"Won't do, the lady won't," said Pinks, lowering his voice to a whisper, and shaking his head. "Lady weighs two hundred pounds and more. A dead weight on the back of any society. Very pretentious, but makes shocking work of the King's English, and discovers low origin in her conversation generally. Puts on finery without regard to color or complexion, told me how many new dresses she had making, has big, fat hands, and wears common gold rings. Worse than all," continued Pinks, raising his hands, "the lady wanted to know if I could tell her how to reform servants, and if I liked rhubarb pies for breakfast."

With such a report from Pinks it was no wonder first-rate society did not take kindly to the lady. The rhubarb pies for breakfast settled the question in Pinks' mind, and he never called again, though he kept up a bowing acquaintance with the lady. Mrs. Chapman now fell back on a reception. A reception would be the thing to make Bowling Green surrender. The day was set and cards sent out, and notwithstanding Mr. Gusher, who was her standing ornament and idol, assisted her in drumming up recruits, the affair turned out to be very unsatisfactory. The nice people she invited sent regrets; and those who did come were second and third-rate people, who never miss a reception on any account, seeing that it affords them the cheapest means of showing themselves. There were cheap people then, just as there are cheap people now, ready enough to put in an appearance at a lady's reception, especially if she gave nice suppers and had daughters to be admired. Nor was it an uncommon thing, even at that day, for a pretentious woman who had just set up in society, and taken to the business of reception-giving, to find herself made the target of a little innocent satire by the nice young gentlemen she had invited to pay her homage.

Chapman differed from his wife, inasmuch as he regarded society as a great bore. Mrs. Chapman, however, was not a little disappointed at the way things had turned. They were flashy and rather fast people who came to her reception; people whom nobody of established respectability knew or cared to know—thoughtless young men, overdressed young women with matrimonial expectations, and a few needy foreigners with small titles. To make the matter worse, some of the lady's guests wore eye-glasses, through which they persisted in gazing at her, and conducted themselves very unbecomingly. Indeed, they eat up all her supper, spoiled her carpet, insulted her servants, and paid her certain left-handed compliments because she had neither coffee nor wine on her side-board. The foreigners, too, were inclined to be merry at the lady's circumference, and at the awkwardness of her movements, as well as to be severe on the style of her dress and the way she wore her hair.

"Who are these people?" enquired a young man, adjusting his eye-glass.

"Very new people," whispered another in reply.

"Vulgar, evidently—just set up to be somebody—don't understand it," rejoined a third, shrugging his shoulders.

Mr. Gusher, who had assisted the lady in beating up her recruits, had assured them that the Chapmans were very distinguished people.

Mrs. Chapman was not more successful in setting up a carriage of her own. She had done a great deal of pushing without affecting a lodgment in the society she had set her heart on. With a carriage of her own she felt that she would be just as good as any of those high old Bowling Green people. She had read of a lady in her carriage driving right into society and forcing a surrender.

Unfortunately the fools were not so plenty as formerly, the demand for Kidd Discovery stock had greatly diminished, and the expense of keeping up appearances in the city had far exceeded Chapman's calculations. Indeed, he had already begun to talk of the necessity of economy. Topman was already drawing heavily on the income of the firm to keep up appearances, and the future must not be overlooked. The lady had, therefore, to content herself with a one-horse turn-out, an establishment not very popular in Bowling Green even at that day. Although the lady had to accept the necessity, there was no getting along without a coachman, and Mr. Napoleon Bowles was engaged to wear a livery and wait on the lady in that capacity. Now Bowles stood about five feet four inches in his boots, was very fat and very short-legged, and very black, for he was a person of African descent and established color. Bowles weighed at least two hundred and fifty solid, so that when he drove his mistress out for an airing of an afternoon the whole establishment made so shabby and yet so comical an appearance as to afford the whole neighborhood a subject for amusement. Nor was there a more self-important person in all Bowling Green than Bowles—except, perhaps, it might be his mistress. But it was only when he got himself into those tight-fitting drab trousers, and that bright blue coat with double rows of brass buttons, and mounted that small, tall hat with the huge buckle in front, that he fancied himself seen to advantage.

Bowles not only became a feature in Bowling Green society, but indeed considered himself necessary to the dignity of the family he was serving, and in duty bound to fight any coachman who would make the slightest insinuations against it. This got him into numerous difficulties, for there was not a coachman in the neighborhood that did not set him down as a fair subject for unpleasant remarks. One called him a dumpling-stomached darkey; while another said he must have been brought up in the family and fed on puddings.

"Can't be much of a family," a third would say, "to have such a short-legged shadow as you for coachman, and only one horse. And such a livery as that! Why don't your mistress dress you like a man?"

Mr. Bowles had several times found himself measuring the pavement and his hat in the gutter, as a reward for his attempts to resent such indignities, which he considered were offered to the family rather than himself. There was so close a resemblance between the circumference of the lady and her coachman as to seriously damage the pretensions of the family, and bring down upon it no end of ridicule.

There was another serious impediment to the lady's pretentions, and that was no less a person than Mrs. Topman. No sooner had the Chapmans set up in Bowling Green than that lady took them into her keeping, promising them no end of introductions to nice people. Now, Mrs. Topman was one of those social afflictions which are found everywhere, whose touch is like contagion, and who take strangers into their keeping only to do them more harm than good. I have called them social afflictions for want of a better term. Mrs. Topman was the highest example of the species. She had been beating about on the outskirts of society without gaining an entrance into it until she was like a faded bouquet that had lost its freshness and perfume. In short, she was a tall, rakish looking craft, with ingeniously painted head-gear, carrying an immense amount of sail, and flying colors not recognized by good society in Bowling Green—at least not on the West side.

CHAPTER XXIII.

MRS. CHAPMAN GIVES A BALL.

It was a cold, dark night in December. The wind was blowing fresh from the northeast, the tall trees on the Battery were in commotion, and the ships in the harbor, seen through a pale mist, were straining at their anchors. A thin, pale mist hung over the sombre old fort on the Battery, over the trees, over the ships, over everything within the eye's reach. And the mist and the solemn beating sound of the sea-wail, in which the sailor fancies he can read all his sorrows, gave a weird and mysterious appearance to the scene. The Battery was nearly deserted that night, for at the time we write of only two old men could be seen, leaning over the railing on the sea-wall and watching in the direction of a ship at anchor in the stream, and looking as if she was just in from sea.

Mrs. Chapman was to give her ball that night. The lady had for several weeks given all her mind and energy to the preliminaries of this grand affair. Who was to be invited, what sort of new dresses she and Mattie would appear best in, who was to provide the supper, and what the whole would cost, were subjects which so engaged the lady's attention that she could think of nothing else. In vain did Chapman demur to the great expense and the folly of keeping up appearances under such circumstances. In vain did he insinuate the probable necessity of inventing a new religion as a means of bringing his revenues up to his necessities. A necklace of pearls and a diamond ring had been got for Mattie, and now a demand was made for a new and expensive dress. If there was anything in the world Chapman admired and submitted to it was his wife. In his thoughts she was above everything else, and he would surrender to her demands, no matter at what sacrifice. As for Mattie, he never seemed to care much about her, nor indeed to regard her with anything more than ordinary affection.

There was no getting along without the ball, Mrs. Chapman said. West Bowling Green had given two or three balls, and had not condescended to send her an invitation. It was very mortifying to get the cut direct in this way. She must bring West Bowling Green down by showing that she could give a ball of her own. And then it would be such a relief to her pride. And, too, it would be just the thing to show Mattie off to the best advantage. Mr. Gusher would shine brilliantly in a ball room, and so would Mattie, and if the young people could be reconciled in that way, why it would be money well spent.

Mrs. Topman was delighted at the prospect, and so was Gusher. And both had been going about among their friends for a week sounding the trumpet of Mrs. Chapman's ball, as well as telling their friends that the Chapmans were rich and very distinguished people. Bowling Green, then, was in a flutter that night. Chapman's house was brilliantly lighted, and carriages began to arrive and set down their gaily-attired occupants ere St. Paul's clock had struck nine. Then there was such a tripping of delicately turned little feet, such a flashing of underskirts, such a witching of perfumed silks and satins, such a display of white arms and white shoulders, as each bevy of beauties vaulted up the steps and were bowed into the house by the polite Mr. Bowles. Bowles felt himself an important element in the dignity of the family that night. His mistress had got him a new blue coat with large brass buttons, and a white waistcoat that reached nearly to his knees, and gave him the appearance of a huge ball of snow surmounted by an illuminated globe painted black. Bowles had delivered most of the invitations, and firmly believed that his mistress was indebted to him for the success of her ball, inasmuch as he had solicited guests worthy of her favor. Nor was he sure that the ball was not given by his mistress to show him off in his new clothes. Bowles had a bow and a smile for each of the guests. "My missus is right glad to sees you—she is. Be a heap o' dancin' did to-night," he would say, as he bowed the guests into the hall.

At ten o'clock the brilliantly-lighted parlors were filled, and presented the appearance of a garden of flowers variously colored. There were merry, laughing voices, graceful forms, young and happy faces, forming the light and shade of the picture presented to the eye. The ponderous figure of Mrs. Chapman formed a sort of central object. The lady was indeed got up in a gorgeous style of dress, for she wore all the colors of the rainbow, without their blending, had flounces nearly to her waist, giving her the appearance of an half-inflated balloon; and she had made a very flower-basket of her head. In short, the lady had made a bold attempt to improve on all known styles of dress, and at the same time to show her contempt for what other people might call taste in such matters. Thus elaborately arrayed she fancied herself as much a lady of quality as any of your fine old West Bowling Green people.

A number of exquisitely dressed young men had gathered about the lady, and although they paid her all manner of compliments, and said various pretty things in admiration of her charming daughter, it was evident that they regarded her as a rare curiosity, whose mental defects were affording them a subject for amusement. There the lady stood, receiving the congratulations of her friends and introducing her daughter Mattie, who was dressed in a plain blue silk with white trimmings, a wreath of orange blossoms on her head, and her golden hair hanging in simple curls down her shoulders. Indeed, the lady suffered by comparison with her daughter, whose charms were made more fascinating by the simplicity of her dress and the quietness of her manners.

In truth, Mattie had no taste for the show and extravagance her mother was so fond of indulging in. Nor could she see what object her mother had, or what really was to be gained by giving this ball. She felt in her heart that it was a piece of extravagance her father could not afford as an honest man, and she saw prominent among the guests persons she had long mistrusted of being his enemies. Gay as the scene was it had nothing in it to interest her. Her thoughts were engaged in something more real and true. They were wandering just then into a distant ocean in search of the object dearest in her affections, wondering how it fared with him. Then the picture of Hanz and Angeline, in their humble little home, revealed itself to her, and her mind filled with strange fancies as to the part she might have to perform in saving them from the trouble she saw foreshadowed in her father's conversation with Topman and Gusher. She little knew what sorrow had been brought into Hanz's home since she left Nyack; nor did it occur to her that old Father Hanz, as she playfully called him, might even then be within the sound of her voice.

The company had all assembled, the musicians were beginning to tune their instruments, and the time for dancing was drawing near. Mrs. Chapman flattered herself that Bowling Green would wake up in the morning to find that she had carried its outworks. But notwithstanding all the pushing she had done, and all the pushing her friends had done for her, she had not succeeded in catching the sort of people she had thrown her net for. There was Topman and Mrs. Topman, moving here and there in all the elegance of full dress. There were a number of others, who were always ready to accept an invitation where there was dancing to be done, or an opportunity afforded to show themselves in their best clothes. They were second and third-rate people, after all—people who get a cheap position in society through their proficiency in dancing, which they accept as the highest object a man or woman has to live for.

Poor Chapman moved about here and there like a raven among birds of brilliant plumage; and never did man look meeker or more submissive. There had been a curious change in his worldly affairs since the time when he preached humility and economy at Dogtown, and was ready to quarrel with any man who did not agree with him that show and extravagance were carrying the country to the devil.

"My wife, my dear wife, gives this ball," he would say, referring timidly to the subject. "My dear wife enjoys these things. Mrs. Chapman is very fond of young society, you see. I hope you are enjoying yourselves. There will be dancing soon—I never dance—and supper at twelve."

There was no man more elaborately got up that night than Gusher. Every hair on his head was trained into exact position, and his tailoring was faultless. In short, Gusher had got himself up with a view to making the greatest destruction on the female heart. He whisked about here and there, making himself useful as well as ornamental, for he felt that he had got the Chapman family on his shoulders, and was responsible for its reputation as very distinguished.

"Miz, you shall permit me ze pleazure, and ze 'onar, to open ze dance wiz you," said Gusher, approaching Mattie with his right hand on his heart, and making one of his extensive bows, "You shall do me ze 'onar, I am sure," he continued, and as he raised his head with an air of confidence, expecting to see her extend her hand, his eye fell on the familiar face of a young man standing at her side, engaging her in conversation. He paused suddenly, his face changed color from pale to crimson, and his manner became nervous and agitated. His whole system, mental and physical, seemed to have received a sudden and unexpected shock.

"Yes, my daughter, you must open the ball with Mr. Gusher. How very kind of you, Mr. Gusher," said Mrs. Chapman, with a courtesy. "It will be so very appropriate, my daughter, for you and Mr. Gusher to lead off." Mrs. Chapman had not noticed the singular change in Mr. Gusher's manner. He, however, recovered himself in a minute, and affecting not to notice the young man at Mattie's side, who still kept his eyes fixed on him, he resumed:

"Do me ze 'onar, Miz, and you shall make me so happy."

"I am sure, mamma," returned Mattie, "Mr. Gusher will excuse me. It was very kind of you to remember me," (turning to Mr. Gusher.) "But really I should appear very awkward dancing with you, who are so good a dancer. I am sure you will excuse me for the opening dance, Mr. Gusher, and I shall have the pleasure, if you will condescend to honor me, of dancing with you during the evening."

"My daughter, my daughter!" interrupted Mrs. Chapman, motioning with her fan, "pray don't be eccentric to-night. Accept the honor Mr. Gusher intended and please me—if only for once."

"I am sure, mamma, I always try to please you," returned Mattie, "and I appreciate the honor Mr. Gusher would do me, knowing how much my dear mamma admires him." Here Mattie paused for a moment and tapped her fingers with her fan, as the young man who had stood by her side turned and walked away for a moment. "It was very thoughtless of me, mother," resumed Mattie, ("you know I am only a thoughtless girl, after all)—but the truth is I am already engaged for the first dance."

"Engaged, my daughter, engaged?" Mrs. Chapman rejoined. "Pray, who to? It was very strange of you!" Here the young man returned to Mattie's side.

"Allow me to introduce you to my mother, Mr. Romer," said Mattie. "Mr. Romer, Mr. Gusher,—a friend of our family." Mrs. Chapman made a courtesy, and the two gentlemen bowed formally and coldly.

"If I mistake not," said Mr. Romer, who was a young man of polished manners, slender of form, with a frank, open countenance, and evidently a gentleman, "we have met before." He kept his eyes fixed on Gusher, as if resolved to read his thoughts in the changes that were going on in his countenance.

"Pardon, pardon, monsieur," returned Mr. Gusher, affecting an air of self-confidence supported by innocence. "I ne-var re-mem-bar as we has meets before. You shall zee I shall make you my respects. We shall meet again, I am sure of zat, zen we shall be such good friends. But I ne-var re-mem-bar zat we meets before."

"You were living in a castle then," returned the young man, coolly, "and I was only an outsider. People who live in castles at times don't remember common people."

It was a strange and curious meeting. Mattie saw there was something embarrassing between the two gentlemen, and came quickly to their relief.

"I am Mr. Romer's partner for the first dance," she said, addressing Mr. Gusher, with a bow. "It was very thoughtless of me. You were so very kind. But I am sure you are too generous not to excuse me."

"It is my great misfortune, miz. But you shall zee as I ne-var intrude myself. I shall have ze pleazure during ze evening." Gusher blushed and withdrew to another part of the ball room, where he captured Mrs. Topman, who was delighted at having such a partner for the first dance. Mrs. Topman was indeed popular as a dancing lady, and nothing pleased her better than to show her skill in the art in company with Gusher, whom all the pretty young girls said moved so nice on his feet.

The music now struck up and fell softly and sweetly on the ear, and the dancing began, and each figure seemed floating in the very poetry of motion, until the bewitching scene carried the mind away captive in its gyrations.

Mattie had never seen Mr. Romer, nor indeed heard of him before that night. She knew nothing of the relations existing between him and Gusher. She was equally a stranger to Mr. Gusher's antecedents. Her mind had, however, for some time been engaged trying to solve the mysterious agency that had brought him into business relations with her father. Being a girl of fixed character and good common sense, it was only natural that she should entertain an instinctive dislike for Gusher, in whom she saw a nature, if not really bad, at least frivolous and artificial.

The unexpected meeting between Romer and Gusher threw a shadow over the entertainment, so far as it affected the latter. Here he had been for weeks sounding the trumpet of Mrs. Chapman's ball, and looking forward to it as the means of making a temple of triumph of himself, and captivating no end of female hearts, Mattie's included; but how sadly he was disappointed. It had suddenly thrown around him a chain of difficulties that might blast his ambition, destroy all his hopes, and cause the veil he supposed was forever drawn over his past life to be lifted. The only way he saw of extricating himself from these difficulties, of cutting through them as it were, was by the force and skilful exercise of great coolness and impudence, and these he resolved to use, and use quickly.

And while the dancing was progressing a number of young fellows, who found more congenial enjoyment in their glasses and cigars, were seated at a table in a room down stairs, which Mrs. Chapman had provided as a sort of free-and-easy for such of her guests as were inclined to enjoy themselves in their own way. Chapman had provided generously, both of wines and cigars, which might have seemed strange to one of his Dogtown acquaintances. He had, however, so modified his ideas as to what constituted strict morality as to believe it would be nothing against a man in the other world that he had drank a glass of wine and smoked a cigar in this.

The young gentlemen were conducting themselves in a manner not recognized in the rules of propriety. Indeed, they had smoked so many of Chapman's cigars, and uncorked so many bottles of his wine, and drank the health of the family such a number of times, that they were fast losing their wits. When, then, Bowles made his appearance in the room, to see if there was anything he could do for the gentlemen, he found them talking so strangely of his mistress, and making so free with her personal appearance, that he considered it an indignity he was bound to defend by putting on the severest look he was capable of.

"Say, Charles," said one of the young men, addressing a comrade as he raised his glass, "who did you get your card through? What sort of a family is it, anyhow?"

"Got mine through Gusher. He's a kind of a spoon, you know. Don't know anything of the fellow, particularly—met him outside, you know. He's mighty sweet on the filly. She's pretty. Would'nt mind being sweet on her myself. I'd be a little afraid the old one would want to throw herself into the bargain. What a crusher of a mother-in-law she'd make," returned the young man.

"An odd-sized lot, anyhow," interrupted a third. "How frightfully the old lady's got herself up, eh? What a melancholy little specimen of humanity she's got for a husband, eh? Who are the Chapmans, anyhow?"

"Devilish new, devilish new," rejoined a fourth. "What a mixed lot they have got for company."

"Fill up! fill up! gentlemen. Here's a bumper to the beautiful daughter. Beauty and modesty carry us all captive in their charms. Let us drink to the daughter." And they filled their glasses and drank Mattie's health.

"When my missus inwites pussons to de ball, my missus 'specs dem ar gemmens what is inwited to presarve dar qualifications. If gemmen am gemmen den dey don't cum'd to my missus's ball to suffocate her!" said Bowles, expressing himself, and assuming an air of injured dignity.

Bowles had to pay dear for his speech in defence of the family, for the young gentlemen surrounded him, and, getting him into a high chair at the head of the table, compelled him to perform all sorts of antics for their amusement, such as making speeches and singing songs. They also made Bowles drink so many times to the lady whose livery he had the honor to wear, that he lost his senses, and fancied himself fighting any man who had said a word against the family. Indeed, it soon became necessary to extinguish Mr. Bowles, and to that end the young gentlemen rolled him up in the table-cover, and put him carefully away in a corner, where he soon went into a sound sleep, and remained until his master woke him up on the following morning.

CHAPTER XXIV.

VERY PERPLEXING.

While these young gentlemen were thus enjoying themselves, and taking such liberties with Mrs. Chapman's favorite servant, Romer entered the room, and was followed in a few minutes by Gusher. They had again met unexpectedly, for there was something nervous and hesitating in Gusher's manner. Romer seemed to be a general favorite with the young men, and they insisted that he fill his glass and join them in drinking the health of the family.

"You will pardon me," said Romer, turning to Gusher when they had set down their glasses; "I took the liberty I did up stairs through mistake."

"It is no matter, mine friend," returned Gusher, patting Romer on the shoulder familiarly. "I ac-cept ze ap-pology. You are one gentleman, I am sure. We shall be very good friends." It was curious to see how quick Gusher regained his confidence and coolness.

"I mistook you for a gentleman I once met in Havana. I understand you have been there," resumed Romer, keeping his eyes steadily fixed on Gusher.

"My farer, he has very large estates in ze Havana. Mine friend, I love ze Havana." Here Gusher put his hand to his heart, and became exuberant. "It make me so much joy to zink of ze day when I shall be back in mine own Havana."

"Knew I had seen you there. You would'nt be likely to remember me, however. Let us fill our glasses, and drink to the pleasant days we have spent there—"

"Oh, it is so many years since I was so happy zare," interrupted Gusher, coolly.

They filled their glasses and drank to the happy days they had spent in Havana. "At least the wine may quicken your memory as to the time we met. About the time I refer to," continued Romer, still watching Gusher's manner carefully, "which was about the time we met, a fellow of wonderful audacity was flourishing, and so attracting public attention by his skill in rascality that little else was talked of. Louis Pinto was his real name; but he regarded names as a matter of no consequence, and used the names of rich and respectable gentlemen whenever a necessity demanded."

"You shall give me zat hand," replied Gusher, extending his hand and taking Romer's, with an air of refreshing coolness. "You bring ze gentleman to my mind. When I shall speak ze truth I shall say he was one grand rascal, I remember him just so well as you shall see."

"I am glad," resumed Romer, "that you know him for a grand rascal. Rascal as he was, I had great admiration for him. He had three remarkable virtues—impudence, coolness, and audacity. I call these virtues because a man possessing them may go through the world and have a history of his own. It was Louis's ambition to do the State some service one day and ornament society with his presence the next. One day he relieved a rich old gentleman of his pretty daughter and twelve thousand ounces, and did both so cleverly that his skill was more admired than condemned. Carrying off the daughter did not seem to offend the old gentleman so much; but his grief was so great over the loss of his ounces that he employed means of recovering them, and with them the thief, whom he had sent to prison to repent of the sin. Louis was rather fond of a change, and accepted prison life as a relief from the labor society required of him, and as a necessary benefit to his health rather than a punishment. He once relieved me of some diamonds, and in such a manner as to make me remember him for his skill."

"I tells you, mine friend," interrupted Gusher, "zat grand rascal 'onar me in ze same way. He gets ze diamond. And I ne-var gets zat diamond back. He make me so much trouble. I am mistake for him so many times." Gusher now proposed that they should fill their glasses again, which they did, the rest of the company joining and drinking to the health of the family.

"That he is taken for you," resumed Romer, "might be considered a compliment, as far as looks go. If I remember right the fellow was exceedingly handsome."

This seemed to excite Gusher's vanity. Laying his hand patronizingly on Romer's arm, he looked up in his face with a smile of injured innocence. "I care nosin for myself; it is wiz mine friend he make me so much trouble."

"You're to be pitied, sir, very much to be pitied. Of course you are not Pinto, and yet the dashing, handsome fellow will insist in trafficking on your reputation. How very aggravating to a gentleman of your position. It requires a genius to do that well. That's what I admired Pinto for. The fellow had such a number of family histories at his tongue's end, and could apply any one of them so cleverly to his own case. In short, he knew exactly how to suit his customer. But you will remember, Mr. Gusher, the most amusing thing of all was the number of fathers he had. To-day he had a Spanish father, who had been through all the wars of Spain; to-morrow his father was a Frenchman who had smelled powder in all the battles fought by Napoleon. They were generals, too. There was one bad feature about Louis's fathers. They were all unfortunate gentlemen, who managed to fight on the wrong side, and got their estates confiscated and their families left destitute."

Romer paused for a moment, but kept his eyes fixed on Gusher. Still there was no change in his countenance. The young gentlemen who had been so merry but a few minutes before, now put down their glasses and listened with intense interest to the conversation.

"You shall zee, mine friend, (wiz your permizion I shall call you mine friend,") replied Gusher, still cool and nonchalant, and again giving Romer's hand a decided shake, "I have hear zat grand rascal tell ze same story so many times. You shall know zat I meets ze grand rascal on Broadway—a few days ago—"

"You met him in New York, eh?" resumed Romer, affecting great surprise. "Looking just as fresh and rosy as ever, I suppose, and as ready to give himself up to the business of ornamenting society." Romer patted Gusher on the shoulder familiarly, and smiled.

"If you should meet him again," he resumed, playfully, "and it is more than likely you will—stop him. He does'nt take offence easily. Keep your eye on him. Tell him you are a friend of his, and have a lady with a fortune you would like to introduce him to. That will gain his confidence. Then slip this card into his hand. It contains my address. Tell him I am an old friend of his, and have some old and important business I would like to settle. Don't let your modesty interfere with your intentions, you know."

Gusher took the card, and after affecting to read the name placed it in his pocket, without exhibiting the slightest change of countenance. "You shall zee I shall do myself ze 'onar of being your diplomat," said he, bowing himself formally out of the room.

"Romer, old fellow, what's up?" enquired one of the young men. "A spoon, ain't he, Romer?"

"Not so much of a spoon, I take it," said another. "Considers himself a planet illuminating the social hemisphere of the Chapman family."

"You must pardon me, gentlemen," said Romer, "for introducing a conversation so strange to you. It refers to a matter which concerns the gentleman and myself, which he perfectly understands, and you may hear more of soon—not now."

Another, and very different scene from that described above, but which forms an essential part of this history, was being enacted just outside. While the sound of the music was reverberating over Bowling Green, and mingling curiously with the sea-wail; while the dance went on, and all seemed gay and festive within, two old men, bent with age and poorly clad, were seen in front of Chapman's house, one of them leaning on a staff. They were the two shadowy figures seen on the Battery in the early part of the evening, looking anxiously out in the direction of a ship at anchor in the stream.

Their manner indicated that they were strangers in the city, uncertain of the location they were in. They would move slowly up and down in front of the house, then pause and listen to the music, the tripping of feet, and the sound of merry voices. The shadowy figures seen flitting through the curtains seemed to bewilder them. Then, after consulting together for a few minutes, and as if armed with some new resolution, they would ascend two or three steps, as if intent on seeking admission to the house. Then their resolution would seem to fail them, they would hesitate, and return slowly and reluctantly to the sidewalk.

Then he of the staff stood in the shadow of the street lamp, and as he did so his kindly but wrinkled face, his white, flowing beard and hair, reflected in the dim light, formed a striking picture of age made touching by sorrow. Then his eyes brightened and his lips quivered, and after looking sorrowfully up at the scene before him for several minutes, he motioned his companion to him, laid his trembling hand on his arm, and said:

"Tar pees no shustice in dis. He prings shorrow hinto mine house, unt shust now his house pees full of peeples what rejoices. I gits mine preat mit t' sweet of mine prow, so ven I ties I ties mit mine conscience so clear as I shays t' mine Got, ven I meets mine Got, dar pees no tirt on mine hands. If I only gits some news from mine poor Tite, Critchel, some shoy comes t' mine poor heart." And he shook his head as he said this, and leaned on his staff, and tears coursed down his wrinkled face.

The old man was overcome, and had no power to restrain his emotions. It was several minutes before he regained control of his feelings. Then he raised his head, and wiping his wet, dripping beard, he pointed with the fore-finger of his right hand upward, and resumed: "Critchel!" said he, in a tone as decided as it was touching, "Critchel! if tar pees un shust Got, un I knows in mine heart as tar pees un shust Got, He come to mine aid, unt He shows he pees angry mit t' man vat shays he pees mine friend t'tay un prings shorrow into mine house to-morrow."

"God will make a just reckoning with us all—depend on that, Hanz," replied the other. "But it will do no good to stand here. We must wait until to-morrow." And the two old men proceeded up Broadway and were shut from sight in the mist. It will hardly be necessary to tell the reader that one was Hanz Toodleburg, the other Doctor Critchel.

Two days before the sheriff of the county had seriously disturbed the peace of Hanz's little house by walking in and making service of a legal document of immense length—Topman and Gusher vs. Hanz Toodleburg—and in which the names were recapitulated so many times, and in so many different ways, as to bewilder Hanz's mind and send him into a state of deep distress. In short, Topman and Gusher, (Chapman's name was not mentioned, and for reasons which any sharp gentleman of the legal profession will understand,) had entered suit against Hanz, charging him with having made certain contracts he had not fulfilled, of procuring money and certain other property for the sale of secrets he did not possess, and indeed of having deceived and defrauded the plaintiffs, and of committing crimes enough to have sent at least a dozen men to the penitentiary. And all this to the serious damage, as well in reputation as pocket, of the highly enterprising and rapidly advancing firm of Topman and Gusher. And the plaintiffs prayed, as virtuous gentlemen are known to pray in such cases, that the defendant's property might be attached, and such damages decreed as in the discretion of the court justice demanded.

The great Kidd Discovery Company was bearing bitter fruit for Hanz. Never before had a sheriff darkened his door, for it had been the aim of his life to owe no man a shilling, and never to quarrel with a neighbor. But here he was with law enough for a life-time, and all for doing a kindness for people he thought honest. He saw Chapman's finger at the bottom of the transaction, but the more he pondered over his troubles the more his mind got bewildered. He knew that before a court his simple story would weigh as nothing against the proof they could bring that he had been associated in some suspicious way with all the circumstances which led to the formation of the great Kidd Discovery Company. There, too, was a paper, bearing his own signature, and indeed a confession of guilt.

In the midst of his grief it occurred to Hanz that a man who had invented so many religions must be something of a Christian, so he resolved to see him face to face, and have an honest talk with him. To that end he persuaded Critchel, who was his friend and adviser always, to bear him company into the city. He forgot that there were religions, based on what are called advanced ideas, and invented so plentifully in certain portions of New England, having little of either heart or soul in them, and which are in truth a cheap commodity, used more to advance commercial than spiritual purposes.

There was still another reason why these two old men were found in the city on that night. Nothing had been heard from Tite, or indeed the ship on which he sailed, for more than a year, and great anxiety was felt for her safety. A report, however, had reached Nyack that day that one of the Hudson Company's ships had arrived at New York, and the hope that she might bring some tidings of the ship Pacific quickened his actions.

CHAPTER XXV.

AN UNLUCKY VOYAGE.

Let us go a little back, reader, and trace the course of the ship Pacific and those on board of her. The iceberg had rendered her almost helpless, and we left her bearing up for Punta Arenas. Having made temporary repairs there she sailed for Coquimbo, where she was thoroughly refitted and provided with new anchors and chains. The great expense and delay incident to this had seriously interfered with the prospects of the voyage, and to such of the crew and officers as were on shares left but little hope of returns. This naturally produced a feeling of discouragement and despondency.

And when the ship was about to proceed on her voyage to cruise among the islands of the Pacific, the second officer disappeared mysteriously, and Coquimbo was searched in vain for him. Tite was accordingly promoted to fill his place. The crew had great confidence in him, for he had shown himself not only the best sailor on board, but had exhibited in cases of great peril such quickness and courage as are necessary to the highest standard of seamanship. Hence it was that the change, while it did not dispel the gloom occasioned by the second officer's mysterious disappearance, gave satisfaction to all on board, except, perhaps, Mr. Higgins, the first officer, who had almost from the day of leaving New York regarded Tite with a feeling of undisguised jealousy.

The lucky old ship Pacific, with her famous old whale-killing captain, had made a bad voyage of it this time.

Fifteen months had passed since she took her departure off the Highlands of New York, and now she had just weighed anchor, and with her canvas spread once more was bidding good bye to Coquimbo, and proceeding to cruise among the islands of the South Sea.

Weeks passed and still the old ship tumbled and rolled about on the placid waters of the Pacific, now touching at a port to get news of the whaling fleet, now anchoring off some island to have a talk or trade with the natives. But all the news the sturdy old captain could get was bad.

Bad luck had followed the whaling fleet through the Pacific that year. The habits of the whale in changing his locality at certain periods are somewhat curious, and afford old sailors a subject for the most wild and unreasonable stories. The sailors, yielding to their superstitions, attributed the scarcity of whales to the appearance of a number of mermaids, whom the natives on various islands had reported, and the sailors sincerely believed, had been seen and heard singing in various parts of the Pacific that year, and under very suspicious circumstances. The sailors had also a superstition that whales entertain so great a dislike for mermaids as to proceed to visit their friends and relatives in another sea as soon as they made their appearance.

Captain Price Bottom declared he was too old a whale-killer to put any faith in the story of the mermaids. Whales, he said, had sense and pluck, and were not to be frightened away by such fish as mermaids. He had his deck cleared, his gear put in order, his boats' crews told off, and officers and men kept practising and made familiar with their duties. Still not a whale showed his head, or blew a challenge to put their skill in practice. The bluff old captain began to feel at last that luck had left him. Morning after morning he would loom up in the companion way before the crew was up, gaze up at the lookout aloft, ask the usual questions concerning the night's sailing, then shake his head despondingly.

"Fifteen months out—sixteen months out—and not a whale killed!" he would say. Then taking the glass he would make a turn or two of the quarter-deck, looking here and looking there, as if to satisfy himself that there was nothing between his ship and the horizon. Then lowering his glass he would nod his head affirmatively, and say: "Mermaids ain't got nothin' at all to do with it. Somebody's been a tellin' them whales I was comin'. Whales has got more sense some years than other years. Know when there's harpoons about as well as any of us, and keeps at a comfortable distance."

One morning he appeared on deck in a more serious mood than usual. Tite was officer of the watch that morning, and the old captain, after pacing up and down the deck several times, apparently in deep study, approached him with his hand extended.

"When I give a young man like you my hand, I gives him my heart, too. If there's a man aboard of this ship what I respect, it's you, Mr. Toodleburg. Yes, sir, I respect you for your mother's sake, as well as for your worth as a sailor and a man." And he shook Tite cordially by the hand, and spoke with such an emphasis.

Then setting his glass down on the binnacle, he took Tite by the arm, and, whispering something in his ear, led him to the taffrail, as if he had something of importance to communicate in private.

"You have a sweetheart at home, I take it, Mr. Toodleburg?" he said, inquiringly, and assuming a very serious manner. "Every young man like you should have a sweetheart at home. Somebody to think about. Somebody to cheer one up. Them we leaves at home is all men like you and me go through these hardships and disappointments for."

Tite blushed and smiled, and made an evasive reply.

"No use denying it, my hearty," he resumed. "Knew ye had a sweetheart thinkin' of ye at home. Show her by yer conduct while yer away that yer worthy of her when yer get home. My sweetheart, God bless her! is all the sunlight I have in a voyage of this kind. My little wife is my sweetheart, she is, Mr. Toodleburg. She an' the two little angels are the sunlight of my heart. There ain't nobody sails the sea has a trimmer little craft of a sweetheart nor I have." He paused for a minute, as if to collect his distracted thoughts. "The man that would bring trouble to her door while I'm away—he would'nt be a man, Mr. Toodleburg," he resumed, still preserving a serious countenance. "Had an ugly dream last night. That's what troubles me. Anything happens to me, Mr. Toodleburg, you're the man I looks to as a friend to my little sweetheart and them two angels at home."

Tite assured him that he would do as he desired, and at the same time tried to dispel from his mind the gloomy forebodings impressed on it by the dream.

"Never had an ugly dream of that kind that it did'nt foretell somethin' bad, Mr. Toodleburg," he replied to a remark made by Tite, that it was not wise to give one's self uneasiness concerning dreams. "There's sharks a' land as well as sharks a' sea. Keep that in your mind, my hearty. And I dreamed that my time had come, and my poor little sweetheart at home was surrounded by sharks ready to devour her. Made my blood boil, it did. Waked up feelin' for a harpoon to throw among 'em. My ghost'll haunt the man that wrongs my little sweetheart.

"That's not all, my hearty. Somebody's brought bad luck aboard—that's certain. A voyage begun in bad luck, as this ere voyage has been, never ends in good luck. But you're young, and so cheer up. Look ahead, and never let present misfortunes discourage you.

"England honors Scoresby to this day. And Scoresby was successful after two voyages that ruined his owners. As to them mermaids frightening away the whales, it's all a superstition. The natives on Queen Charlotte's island have a superstition that there is an island down north of them, called No Man's island—for no man, as they say, was ever seen on it—where there is a subterranean sea peopled by these mermaids; and that these mermaids have built them a palace, where they hold their revels and do all sorts of strange things, even to decoying navigators into it. That story won't do. Don't believe a word of it, Mr. Toodleburg."

That morning about ten o'clock the lookout aloft called, "Whale, O!" The glad announcement sent a thrill of joy over every one on board. The crew turned out with cheerful faces, and every one looked eagerly in the direction pointed to by the man aloft.

"Where away?" was the quick enquiry from the deck.

"Off the larboard bow—three miles. There he blows!" was the response.

A light breeze was blowing, and the ship was bowling off four knots, with her port tacks aboard. There was no one on board more elated at the prospect than the sturdy old captain. Seizing his glass he looked for a moment in the direction indicated.

"There he is!" he exclaimed, lowering his glass. "Clear away the boats and bear away for him, my hearties."

The lashings were cast away, the davit-tackle falls overhauled, and a larboard and starboard boat was launched and manned, and in a few minutes they were dashing over the waves, the men pulling that steady, strong, and even stroke which gives such propelling force to the whaleman's oar. The men on board cheered, and their cheers seemed to quicken the action of the boatmen. The sturdy old captain watched their progress through his glass, every few minutes giving expression to his feelings in words of hope and encouragement.

"An old coaster, that whale is—thirty, yes, nearly forty barrels there. Got pluck, too, that whale has. Can always tell when a whale's got pluck. Them old ones are ugly customers when they gets their pluck up," he would say, nodding his head decidedly and encouragingly.

The ship was now kept away a point or two, and proceeded under easy sail. There was something thrilling in the scene, and every heart on board beat with excitement as the boats went swiftly on, one commanded by the first officer, the other by Tite. Neither of these two young men had seen a whale killed; but there were in the boats old whalemen, who had successfully thrown both harpoon and lance.

The huge monster could now be seen clearly with the naked eye by those on the ship's deck, sporting lazily on the surface, his bright black sides now falling, now rising, like the hull of some water-logged ship, and throwing up thin white volumes of spray, over which the sun's rays reflected with singular brilliancy. Nearer and nearer the boats approached the monster, the first officer's boat being a little ahead. Now the stern boat ceased pulling, and the men laid on their oars. Then the other slackened her speed, and began pulling with cautious and quiet stroke. The lookout announced that the head boat had made the whale, and the men climbed the ship's rigging to witness the struggle. They were doomed to temporary disappointment, however, for the whale, suddenly discovering his pursuers, made a vault and a plunge, tossed the sea into commotion, and disappeared.

"That's what comes of sendin' an amateur after an old whale," said the captain, thrusting his hands deep into his nether pockets, shrugging his shoulders, and pacing nervously up and down the deck.

A signal was now made from the ship directing the boats what course to keep, for experience had taught the old captain what course the whale would take, and where he would be most likely to appear again. It was nearly half an hour before the monster lifted his huge, dripping sides above the surface again, but so near the first officer's boat that a harpoon was let go. They had fastened to him, and the scene became more exciting.

"Bad strike," said the captain, shaking his head and stamping his feet. "That whale's going to die hard." The harpoon, in short, had fallen weak, had failed to touch a vital part, and had made one of those wounds which excite a whale to attack his pursuers.

The word "astern" was given as soon as the harpoon was thrown. The monster threw up a thin wreath of slightly discolored spray, and set off at a velocity of speed almost incredible. Away he went, the boat following in his wake and cutting the water like a thing of life—the boat-steerer and line-tender carefully watching every movement, for the lives of all on board depended on their vigilance. The whale struck his course directly across the ship's bow, less than a mile away. The boat Tite commanded followed, with all the strength her crew could put on their oars.

It was easy to read in the captain's manner, however, that all was not going well with the boats. He quickly ordered a third boat launched, supplied with gear, and the best oarsmen on board to hold themselves ready to man it.

"Thar'll be a fight when that ar whale rises," he muttered, rather than spoke. "Wants a lance in the right place, and a man to put it there. Mr. Higgins ain't the man for that work."

The boat's speed began to slacken. The sharp, whizzing sound, caused by the rapid paying-out of the line and its great tension, gradually subsided. It was evident the whale was coming up to blow, perhaps change his course, perhaps attack his assailants. He had crossed the ship's course, and the head boat was nearly two miles off the starboard bow, the stern boat rapidly coming up.

The water just ahead of the boat began to quiver and curl into eddies, then the huge monster lifted himself, as it were, high above the surface, struck his flukes, and lashed the sea into a foam. This lasted for several minutes, the boat pulling for him with all the strength of her oarsmen. But when nearly alongside of the whale she suddenly slackened her speed, then stopped, then went "astern hard." It was evident to those on board the ship that something was wrong, for the boat seemed to be manœuvring more for her own safety than to gain a position from which a lance could be hurled with effect.

"Too many landsmen in that boat!" said the old captain, who had been carefully watching every movement through his glass; now hoping, now fearing. He shook his head doubtingly, and paced the deck nervously for several minutes. Then, as if there was something it was necessary for him to set right, he turned to the officer of the watch, and ordered him to have the third boat manned. In another minute he was standing in the bow, lance in hand.

"Pull away for him, my hearty bullies," he said; and the men plied their oars, and away the boat went, skimming over the water like a sea-bird. There was resolution and courage depicted in every feature of that bronzed face.

The whale had now turned and was proceeding with open jaws to attack the first officer's boat. Another minute and he would have destroyed it, and perhaps all on board. Just at that moment Tite's boat came up, and with a quick, bold, and dexterous movement, rounded close under the whale's off side, and with a strong arm sent a lance home. That lance made a deep and fatal wound. The enraged monster forgot in a moment the object he was in pursuit of, threw up a volume of deep red spray, then making a desperate plunge, disappeared. He had no intention of giving up the battle, however. He merely sought relief for his wounds in deep water. The boats now waited and watched for the result. After waiting nearly twenty minutes the monster rose again, directly ahead of the captain's boat, and so near as to dash the spray into it.

"Take that!" said the old captain; "that iron'll stop your fightin'." And he hurled his lance, with quick and deadly aim, giving an order at the same time to "astern hard." But before sternway could be got on the boat, the infuriated monster made a sudden turn, dashed upon and stove it into fragments.

The famous old whale-killer had hurled his last lance, had killed his last whale. The dying monster, in making a last struggle with his enemies, had struck the captain with his fluke, and he sunk never to rise again.

CHAPTER XXVI.

DUNMAN'S CAVE.

Flags hung at half mast the rest of that day, and minute guns were fired at sunset. And there was something sad and solemn in the dull, booming sound as it echoed and reechoed over that broad and mysterious sea. And when night came, and drew a dark curtain around the ship, and her timbers murmured and complained, and every sail stood out in shadow against the clear sky, and the surface of the water seemed alive with sprites, flitting and dancing here and there, groups of sorrowing men were seen gathered about the decks, giving expression to their grief at the loss of their old captain.

"God bless him! He was good to us all. There'll be no more whales to kill where he has gone." These were the words of regret that fell from lips that rarely invoked a prayer.

At midnight, when the bells had struck, the crew gathered together on the forward deck, and while one held a lamp another read the Episcopal service for the burial of the dead. And as the light at times reflected each figure of the group, giving it a phantom-like appearance, the picture presented was sad and impressive—such as can only be seen at sea, where each sound calls up some memory, and the sailor fancies he can see the spirit of some departed friend in every flitting shadow.

Officers and men alike began to feel how great was their loss. They were alone, as it were, on this broad and mysterious ocean, and they had lost that odd old man who was their guiding spirit, and who never failed them as friend and protector. All through that night the men watched and strained their eyes in every direction, expecting to see the old sailor rise on some crest; and more than one sailor that night cheered his drooping feelings with the firm belief that some mysterious agency would give them back the old captain before morning.

There was no one on that ship, however, who felt the loss more seriously than Tite. It seemed to change all his prospects, to throw a shadow over his future. He paced the deck, silent and thoughtful, until long after midnight. To him the captain had been not only a friend, but a father. Between them there had grown up the strongest of attachments. Tite had looked forward to the time when this odd old man would have lifted him into the confidence of his owners, and perhaps secured his future prosperity.

All his hopes and joys seemed blasted now. Love, too, had been playing its bewitching part; amidst all these drawbacks and disappointments, love had been prompting his ambition with her dreams of a happy future. Mattie's image, so bright, so beautiful, had been with him everywhere, prompting his thoughts and actions as only the woman you love can, and making him more ambitious to secure that golden future his fancy had pictured. Never before had his courage failed him. No matter what the danger, he had felt that she was at his side, encouraging him. Now the gloomy thought of returning home penniless, with, indeed, nothing but his adventures and misfortunes to offer her and his aged parents, began to prey upon his mind, to make him sad and despondent. Then the advice so often given him by the old captain, never to get discouraged, not even under the most adverse circumstances, and that the brightest day was sure to follow the darkest night, would cheer him up.

When the whale had been taken aboard, the ship, under her new commander, Mr. Higgins, stood away into the North Pacific, where she cruised along the land, in the direction of Behring's Straits, for several weeks. The prospect not seeming to brighten much, Mr. Higgins thought he would try an experiment in what he called "high latitudes," and to that end headed the ship for the Auckland Islands. Now the crew had but little respect for their new commander, and no confidence whatever in his skill as a navigator.

After proceeding in this direction for ten days, one morning about four o'clock the lookout called the attention of the officer of the watch to strange sounds heard close ahead. It resembled the dull, sluggish sound of breakers on shore during a calm. The sounds became louder and seemed to be approaching the ship, but as her reckoning gave no land anywhere near, the cause of the sounds began to excite great alarm. The captain was called and the crew turned out, and an effort made to put the ship on the other tack, but it was of no avail. An almost dead calm prevailed, and the ship refused to obey her helm. In short, the ship was being carried rapidly forward in the grasp of a strong under-current. A heavy fog hung like a pall overhead, enveloping the ship's royals and top-gallant sails; and as the noise increased a strange feeling of awe and fear came over the crew, exciting their superstitions to the highest pitch.

As the ship went on the sounds began to resemble the dashing and surging of a heavy body of water forced by a strong tide through a narrow gorge. Still nothing could be seen of land, which increased the strange sensations produced by so singular a phenomenon. Nothing either crew or officers could do would improve the situation, for in the ship's condition they were as helpless as children. The lead was cast, and sixty fathoms called. It was now evident that there was land close by. But the trail of the line only showed the more clearly that the ship was at the mercy of some rapid and dangerous current, perhaps being drawn into some whirlpool. Now the fog seemed to lift, and long lines of light were seen ahead, but it was only to be succeeded by greater darkness. Then the sounds began to change and vary; and while what seemed voices were heard singing and sighing overhead, the deep rush and roll of waters below had a strange and bewildering effect on the feelings. Now the moon seemed to be rising through the fog ahead, and a pale, white light gleamed for a few seconds, then disappeared, and all was dark again. And as the ship advanced, the bold outline of a high and nearly perpendicular bluff revealed itself above the fog, and had the appearance of hanging directly over the ship. There was no mistaking the danger now. In a few minutes more the ship was between walls of rock three hundred feet high, drifting swiftly through a narrow channel of deep and agitated water into a dark and dangerous cavern.

The ship passed in under full sail; the atmosphere changed and became singularly oppressive; the very blood chilled; fear seized on all on board, and men who a short time before were full of courage and strength now became as helpless as children. The current was less rapid inside, but the noise increased and became even more bewildering; while the barometer would rise and fall quickly, and the compasses became agitated under the influence of some strong magnetic disorder. Every few minutes deep and rumbling sounds would break in the distance, roll along the cavern, and echo and reëcho through the great arches overhead. And these would be succeeded by soft, flute-like voices, mingling in chorus. The effect of this, in so dark and dungeon-like a place, where the mighty hand of Nature had performed one of her wildest freaks, was bewildering in the extreme, and gave wing to the strangest fancies. Hardly a word was spoken; not a brace manned, nor a sheet touched. The ship moved along as if directed by some unseen hand, for there was no wind in that deep, dark cavern. Then the water became broken, and the surface checkered with phosphoric lights, flitting and dancing, like so many sprites on a revel. The arch overhead became covered with a pale light, which seemed to struggle against the darkness; then stars, or what appeared to be stars, were seen, as through a mist. Then they would suddenly change into every variety of color, and reveal the existence of massive columns of basaltic rock supporting the arch. Still the distracting sounds were heard, but no order was given concerning the ship, scarcely a word exchanged between the men. They felt that they were drifting into some unknown sea, perhaps some place of enchantment, where death was certain, and from whence nothing more would ever be heard of them.

Could this be the mermaid's retreat of which the old captain had spoken, and of which the natives on Queen Charlotte's Island had such a strange superstition? Tite thought to himself. All the pleasant associations of home, all that he loved there, and all that he had hoped for, now rose up in his mind like a sweet and beautiful dream, only to be overshadowed by the terrible thoughts this strange and gloomy place had impressed upon him. There was no hope for him now; he felt that he should never enjoy those scenes again. But what was that to the anguish of his poor old parents, who would linger on week after week, month after month, and year after year, wondering and waiting in vain for some news of him, and dying of hope deferred.

While he was thus musing a pale, aurora-like light broke in the distance, directly ahead of the ship. Now it opened gently, now shut again. Again it glimmered and gradually expanded until the whole cavern became aglow with light, and presented a scene of such enchanting beauty that all on board were spell-bound with admiration. Massive columns, grand and impressive, rose on every side to the very roof, and reflected all the colors of the rainbow. And through them the gallant old ship continued to sail, like a phantom.

This bright, bewitching scene continued for about fifteen minutes, when the light gradually died away, and all became dark and solemn. Then deep, plunging sounds of falling water indicated with startling effect that the ship was approaching a mighty cataract, down which she must soon plunge to her destruction. These sounds, made more terrible by the darkness, were like death-knells, calling the men to prepare to meet their doom.

And while all on board were contemplating these sounds, the ship suddenly careened a-starboard, a harsh, grating noise was heard overhead, and quantities of broken crystallites began falling on deck. This was followed by a crashing sound, and the ship righted. The topmasts had fouled, and one after another were carried away and now hung, a dangerous wreck. Then her gib-boom came in contact with one of the columns, and met the same fate. The ship now swung round and struck with a violent shock on a sunken rock, and almost simultaneously her mainmast went by the board, she began to fill and settle down, and soon became a forlorn wreck. A short consultation was held between the officers and men as to what was best to be done. There was, however, no alternative but to take to the boats, and make the best effort possible to save life. There was no time to lose. Five boats were quickly launched, and manned, and supplied with such provisions and water as could be procured in the hurry of the moment. An officer took command of each boat, and Tite managed to secure six of the best oarsmen on board. There was no excitement, no disorder. Everything was done with as much order and regularity as if nothing had occurred to interrupt discipline.

And now when the five boats were ready, and the order given to "pull away," each man seemed to pause and take a last fond look at the old ship, as if a lingering affection caused him to part from her with reluctance. And as they stood taking this last look, the light again broke forth, giving to the strange scene a weird and bewildering effect.

The boats now pulled away, Tite's boat taking the lead. They had agreed to keep together as much as possible, (and to that end made signals at short intervals,) gain the ocean and seek relief along the shore. Darkness soon shut in again, however, and the noises were so bewildering that the signals from the boats could not be understood, and they separated never to meet again.

We must now follow the fortunes of the boat commanded by Tite. He had been fortunate enough to secure a compass, which, though it did him little good while in the cave, would be of great assistance to him outside. The question as to how the entrance of the cave bore, and the surest way of gaining it, was of most importance now. Tite estimated that they were at least ten miles from it, and that by steering directly against the current, they could not fail to make it. After pulling steadily for four hours, stopping only once to refresh themselves, they came in sight of the entrance, and saw daylight beyond. A feeling of joy now came over the men, and three hearty cheers were given that echoed curiously through the arches overhead. Still there was another and serious obstacle to contend with. A boar, or tidal wave, had made at the entrance, and was rushing in with a roaring noise and such force that the boat could not have stemmed it for a minute. It was therefore, necessary to seek safety behind some high rocks on one side of the entrance, and wait a change in the tide. After waiting in this position for nearly an hour they again put out, and headed for the entrance. A rapid current was still setting in, and the men had to pull with all their strength to stem it and gain the ocean.

When they had gained the ocean they felt as if they had been suddenly transferred to another world. After waiting several hours, and none of the other boats making their appearance, Tite headed his boat west and stood down the coast, close in shore, in the hope of finding a safe landing place, perhaps a friendly settlement. An almost perpendicular bluff of rocks, more than two hundred feet high, forming a walled coast, such as is seen in the Bay of Fundy, and at the foot of which the sea dashed and broke, rendering it impossible to make a landing, extended as far as the eye could reach. Along this frowning coast the boat swept until nightfall; but not a human being was seen, nor a place where they could land safely discovered.

Three days and three nights they coasted along this bold sea-wall, and now their provisions and water had given out, and such was their suffering from thirst, hunger, and cold, that two of the crew died from sheer exhaustion. Indeed, it was only extraordinary exertion on the part of Tite, and his manner of encouraging the others, that kept them from giving up in despair. Early on the morning of the fourth day an indentation in the land was discovered, sloping into a quiet little valley, a place of welcome to the weary, through which a stream of water winded down into the sea. Each heart now beat high with joy. Deliverance had come at last. The boat's head was directed toward the beach, but the wind had freshened, and a heavy surf was beating on shore, and unless the boat was skilfully handled there was great danger of swamping.

Still the boat was kept on, and in less than half an hour from the time the beach was discovered the boat was plunging through the breakers.

On entering the surf an immense roller overtook the boat, lifted her high up on its crest, and, owing to some unskilful management, she was capsized. The crew were tossed into the boiling surf, and left to struggle with the receding waves for their lives. Tite's first thought was to secure the boat, and seizing hold of the line he made a desperate effort to gain the beach, and was successful, as were two of the men. The others were too weak to make much of a resistance, and were carried away by the undercurrent, and nothing more was seen of them.

CHAPTER XXVII.

OLD DUNMAN AND THE PIRATE'S TREASURE.

With only the drenched clothes they stood in, no means of lighting a fire, and death from starvation staring them in the face, these three shipwrecked men stood upon the beach of this strange island, still hoping and wondering what was to be the next change in their condition. Was the island inhabited? By whom? What was the character of the natives, and what sort of reception would they meet when found? These were the questions which engaged their thoughts as they stood on that lonely beach, hoping against hope, and every minute fancying some friendly sail heaving in sight to relieve them from their perilous position. After the darkest night comes the brightest day. This was ever uppermost in Tite's mind, and he endeavored to impress its teachings on the minds of his companions, who were fast yielding to their fears, and would have given up in despair had not his stronger resolution encouraged them still to hope for deliverance.

There was an abundance of small shell-fish along the coast, and on these they subsisted. It was agreed to remain near the boat during the day, as a precaution against an attack from the natives, who might have seen them approach the coast, and perhaps be watching their movements near by. But the day passed and not a human being was seen. At nightfall a couple of goats and a pig, and some fowl that appeared to be keeping them company, emerged from a thicket on a hillside, descended into a valley or ravine, and drank in the brook. The sight of these animals filled the hearts of the shipwrecked men with joy. It was to them a proof of civilization. New hopes, new joys, new strength came with the sight of these animals; and they advanced cautiously toward them. But the animals were shy, and scampered away up the hill at the first sight of the strangers.

There was a high hill near by, and, encouraged by the sight of these animals, Tite started off just at dusk to ascend it and survey the surrounding country, leaving his comrades on the beach to guard the boat. It was quite dark when Tite reached the top, but the stars were out, and the atmosphere was clear. Not a habitation was to be seen, nothing but a wild, unbroken forest as far as the eye could reach. He watched there for an hour or more, his eyes quickened by anxiety, and his mind becoming more and more excited, until his fancy pictured in every shadow some moving object. Then, as his eye traced along down the deep ravine, he discovered, or rather thought he discovered, a pale wreath of smoke curling lazily upward, not more than a mile from where his comrades lay. What at first seemed only a fancy, now became a reality, for the smoke increased in volume, and indicated with certainty a habitation of some kind.

Descending the hill as quickly as he could, he found the two men fast asleep, overcome with fatigue and excitement, and it was with great difficulty that he could awake them. When, however, he told them what he had discovered, their hearts filled with joy, and they sprang to their feet ready to follow him. Still they entertained a lurking fear that the smoke might mark the bivouac of some savages who had watched their movements during the day, and lighted this fire to cook the evening meal.

They followed the stream about two miles up the ravine, picking their way over rocks and through a thick wood, until they came to a little gurgling brook, cutting its way through a deep dell running at right angles with the ravine. Here they rested for a short time, and carefully surveyed the scene, excited by strange thoughts. A light suddenly flashed from the opposite bank, not more than forty yards ahead. This evidently marked the object of their search. Then those familiar sounds made by goats, fowls, and pigs were heard. Crossing the dell they advanced cautiously in the direction of the light. They had not gone far, however, when an opening in the woods was discovered, in the centre of which a small, rude cabin, built of stones and mud, stood. A bright fire was burning inside, smoke was issuing from the rude chimney, and the light shining through two square openings in the sides, was reflecting curiously over the scene outside.

Again the three men halted, and stood viewing the scene in silence, now hoping, now fearing, now wondering what sort of beings inhabited this strange place. Still the domestic animals kept up those noises, so familiar to Tite's ear when at home. And these were broken at intervals by what seemed the barking of a wolf. Now a strange and shadowy figure passed and repassed in the cabin, its uncouth form reflecting every few seconds in the light. Should they advance, enter the cabin, and see who this strange being was, or return to the beach and wait until morning? This was the question which occupied their thoughts now. Impelled as well, perhaps, by anxiety as necessity, Tite resolved to push on to the very door. Leaving the men with orders to follow him at a short distance, he proceeded on cautiously until he reached the edge of the opening in which the cabin stood.

He was now within a few paces of the door, when the fowls, which seemed to abound in the vicinity, discovering him, sounded the alarm. The cabin door now opened, and there stood, in the shadow of the light, the figure of an old man bent with age, and dressed in the skin of a wolf, the long fur of which gave him more the appearance of an animal than a human being. His face was like colored parchment, his mouth and cheeks wrinkled and sunken, his eyes small, black and bright, his long, white hair and flowing beard, his bony hands, which he raised every few moments and held over his long white eyelashes, as a shield to his sight, gave him a strange and witch-like appearance.

There the two men, the figure in the door and Tite, stood for several minutes gazing in silence, but with a look of astonishment, at each other. The animals and fowls had gathered in a group about the old man, alarmed at the sight of a stranger. At length a thin, shrill voice broke the silence by enquiring: "Who is it that comes here to disturb my peace?"

"We are friends," replied Tite, "shipwrecked sailors, in search of shelter and food."

The cabin door now opened, and there stood, in the shadow of the light, the figure of an old man bent with age, and dressed in the skin of a wolf..

"Heaven pity you, and forgive me," returned the old man, his eyes beaming brighter and his whole manner becoming more earnest. "Heaven forgive me, you shall have both, and be welcome in my palace. Heaven forgive me, for this is my palace and I am king of this island. Come in, and such as I have you shall share with me." And he advanced, took Tite by the hand, and led him into his cabin, the two men following. Spreading seal and wolf skins on the floor, he bid them be seated, while he prepared food for their supper. His motion was a shuffle rather than a walk, and he moved about the cabin more like an animal than a human being. He seemed to have an abundant supply of dried fish, fowl, and fruit; of vegetables and roots, from which he made a beverage that filled the place of coffee. And with these and some goat's milk he soon set before them a supper, saying as he invited them to partake, "Heaven forgive me for all my sins, and they are many. Your are countrymen of my own, and speak the same language. Ah, I had almost forgotten it, as the world has forgotten me. Now it all comes back, and makes me feel happy. I am old, very old now. Heaven forgive me. There will be no more of poor old George Dunman soon. When he dies he will die with great sins on his head. If sin can be washed out with sorrow, Heaven knows I have had sorrow enough." He advanced towards Tite, and laying his hand gently on his shoulder, looked earnestly and intently into his face: "you are young, very young," he said, "crime has made no wrinkles in your face yet. Mine is full of age and crime, and a heart filled with remorse, have burned their deep seals into mine. Look you, young man," and he pointed to his eyes, "these eyes were not made to weep. But this poor heart of mine is crushed with its crimes." Here he pressed his right hand to his heart, and raised his eyes upwards, as if imploring Heaven's forgiveness in silence.

This continued invoking Heaven's forgiveness excited Tite's curiosity to know something of the old man's strange and wonderful history, for he already began to feel that there was a terrible crime at the bottom of it. When they had partaken of supper and were all seated around the fire on their skins, and nothing but the music of the brook was heard outside, the old man requested Tite to give him an account of his voyage, together with the place and manner of their shipwreck. Tite was glad to comply with the old man's request, for it afforded him an excellent excuse for making a similar one.

The reader has already been made familiar with Tite's unfortunate voyage, hence it will not be necessary to repeat it. The recital interested the old man deeply, and when he had reached that part which described their troubles in the cave, the old man's eyes sparkled, and his whole nature seemed to warm into enthusiasm.

"There's where my ship lays, guns and all," he said, pressing his hands on his knees. "My men used to call this island 'No Man's Island,' and they named that place 'The Cave of Enchantment.' Then they named it after me. The natives on an island ten leagues from this have a queer superstition concerning it. They call it the devil's last resting place, and assert that it is peopled by mermaids, who get honest navigators into it, and then destroy them. My ship lays there, guns and all," he repeated.

When Tite had finished his story, the old man began his by saying: "Heaven forgive me, for I am a great sinner, and have much to answer for in the next world. I was born in Bristol, England. My father was a clergyman of the established church. I have no remembrance of my mother, for she died when I was an infant. When I was fifteen years old I was sent to sea as a means of bettering my morals. I served first on board an Indiaman, made two voyages to China, and was wrecked on the coast of Malabar; and when I got home my father or friends procured me the position of midshipman on board a man-of-war. I served on board the frigate Winchester, and other of His Majesty's ships, I did, for fifteen years, and was only a midshipman at the end. Heaven forgive me for my sins. It seemed there was no promotion for me. I was then transferred to His Majesty's packet service, and assigned to the brig Storm, carrying six guns, and the mails between Plymouth and the North American provinces. She was a beauty of a craft, that Storm was. She used to carry a crowd of canvas, and jump the seas like a sea-bird. I was four years first officer of that craft, was proud of what she could do, and the devil took advantage of my ambition, and created within me a longing to be in command of her, and make myself heroic by roaming unrestrained on the free sea. That feeling kept increasing until it become a passion with me. Then it was my misfortune to fall in love. Yes, love was a misfortune to me. I had courted and was engaged to the daughter of a rich old man who had made all his money in the West Indies, and still had plantations there.

"We were to be married on my return, after a voyage to North America. But I returned to find her married to a young officer who had sailed companion with me on board man-a-war, and who had professed great friendship for me only to deceive me. He had professed to be my friend and confident; and it was this that carried the knife of disappointment to my very heart. I was denied an interview with the woman I had loved, even worshipped. The man who had professed to be my friend now turned his back on me, and denied me even an explanation." All the fire there was left in the old man now seemed to kindle into a blaze, and the fiercer elements of his nature took possession of him.

"To make the matter worse," he continued, "our good, kind, and brave captain was relieved, transferred back to the navy, and this man, who had outraged my confidence and made my life wretched, appointed to fill his place. I resolved to be revenged. But how could it be got? How could I punish the man who had so wronged me without rebelling against my country, against God's laws, and against society? The devil told me it could be done.

"As it was not a question of conscience with me, in the frame of mind I was then in, there was no trouble in following the devil's advice. I conceived a plan for sending this captain out of the world by the shortest road, seizing the ship, and roving unrestrained upon the free sea. It was soon found that there was enough on board to join the enterprise and share the spoils, and the plan was carried out when we were half voyage over. That was fifty years ago. I shall never forget the terrible struggle of that night, nor the bloody work that was done. Heaven forgive me. When I had got command I ran the Storm into the Caribbean Sea, landed all who were suspected, as well as such as more openly opposed the enterprise, on an island, and then put away for the Pacific via Cape Horn. When we got into the Pacific, we hoisted—." The old man paused suddenly and hung down, his head. "Heaven forgive me for my crimes," he resumed, evidently in doubt about acknowledging the full force of his crimes.

"I may as well tell you it all—shake the load free from my conscience, and ask you to join me in invoking Heaven's forgiveness. We hoisted the flag that sees an enemy in every other flag, and for three years the Storm scourged these seas from Cape Horn to Sands' Head. When ships, sent in pursuit of us, were searching along the west coast, we were making war on commerce on the coast of China. We had a name for every sea we entered, so as to make our pursuers think there was more than one vessel, and so divide their attention.

"Yes, for three years we scourged these seas, and made war on land as well as sea—capturing, plundering, murdering—yes, committing crimes that shame manhood, and make me fear the vengeance of a just God. And all for gold, gold, gold. And what good can gold do a man with a conscience haunted by crimes committed in getting it? Gold can do me no good; but man is a mean animal at best; and you can so teach him in crime that he will commit the most revolting out of sheer wantonness.

"We soon had more gold and jewels than we knew what to do with. Some of our men left us and went home with enough to make them rich for the rest of their lives. And we have buried enough on these islands to buy a city. Gold lost its charms with us, and crime became an excitement and an entertainment.

"We discovered this island while cruising from one ocean to the other, and found on it some sailors, whose vessel had been wrecked near where you landed. They had been seven years here, and it is to them we are indebted for these animals and fowls. They lived contented, for they had given up all hope of getting away, and are all dead now. We made this place a retreat, had a settlement here, after the wreck of the Storm in the cave, of forty men. They are all dead but me. I have been here forty years—nine of them passed alone; and now my time has almost come. I took the name of George Dunman because I had disgraced that of my parents, and because I am an outlaw, and I want to die here and be forgotten."

It was after midnight when the old man finished his story. His manner became nervous and restless, and it was evident there was something more he wanted to disclose, but hesitated to do.

The strangers accepted the old man's invitation, and took up their abode under his roof, finding plenty of food and kind treatment. But they soon became weary of so monotonous a life, and longing for some means of reaching their homes and civilization, would visit the coast nearly every day, in the hope of seeing some friendly sail and effecting their deliverance. This anxiety to get away on the part of his new friends so preyed on the old man's mind that his strength began to fail fast, and at the end of two months it became evident that his sands of life had but a few more days to run.

Two months passed, and the weather was becoming cold. The old man was up earlier than usual one morning; still he seemed more feeble. He tottered about the cabin, his frame shook and trembled, and his whole system seemed to be under some new excitement. He had formed a strong attachment for Tite, whom he now approached with his hands extended. "Like you," he said, grasping his hand firmly and looking up imploringly into his face, "I was young and handsome once. I am old and ugly now. Crime has written its ugly finger all over my face; has thrust its poison into this poor heart of mine. Never let it lay one ugly finger on your face. Make yours a life of joy, so that you may die happy. Oh, these poor old gray hairs of mine, this head that has sinned so much." And he raised his hard, bony hand to his head, and tossed the long white hair back over his shoulders.

"Come with me, come with me, young man," he resumed, grasping Tite by the arm nervously and tottering to the door. When they got outside he whispered in his ear: "You shall see where it is buried before I die. It has made my life wretched; it may make yours happy." He paused for a few seconds, and looking back, saw the two men standing watch at the door. "Come," said he, beckoning to them, "you may as well come, too."

The men joined them, and when they had reached a spot about twenty rods from the cabin, they came to a square pile of stones, in a dark wood on the side of a hill. The old man sat down, and resting his arms on the stones, continued: "Here, buried three feet below these stones, is gold and silver enough to make you all rich for life, and perhaps happy. Churches, convents, ships, and even life itself have contributed to it. All I now seek is peace in Heaven; and yet I cannot get that with this gold, for it is the price of crime and death. Take it, take it; and when my life of sorrow is ended, and these poor old bones shall move no more, divide it among yourselves; and if Heaven sends you a deliverance from this lonely island, so live that it may bring you blessings, not curses, as it has done me."

Three days after what I have described in the above paragraph took place, Tite and the two sailors returned from the coast and were alarmed to find the cabin deserted. They waited for a short time, and then searched the woods in the vicinity, but could find nothing of the old man. The compasses were there, and his nautical instruments were still hanging on the wall, and the fire was nearly burned out. It had been his custom to have supper ready punctually when they returned. There was now a strange and mysterious stillness about the place. Even the fowls and the animals seemed silent.

On proceeding to the spot where the treasure was buried, they found the lifeless body of the old pirate. Old Dunman was dead, and lay there, with two of his pet goats nestling at his side.

CHAPTER XXVIII.

MR. GUSHER SUSTAINS HIS CHARACTER.

"Husband, dear; husband, dear," said Mrs. Chapman, for I must again return to that lady, as she addressed her meek-looking little husband, "how distressing it would be if Mr. Gusher should turn out not to be Mr. Gusher. He is such a nice young gentleman, and so popular in society. If he should turn out to be somebody else? He has been such a favorite at our house, you know. I am sure I should never survive such a scandal as that. I am sure it would kill me—at least I should faint; I feel as if I should faint now!" "Pray don't faint, pay dear," interrupted Chapman, submissively, as she handed him a letter she had received that day from Mr. Romer. And as she did so, she got up and paced the room in a state of great agitation.

"Never faint, my dear," resumed Chapman, "until you know what you are fainting for. There is nothing to be made by fainting or borrowing trouble." This conversation took place in the parlor one evening about three weeks after the ball. Chapman read and reread the letter, and then remained silent for several minutes. "Very strange, if true, my dear. But there may be a personal difficulty at the bottom of it, and the young man has taken this method of damaging Mr. Gusher's character."

Mr. Romer presented his compliments to Mrs. Chapman, and, seeing the intimacy there was between her family and a person calling himself Philo Gusher, begged to inform her that the name of that individual was Louis Pinto, a notorious and well-known impostor, who had fled from Havana, where he had been several times imprisoned, to escape punishment for his crimes.

"Anything but that, my dear husband. I am sure my pride would never survive it. And to happen just when society—yes, my dear, the very best of your Bowling Green people were beginning to leave cards. Another ball and we should have brought the best of them down."

"Another ball, my dear?" returned Chapman, with a sigh. "A ball a year ought to satisfy any respectable family." Chapman was indeed becoming alarmed at his wife's extravagance and weakness for society. Her worldliness he feared would bring him to grief ere long. The last ball had entailed the expense of new carpets; and the young gentlemen had quite taken possession of the house, which they held until after daylight, and then went home in a very unsteady condition of the limbs. To make the matter worse, Bowles had been very much demoralized ever since, and now demanded another horse or his discharge. He had no complaint to make either about his pay or livery; but to have it thrown up to him every day, and by all the coachmen in the neighborhood, that he was in the service of a one horse family, was more than his proud spirit could bear.

Chapman held that dancing was not the profession of a gentleman, and that balls had done nothing for the great moral progress of the world. In fine, his mind had been engaged for some time back on something more serious; and he delighted his wife by telling her that he had been working up a great scheme for freeing and vitalizing all mankind.

The door bell rang, and in another minute Mr. Gusher, all serene and elegant, was ushered into the lady's presence. Never was young gentleman more exquisitely upholstered.

The lady extended her hand and received him cordially, saying she had been looking for him with unusual anxiety.

"I am very glad you have come, Mr. Gusher," interposed Chapman. "My dear wife is oppressed with a little matter I am sure you can relieve."

Mr. Gusher turned and thanked them for the high compliment thus paid him. "You shall ze as I shall be so grateful for dis 'onar. And your daughter—she is well?"

"Very well—she was speaking of you kindly to-day. Here is something that reached me to-day, Mr. Gusher," she resumed, rising from her chair and handing him the letter, with a dignity of manner quite uncommon to her: "I am sure you will pardon me, sir, but it contains matter which, as a friend of yours, I have taken the liberty to submit. I make it a rule to stand by a friend, you know."

Gusher took the letter and began reading it with an air of unconcern. Then breaking out into a hearty laugh, he replied: "Zis grand rascal as write dis lettar is one par-tick-lar friend of mine—"

"I am sure, sir," rejoined Mrs. Chapman, "he is an enemy of yours, and no friend. That you can explain it all satisfactorily, I have no doubt."

"Pardon, madam, pardon; this grand rascal I call him one friend. Ze 'onar, madam, he is so much dear to me as my life. Oh yes, you shall zee as my 'onar and mine country is more dear to me zan my life. Zis grand rascal, he is my friend be-cause he do me zis injury so many times, and in ze end he do me so much good. You shall zee zar was a lady. Zat lady, ze grand rascal as writes zis letter—it is so many years ago, as I almost forget—pays to her his compliment. Pardon, madam, zat lady prefar me to ze gentleman. Zen zat gentleman he pays to me his compliment like one grand rascal. He persecute my 'onar, and he make me so many friends—"

"Really, Mr. Gusher," interrupted Mrs. Chapman, encouragingly, "then it is all the result of jealousy? I had a suspicion that there was something of the kind at the bottom of it."

"You shall zee, madam, it was be-cause ze lady prefar me. Zen I give ze grand rascal one pistol." Here Mr. Gusher flourished his right hand. "You shall give me ze satisfaction as one gentleman he give to ze oser, I say. I gives to ze grand rascal one small sword. I say I shall have ze satisfaction one gentleman he will give to ze oser. No, madam, ze grand rascal, he is one small coward. He will not give me ze satisfaction. I shall show you as this grand rascal tells not one word of ze truth."

"I told you, my dear," said Chapman, "that Mr. Gusher was a gentleman, and would explain it all to your satisfaction."

Mrs. Chapman expressed herself highly gratified at what she had heard. But in order to put the matter beyond question, and to prove to her entire satisfaction that he was not only an innocent, but a much injured gentleman, Gusher returned on the following day armed with a large number of letters, some of them sealed with great seals, the writers setting forth that they had known the young gentleman from his birth up, that he was of irreproachable character, and his parents very distinguished people.

Of course the Chapmans were entirely satisfied. Indeed Mr. Gusher so turned his guns on Mr. Romer as to make his position extremely uncomfortable. Both were guests at the old City Hotel, where Gusher was a great favorite with all the young ladies, and to whom he related his difficulty with Romer. In short, he so enlisted their sympathies in his behalf that they were ready to join him in ejecting Romer from the house as a slanderer. One said what a mean thing he must be to slander the handsome young foreigner in that way. A second tossed and turned her head aside when she met him, and pouted her pretty lips to let him know what she meant. A third refused to return his bow, while a fourth gave him the cut direct. There was no standing up against such a storm of female indignation as he now found blowing about his ears. He saw, also, that to have attempted to sustain his charges with proof would only be sheer folly. In short, there was nothing for the plain young outspoken American to do but surrender the field to the handsome young foreigner and his female admirers, seek respectful treatment beyond the sound of their voices—and wait.

CHAPTER XXIX.

CHANGED CIRCUMSTANCES.

Oh, what a sweet charm there is in hope. How it beguiles the ambitious lover, causes him to build castles he finds crushed at last under his disappointments. How gently it lifts the drooping heart into an higher realm of cheerfulness, still gilding and brightening the future. Day after day and week after week it carries the timid, desponding soul over its sea of trouble and disappointment, and pictures its love-dream in colors more and more beautiful. How it ensnares us, and then betrays us with its false visions of future bliss. It beguiles both you and me with its featly spun tales of fame and riches, which it weaves so ingeniously into its fascinating web.

Such were the thoughts invading Mattie's mind as she sat at the parlor window one morning, looking out over Bowling Green, contemplating the strange influences by which she was surrounded, and wondering what the future would bring her. There was something so earnest and yet so kindly in that pale, expressive face, and those soft blue eyes.

She had counted the days since Tite sailed. It was nearly three years ago, and only one letter had been received from him. There was a report in circulation now that the ship, with all on board, was lost. And although this report could not be traced to any reliable source, it was credited by the owners, who had heard nothing of the ship since she left Coquimbo.

The love Mattie bore Tite burned as brightly now as on the day when first it was kindled. She had thought of him always, dreamed of him, prayed for him, for she had the heart of a good and true woman. Yes, she had followed Tite in her love-dream through all the strange depths of that mysterious ocean. But the more she traced for him the more it seemed to deepen her disappointment. Still hope flattered her lingering love, cheered her, and brightened the star of her future. Hope came to cheer the heart that had longed for relief so lovingly, that had begun to yield to the stormy forebodings which hope deferred oppresses the soul with.

Notwithstanding all this, fear at times seemed to get the better of her resolution. How she had watched and waited, and yet there was no tidings of his coming.

Was Tite lost? If so, how, and where was he lost? Must she give him up as gone forever? Must she give him up, and see him, and hold sweet communion with him, only in her love-dream, among the flowers fancy pictures in the garden of our hopes? Must she forget the idol of her love, transport her affections, yield to her mother's wishes, which were daily becoming more pressing, and marry Mr. Gusher, a man she did not even respect, much less love? In gratifying a mother's ambition she might, perhaps, make her own life wretched. If Tite was lost, what was to become of his aged parents, Hanz and Angeline? Their welfare seemed to concern her even more deeply than that of her own parents. Hanz had found means of communicating with her, had made her acquainted with all his troubles, and now the day set for a hearing of his case was near at hand.

Mattie knew nothing really bad of Mr. Gusher. He had seemed to her one of those uncertain characters who float about on the surface of society without having any fixed position in it, who have no legitimate occupation, depend on chance for everything, and lead an artificial life generally. Such men, it had seemed to her, were poor companions to sail down the stormy sea of life with. In Tite she saw something real, good, substantial; one of those young men who prosper and build up their own fortunes and future, because they apply themselves steadily and energetically to the legitimate pursuits of life.

The door opened suddenly, and Mattie's reverie was interrupted by her mother, whose portly figure quite filled the space, for, in truth, the lady had enlarged her hip circumference with an unpardonable amount of padding. Mrs. Chapman expected distinguished company that day, and had arrayed herself in a tantalizing amount of finery. For the first time, too, she had put her hair up in puffs, which was the fashion of the day in Bowling Green. Indeed the lady flattered herself that there was nothing in Bowling Green that could excel her in the magnificence of her upholstery.

"Expecting company to-day, very distinguished company, too," said Mrs. Chapman, advancing and bowing her head oppressively, "and how very annoying not to be dressed as one wants to be." After viewing herself in the glass for several minutes, turning first one side and then the other, viewing and reviewing her skirts, and training her puffs into more exact platoon, she turned to Mattie, and resumed, "Now tell me, my daughter, how do my skirts hang? Does my dress become me? Do puffs become me? You see my face is a little broad—puffs will, I am afraid, make it look disadvantageously broad. Tell me now, my daughter, am I presentable?" Mrs. Chapman waited with an air of self-admiration for a reply. "You have such good taste in such matters, my daughter;" she concluded.

"Why, mother," replied Mattie, smiling and viewing her mother from head to foot, "how very worldly you are getting, and so vain. Never saw you look better—and so young."

"I appreciate the compliment, my daughter," returned Mrs. Chapman, dropping a bow and a courtesy. "A woman of my complexion may be excused for refusing to get old."

"I was only joking," resumed Mattie, laughing heartily. "My dear mother takes everything so serious—"

"Come, come," interrupted Mrs. Chapman, her face coloring, "does my dress become me? Am I presentable?"

"You are elegance itself, my dear mother, and would be presentable anywhere," returned Mattie, with a merry twinkle of the eye.

"That's what I wanted to know," said Mrs. Chapman with a bow, and a slight motion backward. "And now, my daughter," she resumed quickly, "this is a good time for having a very serious talk on a very important, but very different matter. What we were talking about yesterday, you know. I hope you have made up your mind to banish Toodleburg." Mrs. Chapman drew herself up into a stately attitude, and assumed a look of uncommon severity. "You know how much your parents dote on you, my daughter, and how much depends on you to give the family a firm standing." The lady tossed her head haughtily and pretentiously. Mattie remained silent and thoughtful.

"Toodleburg's at the bottom of the sea—that's my opinion. And if he stays there it wouldn't distress me—it wouldn't," resumed Mrs. Chapman, giving way to her temper and becoming more earnest. Just then tears gushed into Mattie's eyes, and as they coursed down her cheeks told the tale of her sorrow.

"What I said was intended for good advice, my daughter, not to wound your feelings," continued Mrs. Chapman. "Even if the young man should not be at the bottom of the sea, we should never be presentable with him attached to the family—never in the world. Such a name, and such common people for parents! What would Bowling Green say, my daughter? We must all yield to the force of circumstances; and the circumstances are all against this Mr. Toodleburg tumbling himself into our family." She paused suddenly, and again viewed her ponderous figure in the glass, now adjusting one side of her skirts and then the other. "I wonder if this dress really does become me? Green and orange are in harmony with a complexion like mine," she said, turning to Mattie, and waiting for a reply. But Mattie was trying to relieve her feelings of the grief that was filling her eyes with tears.

"To return to what I was saying, my daughter, sentimental marriages, I was going to say, (well, I will say it,) are fools' marriages. Yes, they are. Your father understands that. Never would have got him—never in this world—if I had been given to sentimental love. Toodleburg's a good enough young man in his place—but he's never, never coming back, my daughter. But even if he was to come back, there's no place for him in our family. View these things, always do, through the eye of philosophy—I do." Mrs. Chapman again paused, bowed her head admonishingly, and extended her fat, waxy hands. Mattie still remained silent.

"After all the polishing you have had, my daughter, to let your mind run to such an unpolished young man. Drag a family down when a family is going up, and there's the end of that family—with society I mean." Mrs. Chapman tossed her head, and again returned to the mirror, saying as she viewed herself in it: "Drag a low bred fellow into a well bred family, I repeat, and down that family goes."

"Well, well, my dear mother shall have it all her own way," replied Mattie, cheering up and assuming an air of indifference. "Anything to relieve your anxiety, my dear mother. How nice it would be to have a husband you admire so much, and to think that I obeyed your wishes in everything. The fact is I had a very serious talk with Mr. Gusher yesterday—"

"You didn't offend him with your eccentricities, I hope?" Mrs. Chapman interrupted, enquiringly. "Mr. Gusher is such a polished gentleman, and so very sensitive."

"I don't know how sensitive he may be, mother; but I told him just exactly what I thought, as I would have told any one else. I told him how much you admired him, and what a favorite he was generally; and that if I consented to accept him for a husband, it would be solely to accommodate my dear mother—"

"How very obstinate my daughter is," interposed Mrs. Chapman. "How very distressing to have a daughter always in rebellion."

"I am sure you would not have me flatter Mr. Gusher with a falsehood, mother," resumed Mattie. "I tried to impress him with the fact that I was not good enough for so accomplished a gentleman; but he insisted that I was, adding that he cared nothing for riches or station. As for loving him, I told him plainly I didn't think I ever could, though there was no knowing what changes time might work in my feelings. I gave him my hand, nevertheless, and told him if he took me it must be with the consequences."

Mr. Napoleon Bowles announced visitors, and this put an end to the conversation. The reader must know that this was not a voluntary yielding on the part of Mattie to the wishes of her mother. She only adopted this course as part of a plan by which she hoped to gain time, during which Tite might return, and thus afford her the means of averting a dilemma into which her mother was forcing her.

CHAPTER XXX.

A TERRIBLE CALAMITY OVERTAKES THE FAMILY.

It was not to be expected that so pushing a woman as Mrs. Chapman would be turned from the object she had set her heart on by the interposition of ordinary obstacles. She had taken good care to have the engagement pretty well trumpeted over Bowling Green; and in less than three months from the time what is described in the foregoing chapter occurred, the lady had a day fixed for the wedding ceremony, which, she declared should be on such a scale of magnificence as would astonish all New York, to say nothing of West Bowling Green. And now she was distracting her wits, and the wits of her friends, over what she called the preliminaries extraordinary. Weddings, the lady said, must be illuminated according to the position of the family. And to that end an additional amount of elegant furniture was got for the house, a new carriage was ordered, and Mr. Napoleon Bowles was to appear in a new livery, with top boots. Nor was the family finery to be neglected, for at least a dozen dressmakers had been employed for a month plying their needles. In short, this great coming event in the history of the Chapman family had afforded Bowling Green enough to talk about for a month.

The lady's meek looking little husband pleaded in vain for economy; suggested in vain his almost empty pocket. "A quiet family wedding, my dear, with a few honest-hearted friends invited, will be so much better, you know;" he would say, submissively. "You know what nice quiet weddings we used to have at Dogtown, and how cheap they were."

"Don't mention Dogtown, my dear; pray don't, my darling," the lady would reply, a curl of contempt on her lips. "We live in New York, now. I wish we had never known Dogtown—only common people marry in that way in New York. Never bring Dogtown into the house again, my darling."

"Have it all your own way, my dear," Chapman would conclude, knowing there was nothing for him to do but surrender submissively.

St. Paul's Church was to be decorated with flowers, for the young people were to be married there, surrounded by gay and admiring friends, who were to make the picture bright and sunny with their smiles and congratulations. And there was to be a grand reception and a sumptuous supper at the house; and the happiness of bride and bridegroom was to be drunk in sparkling wine; and music and dancing was to animate the soul and add charms to their joy-dream.

Mrs. Chapman, I may add here, had a great weakness for distinctions. She had cards printed in gold, in blue, and in red. Such as received cards printed in gold were to consider themselves particularly honored. In short, she divided her guests into three classes—select friends, friends, and acquaintances, and sent them cards accordingly. This manner of distinguishing between guests got the lady into a deal of trouble, and gave rise to much ill-feeling between those who held cards printed in gold and those holding ordinary red ones. Beau Pinks had been honored with a card printed in gold, which he said was a proof of the high esteem he was held in by the lady. In truth, the Beau took great pride in showing this card to the best Bowling Green society, and, with a suggestive nod of the head, saying he had got his best clothes ready, and was waiting to put in an appearance. Mrs. Chapman had always regarded Pinks as a valuable capture, and if he came to the wedding, why, that would in part be gaining the advantage she desired, and in a measure pay off the old score she had against a few of these nice old Bowling Green people.

It must be said to Pinks' credit that he never declined an invitation to a wedding, and rarely missed a chance to mourn at a friend's funeral.

And while Mrs. Chapman seemed to think of nothing else, and talk of nothing else but this great coming event, Chapman had been noticed to wear a more serious look than usual, and indeed to be in a more thoughtful mood. Indeed it was evident there was something on his mind causing him deep anxiety, even distress. It was noticed, too, that he had for several days gone to business earlier than usual and returned later. And when Mrs. Chapman requested an explanation, he would reply by saying: "Matters at the counting-house require examining into, my dear." In truth, the financial affairs of the great Kidd Discovery Company had begun to exhibit those infirmities which are a sure sign of speedy wreck.

And now the day was come when Mattie was to be married to Mr. Gusher. It was three years to-day since Tite bid her good-bye and sailed on his voyage, and it was to be her wedding-day. How strange the changed scene seemed to her.

It was one of those soft and balmy mornings in May, when nature seems to enchant us, and hold sweet communion with us through all her beauties. There was not a ripple on the water; white sails dotted the calm surface of the bay, which seemed like a silvery lake quietly sleeping in the embrace of pretty green hills, softened by the golden gleams of the rising sun. The trees were in blossom; birds were filling the air with delicious melody, but not a leaf stirred.

The Chapman family were up before the sun that morning, and the whole house was astir ere Bowling Green had fairly waked up, or the din of Broadway had broken the stillness. Chapman had spent a restless night, and seemed sad and downcast, as if some trouble he would fain conceal was weighing on his mind. He breakfasted alone that morning, and went to business an hour earlier than usual, promising to return at one o'clock. He returned, however, at twelve, and in such a state of distress as to alarm the whole house. Indeed he entered the house more like a madman than a philosopher, and so alarmed Bowles by the wildness of his manner and appearance, that he proceeded in a state of great excitement to inform his mistress. When, then, that lady entered the parlor she found her husband stretched on the sofa, with his right hand pressing his forehead, and apparently in a state of great distress. To her repeated enquiries as to what produced this great distress, he would only answer by shaking his head and giving vent to the most pitiful groans.

The lady could not fail to see that some great misfortune had overtaken her husband—something that might blast the dream of her golden future.

"I hope, my dear, it is nothing that will interfere with the wedding to-day?" she enquired, her face already beginning to give out signs of alarm.

Chapman made no reply, but got quickly up from the sofa and paced the room hurriedly, his hair tossed in to disorder, and in a state of frenzy.

After pacing up and down the room in this manner for two or three minutes, which seemed like hours to Mrs. Chapman, who had kept her eyes fixed on his every movement, he approached the lady, and with a wild stare, muttered rather than spoke: "A funeral, funeral, my dear—not a wedding to-day." Chapman pressed his hands to his head again, and wept like a child. "Boundless iniquity," he resumed, "fraud—deception—crime— disgrace—folly—extravagance—disappointment—poverty. What a sham the world is! All, all is gone! No need for a clergyman here to-day. The sheriff will be here in an hour."

"My dear, my dear, do explain yourself, so that I may understand our position;" Mrs. Chapman interposed, her whole system yielding to the force of excitement. "If the trouble is only of a transient nature, we may still give the wedding—"

"Wedding! my dear," interrupted Chapman, wiping the tears from his eyes. "There can be no wedding in this house to-day, for Gusher has turned out an impostor, and is in prison—." Before he had time to say any more, the lady threw up her arms with an exclamation, shrieked and swooned. Chapman attempted to catch her in his arms as she was falling, but she carried him to the floor under her great weight, and indeed caused him to feel alarmed for his own safety. Fortunately, Bowles entered the parlor just as his mistress fell, and seeing the danger his master was in, ran to his relief, and after extracting him from his perilous position, assisted in getting his mistress safely on the sofa, where restoratives, such as are common where ladies are given to such ills, were applied.

Chapman was indeed a man to be pitied. He had now more than his head and hands full of trouble. The care it was now necessary to bestow on his wife (for she was above all else in his mind) in a great measure relieved him of the excitement caused by his great financial misfortunes. When, then, Mattie entered the parlor and found him comparatively calm, she fancied her mother had swooned from over-exertion on her behalf. Taking a seat beside her mother, she kissed and kissed her cheek, and proceeded to bestow upon her those attentions her case demanded, and in so kind and gentle a manner as to show how deep and true was the love she bore her.

Chapman soon relieved Mattie's mind, by telling her all that had happened. As he concluded she grasped his hand firmly and imprinted a kiss on his cheek. "Heaven be thanked, father," she said, "it is a kind Providence that directs all our destinies. I am free now. You are free—free in your intentions—free in your conscience. I am happy now—happy because I shall not have to interpose my oath against yours. You shall know what I mean by that hereafter."

While this was going on up stairs Bowles, his eyes protruding, and in a state of great alarm, entered the kitchen, where Bridget, the cook, and Kitty, the chambermaid were at work, and stammered out: "Der don't be no weddin' in dis house to-day—peers to me—no how. Quid mortibus, portendibus—my missus am most dead."

"To the pots wid yeer latin, ye nager," said Bridget, seizing the tongs and holding them threatingly over his head. "To the pots wid yeer latin, ye nager. Spake so a dacent woman can understand what ye mane." To appease Bridget's wrath and save his head, Bowles condescended to use plain English in describing what had happened up stairs.

"Much good may the faint do the big, auld woman," said Bridget, with an air of indifference. "The divel takes a mighty good care of his own."

"Quid—mortibus—portendibus," repeated Bowles, as Bridget ran to the door with the tongs upraised, causing him to beat a hasty retreat.

"Bad luck to such a nager!" exclaimed Bridget, as Bowles shut the door. "Shure he thinks more about his latin and his livery an he do about his priest."

"Chapman, my dear Chapman, how crushing this all is," the lady whispered, as she began to recover her consciousness. "I feel more dead than alive—I do. Send Bowles out. Do what you can to soften the disappointment. Tell those who come it was all owing to unforeseen circumstances. Oh, my dear daughter," she put her arm around Mattie's neck, drew her to her and kissed her, "how can we look Bowling Green in the face after this? We never shall, and yet your father is a scholar and a gentleman."

Chapman's excitement began to return with his wife's recovery; indeed it soon became her turn to soothe his troubled mind.

"Gusher—the handsome young gentleman—is in prison, eh, and turns out to be—"

"My dear wife," interrupted Chapman, again giving way to his feelings, "he turns out to be Louis Pinto, an impostor. That's the whole of it—except what there may be in this paper." He drew a newspaper from his pocket, and pointing to an article headed: "A Notorious Impostor caught at Last," said: "There, my dear, read that." It gave a very long account, or rather history of the prisoner's exploits in Havana and New Orleans, his operations in New York, financially as well as socially, and indeed all the circumstances attending his career since he arrived in the city, his connection with the great Kidd Discovery Company, and not forgetting to mention that he was to have been married this day to a lovely and interesting young lady—the daughter of a highly respectable family.

"Have read enough, my dear," said Mrs. Chapman, putting the paper aside quietly. "Smelling salts, the ammonia, my daughter," she whispered to Mattie, and motioned her hand to bring them quickly. "I shall faint again, I am sure I shall."

"Don't let it worry you so much, mother," replied Mattie, as she handed her the phial. "We ought all to be thankful that we have escaped with no worse disgrace. I at least am thankful."

Mrs. Chapman shook her head, but made no reply for several minutes. Then turning to her husband, she pressed her hands to her head and resumed: "My pride is crushed, and my courage all gone, gone, gone. Bigelow Chapman, my dear, when I married you I knew you were intellectually great, and I looked forward to a brilliant future. The house is all dark now."

"Extravagance, my dear, extravagance," said Chapman, shaking his head suggestively. "It is a master that will break down the best of us." Topman and Mrs. Topman have been indulging in extravagance; Gusher has been spending all the money he could get, and all the young men in the office went to doing the same. "And you, my darling—you know you havn't lived—." Chapman was going to say, "so economical."

"But, my dear," rejoined Mrs. Chapman quickly, and evidently inclined to change the conversation: "It was not me who introduced the handsome young gentleman into the house."

"No, my dear—you only encouraged him when he was in," replied Chapman, submissively. "I didn't tell you all, my dear, Topman is a forger, and is not to be found. And, and the worst of it is—and that is what has caused all the trouble—the great Kidd Discovery Company is dead! That's where it is!"

"Dead, my dear, dead!" reiterated the astonished woman. "We call it gone up in Wall Street—"

"Couldn't you contrive some way, my dear, to lighten the disgrace?"

"Wall Street is in a state of excitement, the sheriff is in possession of everything, and beggary stares me in the face—"

This conversation was interrupted by loud ringing of the hall bell, and in another minute Bowles opened the parlor door and the sheriff and one of his deputies entered, and commenced their business. "Beg your pardon," said the sheriff, bowing politely, while his deputy deliberately took a seat and began a survey of everything within sight. "You must excuse any lack of ceremony on our part. It is a part of our duty to do these things, and we try to relieve them as much as possible of their painful features." Then taking Chapman aside, he suggested that the ladies better be got up stairs. And while this was being done the deputy entered the back parlor, and placing his hat on the pier table, began taking an inventory of all the furniture.

"You will find my deputy a gentleman," said the sheriff, addressing Chapman when the ladies had left the parlor, "and if not such a companion as you would prefer, I am compelled to leave him with you, and hope your esteem for him will improve on acquaintance. He will take a schedule of everything, and anything missing thereafter you will be held responsible for." Thus saying, the gentleman bid Chapman a polite good morning, and hurried himself out of the house.

Again the hall bell rang. This time Bowles brought in an unsealed note, grimy and discolored. Chapman immediately recognized it as from Gusher. He carried it up stairs to his dear wife, who read it aloud, for it was addressed to her, and read thus:

"Pardon, madam, pardon. Zis one circumstance, he is so very disagreeable. My compliment to ze family, an Mr. Gusher, he beg to say as he shall be compel to forego ze pleasure of is marriage zis day wiz your daughter. He is one grand rascal what make me so much trouble. So many friend come to see me to-day. But ze suberscribed condition of my accommodation shall prevent ze carry out of my obligation wiz your lovely daughter. You shall zee, madam, as I am a man—yes, madam, a gentleman of 'onar. I shall get all my enemies undar my feet. Zen I shall do myself ze 'onar to marry your lovely daughter. Allow me, madam. I shall subscribe myself your friend.

"PHILO GUSHER."

"Impudence to the very last," said Mrs. Chapman; "he has brought this disgrace upon us, and now insults us in this way." When Chapman returned he found the parlor doors locked, and was informed by the sheriff's deputy that he must confine himself to the kitchen and one room up stairs.

CHAPTER XXXI.

A VERY PERPLEXING SITUATION.

Wall Street was in a great flutter that day. A forgery, a defalcation that to-day would cause but a ripple on the surface, would have at that day sent the street into a tempest of excitement. A sheriff's deputy stood at the door of the office of the great Kidd Discovery Company, and a crowd of anxious and excited people, who had invested their money and now found they had lost it all, and had been made the victims of an aggravating fraud, surrounded the building. Threats and imprecations, enough to have sent a much more respectable house to the bottom of the sea, were heaped on the firm of Topman & Gusher. Nor indeed would it have been safe for any one connected with that enterprising firm to have shown his head in that assembly just at that time.

"Gentlemen will understand that this consolidated establishment is in a very unconsolidated condition. No further business will be done until its affairs are compromised;" the sheriff's deputy would announce, in a loud voice, as he endeavored to keep the crowd back. "There's only an empty safe, gentlemen, and some handsome office furniture," he would ejaculate. "You can't have them, you know."

Extravagance had indeed swallowed up all the substance and left only these insignificant things for the crowd of anxious creditors to feast their eyes on.

Rumor after rumor rang through Wall Street, each in turn increasing the amount of Topman's forgeries, and adding new names to the list of his victims. Bank ledgers were examined to see if the name of the firm appeared on them, and portly old directors put on their spectacles and congratulated themselves that the concern did not owe them a shilling. Groups of excited men stood at street corners discussing in animated tones the great event of the street. Everybody knew it must come. Nobody expected it would come so soon.

The strangest thing of all was that no one knew anything of the antecedents of either member of the firm, or what the great Kidd Discovery Company was really based upon. Enterprising gentlemen had bought and sold the stock, and made and lost money by it. That was all they knew of it. The morning papers had given them an interesting account about Gusher; now some one was needed to tell them all about Topman—where he came from, who he was, and where he was to be found. There was enough to call him rascal now. Even those who had ridden in his carriage, and enjoyed his dinners, and indeed thought him the best of fellows a few weeks before, were now ready to give him the hardest of kicks.

In truth, the firm was a mystery in Wall Street, and its largest creditors were in the greatest darkness concerning it. Some one has truly said that in a great commercial city men are known only by their enterprises and their successes; that their antecedents become lost in the magnitude and rapidity with which events revolve. This is particularly so with us. The firm of Topman & Gusher had fixed itself in Pearl Street, and gone quietly into business without friends, acquaintances, or endorsers; and in a single year had secured both credit and respectability. And it had done this on what is too frequently mistaken for energy and enterprise—show and pretension.

Upon Chapman's shoulders, however, the crushing effect of this great disaster fell heaviest. Stripped of all he had, ruined, disgraced, he stood like one amazed at the suddenness of his own fall. He had built his castles on sand, and now found them tumbling down, and crushing him under the ruin. His avaricious nature had led him, not only to wrong, but to bring distress and ruin on the unsuspecting and simple-minded Dutch settlers. The wheel of fortune was turned now. He had himself been ruined, betrayed, and disgraced by the very men he had put confidence in and made partners of his guilt. He also had set a snare and invented a plot by which he expected to strip honest old Hanz Toodleburg of his property, and now he had been caught in it himself.

His daughter, Mattie, had already disclosed to him the fact that she had overheard the conversation between him and Topman, relative to the manner of entrapping Hanz, and knew the secret of their plot. And she had appealed to him to save her the pain of bearing testimony that would conflict with his, to save an honest old man from poverty. The man of great progressive ideas now found it necessary to invent some way of escaping from what he saw would be worse than ruin and disgrace—a criminal's doom. His name had not appeared in the suit Topman & Gusher brought against Hanz Toodleburg. Oh, no. Chapman was needed as a witness to prove the signing of the papers, and all the circumstances relating to the sale of the secret of Kidd's treasure. Poverty and misfortune had now stepped in to purify and direct a smitten conscience.

He could not see his daughter further disgraced. Nor could he meet her in a court, giving testimony in conflict with his, and exposing his crime. He could only escape by coming out boldly, and doing justice to the old man he had tried so hard to wrong. It would also be to his advantage to assume this virtue, for if the case were decided against Hanz he would gain nothing. The creditors would in that case get all the property, whereas, if he confessed his partnership in, and exposed the plot, and defeated the creditors, some benefit might result from it—at some time. The son might still be alive, Chapman said to himself, and if he should form a connection with the family at some future day, (and there was no knowing what might happen,) why it was better to protect Hanz and the property now. He well knew that Mattie had fixed her affection on the young gentleman, and if he should ever return, nothing her mother could say hereafter would prevent their marriage.

CHAPTER XXXII.

HARVEST SUNDAY.

October was come again, the poetry of summer had almost departed, and it was a quiet Sunday morning in the country. The bell on the little old church by the hillside, at Nyack, was calling the plodding Dutch settlers to morning service. The hard, hollow sounds of the old bell echoed harshly over the hills, and yet there was something in its familiar sounds, and the quiet pastoral scenes it was associated with, that always moved our feelings, and prompted us to give them a pleasant resting place in our love.

Cattle were resting in the fields, and their yokes hung on the gate posts that day. A soft, Indian-summer glow hung with transparent effect over the landscape; and a gentle wind whispered lovingly over the Tappan Zee. Autumn, too, had hung the trees in her brightest colors.

It was Harvest Sunday, a sort of festive resting-day with the Dutch settlers, who had gathered about the little church in great numbers, young and old, all dressed in their simple but neat attire. Others were quietly wending their way thitherward, along the lanes and through the fields. There they gathered about the little old church, a smiling, happy, and contented people, and waited for the Dominie, for it was their custom to meet him at the church door, and after exchanging greetings, follow him like a loving flock into their seats.

The Dominie was to preach his harvest sermon, and his flock was to join him in giving thanks to God for the bounties He had bestowed upon them. He had, indeed, blessed them with an abundant harvest that year; and now they had come to thank Him and be joyful. Conspicuous in the group was the little snuffy doctor, Critchel, looking happy among the people whose ills he had administered to for half a century. On Harvest-Sunday he could kiss and caress the bright faced little children he had helped bring into the world as fondly as a young mother. There, too, was the schoolmaster, with his ruddy face and his seedy clothes, ready to do his part in making Harvest-Sunday pass pleasantly, for indeed the crop was a matter of importance with him. And there was Titus Bright, for the merry little inn-keeper would have considered such a gathering incomplete without him. Titus was not so well thought of by the Dutch settlers since he gave up his little tavern for a big one, and had taken to boarding fine folks from the city.

And now the appearance of Hanz and Angeline, advancing slowly up the road, for Hanz walked with a staff, created a pleasant diversion. Several of the young people ran to meet them, and greeted them with such expressions of welcome as must have filled their hearts with joy.

When they had nearly reached the church, Critchel proceeded to meet them with his hand extended. "Verily, good neighbor Hanz," said he, after greeting the old people with a hearty shake of the hand, "the people have had strange news to talk about for a week past." Critchel shook his head, looked serious, and taking Hanz by the arm, drew him aside. "This Chapman has fallen to the ground, they say."

"Mine friend Critchel," returned Hanz, leaning on his staff, and casting a look upward. "I tolds you tar pees un shust Got; and now you shees how dat shust Got he pees mine friend."

"Aye, verily," rejoined Critchel, "and he lets them what builds castles and lives like lords suffer their disappointments. Poor people like us, who work with their hands, stick to their lands, and pay their debts, have their castles in peace and contentment."

"Tar pees shust so much wisdom in vat you shays, mine friend Critchel. In dis world tar pees nothin' sartin. Dis Chapman, he puts his money in his pocket, and ven he gets his money in his pocket he gets rich and prout. Zen he goes to t' city so pig and prout as he can pe. Now he comes pack from t' city, mit his pig vrow, and tar pees nobody as makes one pow to his pig vrow. Above tar pees one shust Got, Critchel."

The misfortunes of the Chapman family, my reader must know, had been furnishing Nyack something to talk about for several months. But it was only with their return to town, which important event took place one morning during the last week, that the quiet of Nyack was disturbed and the gossips sent into a state of excitement. The family, indeed, returned as quietly as a family in misfortune could be expected to do, and put up at Bright's Inn, where, it was given out, they would live on the wreck of their fortune until Chapman could see his way clear for a new start in the world. But little was seen of Mrs. Chapman, of whom it was reported that she desired to live in retirement, and did not see visitors.

The lady, however, had resolved that Nyack should not turn up its nose without being kept in mind of the high social position the family had held in the city. And as a means of making the desired impression, and also of finding relief for her injured feelings, she had brought Napoleon Bowles into "retirement" with the family. And that faithful domestic accommodated his pride of a Sunday by dressing in his livery and top-boots, and walking out, to the astonishment and amusement of a crowd of curious urchins, who were sure to gather about him.

As for Chapman, he went about the town as if nothing had happened, renewing acquaintances, and declaring there was no honester man in the settlement than Hanz Toodleburg; that the charges against his honesty, and his connection with the Kidd Discovery Company, were all scandals, got up by bad men; and that he had been deceived by them himself.

During the few days Chapman had been in Nyack, he had made himself appear so good a friend of Hanz that the honest settlers not only began to express sympathy for him in his misfortunes, but to enquire what they could do to put him on his feet again. When, however, he told them it was not their sympathy he wanted, but their money to assist him in building a steamboat two hundred feet long, and that he had matured a plan for a railroad, so that they might ride from Nyack to New York in an hour, they became alarmed, put their heads together wisely, and declared the man mad beyond cure.

Here I must leave Chapman waiting to see his way clear. He came of that old round-head stock which, wanting its way always, ready to meddle with everything, never contented, ready to play the sycophant to gain power, selfish and arrogant in the use of it, is, nevertheless, found giving shape, action, and momentum to all our great enterprises. Out of all the trouble Chapman had caused Nyack, there had come some good that would be turned to account in the future. Misfortune had bowed, not broken his spirit. He was again prepared to invent a new religion, to build a church, to keep a boarding-house, to start a bank or run a steamboat—and all with modern improvements.

The little church bell was still ringing, and the crowd still kept increasing in numbers and cheerfulness. "The Dominie's coming! the Dominie's coming! The Dominie's coming!" was lisped by a score of lips, as the attention of the people was attracted down the road. There the old Dominie came, mounted on a clumsy-footed, big-headed, bay cob—a little bright-eyed girl, whose face was full of sweetness and love, and dressed in blue and white, riding behind him. His broad, kindly face, shadowed by a wide-brimmed hat, his flowing white hair, his quaintly cut coat, with the ample side pocket, and his long, white necktie, presented a picture so full of truth and simplicity as to be worthy of being preserved on canvas. He was, in truth, a figure belonging to an order of things that was fast passing way—at least along the banks of the Hudson.

Children clapped their hands and ran to meet him; girls greeted him with offerings of flowers; and when he had dismounted, both old and young gathered about him, lisping him a welcome and shaking him by the hand. There was nobody like Dominie Payson, and the love these people bore him, and now gave him so many expressions of, was true and heartfelt. And when he had kissed the children, and exchanged greetings and kind words with their parents, he proceeded into the church, followed by his flock. His sermon was, perhaps, one of the oddest ever listened to, for after returning thanks for the bountiful harvest, and extending on the goodness of God, and advising his flock to stick firmly to their farms and their religion, that being the only true way of getting to Heaven, he turned his guns against Mr. and Mrs. Chapman, though he never once mentioned their names. He urged his flock to keep in mind always how much better off they were, how much more happy they were than those men who came to town with the devil and a number of strange religions in their heads. Such people, he added, always had the devil for a friend; and it was the devil who assisted them to get poor people's money. And with this money they dressed their wives in silks and satins, built big houses, and lived like people who were very proud and never paid their debts, nor did a day's work on the roads. It was all well enough for these men to talk of Heaven and put on pious faces, but Heaven would take no notice of them while they gave themselves up to the temptations of the devil and built steamboats and founded railroads, to kill honest people with, and ruin the country.

"My friends," said the Dominie, resting for a moment, and then charging his guns for another fire at Chapman, "you have seen a man ready to sell his soul for money enough to build a steamboat. Now he wants to build a railroad to get you out of the world quicker." The Dominie shook his head, wiped his brow, and again paused for a few seconds. "Let them dress their wives in satins and silks, let them ruin their country with their steamboats and railroads, let them build their big houses, go to the city, get proud, waste all their money in folly and vice, and return among honest people with a sheriff at their heels, because they don't pay nobody—but don't you go and do it. My friends—there will be an account to settle with these people who swell themselves up so big, when roasting-day comes. You that have wives—look to them. Keep their hearts pure and simple. Don't let them spend your money in silks and satins. If you do, the sheriff locks up your door and puts the key in his pocket." Thus the Dominie concluded, reminding his hearers that, as it was Harvest-Sunday, they must not forget to be liberal with their sixpences when the box came round.

His hearers were greatly delighted, and declared they had not heard him preach so good a sermon for many a day. And when he came down from the pulpit they congratulated him, and sundry extra pecks of wheat were promised as a reward for the light he had favored them with.

The day wore away pleasantly, and when evening came, when the gleams of the setting sun tipped the surrounding hills with golden light, and dusky shadows were creeping up the valley, the reader, if he had looked in at Hanz Toodleburg's little house, might have seen one of those quaint but pleasant pictures which are a fit ending of such a day.

There, grouped around his table, sat the Dominie, Doctor Critchel, Bright the inn-keeper, and the schoolmaster, for Hanz had invited them to sup with him, and Angeline had prepared the best she had to set before them. There, too, was Tite's empty chair. There it stood, silent and touching, all the pleasant memories it once contained made sad now by the mystery that enshrouded his long absence. There was his plate, and his knife and fork, all so bright and clean, set as regularly as if he were home, and guarded so tenderly. The eloquence of that vacant chair, appealing so directly to the finer sensibilities of every one present, left a deep and sad impression. Supper was nearly over before any of the guests had courage to refer to it. The Dominie at length raised his spectacles and addressing Angeline, said: "Heaven gives to every house its idol. We have been blessed to-day, and made happy. It will yet please Heaven to bring back the idol of this house, and fill that empty chair. I am sure we shall all be glad when the boy gets home."

"When he does, there will be such a time at my house," interposed the inn-keeper, nodding his head approvingly. "There's the parlor for him to do his courting in. And one of the prettiest little sweethearts is waiting to give him such a welcome. God bless her—she isn't a bit like the rest of them Chapmans—she isn't."

"My school don't keep the day he comes home," rejoined the schoolmaster, helping himself to another piece of pumpkin pie.

The mention of Tite's name filled old Hanz's eyes with tears. He buried his face in his hands, and remained silent for several minutes, overcome by his feelings. As soon as he had recovered control of them, he wiped the tears from his eyes, and replied in broken sentences: "I vas sho happy ven mine Tite, mine poor poy Tite vas home. Peers as if now, mine poor poy he never comes home no more, he never prings shoy into mine house no more."

"Always look on the best side of things, neighbor Hanz," replied the Dominie.

"Yah, put I gets sho old now."

"It would not astonish me," continued the Dominie, playfully, "if the young gentleman surprised us all to-night. Stranger things have happened." These remarks excited a feeling of anxiety.

"I was on the other side of the river last night," continued the Dominie, "and the people there had a report from the city that the vessel he sailed in had been heard from." Angeline quietly left the table, for the wells of her heart were overflowing.

"Tar shall come news as t' wessel mine Tite shails in comed pack, eh?" enquired Hanz, fixing his eyes steadily on the Dominie.

"Not that she has arrived," returned the Dominie, "but that there is news of her—"

"Tar pees news," muttered Hanz, his eyes glistening with anxiety. "An nopody tells me t' news before, eh? Tar pees shum news of t'at wessel, eh? Tar don't pee no news of mine poor Tite, eh?" The old man extended his trembling hand and grasped the Dominie's arm nervously, his face became as pale as marble, and his whole system shook with excitement.

"Tar shall come news as t' wessel mine Tite shails in comes pack," he ejaculated, "an tar pees no news of mine poor poy, eh?" And he threw up his arms, rested his head on the Dominie's shoulder and wept like a child. "No, mine Tite he ton't comes home no more," he sobbed.

CHAPTER XXXIII.

RETURNED HOME.

While the scene just closed was being enacted, a glance across the river and down the road that skirts along the Hudson from Yonkers to Tarrytown, would have discovered a light country wagon, drawn by a single horse, and containing two men, advancing at a brisk pace. They had nearly reached Dobbs' Ferry as the sun disappeared in the west.

He who sat beside the driver, with his arms folded, and thoughtful, was a tall, well-formed young man, with light hair that curled into his neck, side whiskers, deep and intelligent blue eyes, a face that lighted up with a smile when he spoke, and which had been fair and handsome, but was now scorched and sun-burnt. His hands, too, were small, but hard and weather-burnt, indicating that he had been accustomed to use them at hard work. His dress was of blue petersham, looking neat and new, the short coat buttoning square across his breast; and a tall hat set oddly enough on a head evidently not accustomed to the fashion that dictated such a covering. A broad, white shirt collar, turned carelessly down, was tied with a black silk handkerchief, the long ends of which hung outside his coat.

There was something mature and thoughtful in his manner, even beyond his years. The driver, an inquisitive fellow, had several times tried to draw him into conversation, that he might find out something concerning him, for he seemed familiar with the names of places along the river, and yet kept up the disguise of a stranger. But on nothing, except the vessels passing up and down the river, did he seem inclined to be communicative. On these he would make such remarks as showed familiarity with the sea. Indeed his mind seemed absorbed in something of deep and painful interest.

They drew up at the little inn with the swinging sign near Dobbs' Ferry, for the driver said his horse was jaded, and needed feed and rest before they proceeded further, and were met by the short, corpulent landlord, who, after ordering the animal cared for, invited them into the house, saying there was a good supper ready.

"It is sundown now," said the passenger, in a tone of impatience, as he alighted from the wagon, and received the landlord's extended hand, "and we are still six miles away. You have forfeited the inducement I offered to quicken your speed; but it is no offset to my disappointment." This was addressed to the driver, who muttered something, about the heavy roads, in reply, tossed his hat into a chair on the porch, and with an independent and half-defiant air, walked into the house and took his seat at the supper table.

"'Tisn't the first time Sam's supped at my house," said the landlord, bowing and inviting the stranger to walk in. "You'll walk in, sir, won't you? There's always a good supper at this house—kept it when King George's troops were about—only four shillin', sir," the landlord continued, bowing and motioning his hand. But the stranger shook his head negatively, drew a cigar from his pocket and politely requested the landlord to give him a light. And when he had lighted his cigar, he drew a Spanish dollar from his pocket, and slipped it into the man's hand, saying it would pay for both their suppers, and he would take his when they returned. He, at the same time, begged the landlord to give himself no concern about him, but to proceed to his supper, which he knew from his appearance he would enjoy.

"Seein' how you're a gentleman," said the landlord, bowing obsequiously, "there's three shillin' more for the horse—that squares it."

"Certainly—I forgot the horse," replied the stranger, drawing a half-dollar piece from his pocket and giving it to the landlord.

"There's a shillin' comin' to you," returned the landlord, putting the money into one pocket, and feeling in the other, "Never mind the shilling," said the stranger, "we will settle that another time."

"Travellers always find a good bed at my house, and enough on the table. That's more than the fellow who keeps the house further on can say," continued the landlord, again bowing and proceeding to his supper.

The stranger now paced quickly and impatiently up and down the little veranda, pausing every few minutes and looking out in the direction of the wagon, as if it contained something he was guarding with scrupulous care. In short, the object of his solicitude was a stout, leathern valise, in the wagon, and which was so heavy that it required the strength of two ordinary men to handle it easily.

Twenty minutes passed and the driver again made his appearance, wiping his lips and buttoning up his coat unconcernedly. "Sorry to have detained you," he said, flapping his hat on. "Landlord says you've settled the shot—won't be long getting there now." In another minute they were in their seats and on the road to Tarrytown.

It was nearly eight o'clock when they reached the old ferry, and found it deserted for the night. The boatmen had ceased their regular crossings nearly an hour before, and were quietly smoking their pipes at home. The moon was up, stars shone brightly in the serene sky, and not a sail specked the unruffled surface of the Tappan Zee. Lights twinkled on the opposite shore, and the little old town of Nyack was dimly seen.

They waited a few minutes, and as no one appeared, the driver went in search of the boatmen, saying a few extra shillings would make it all right with them. And while he was gone the stranger paced nervously and with rapid steps up and down, every few seconds pausing at the pier-head and looking intently in the direction of Nyack. Was it joy he anticipated, or disappointment he feared? Something was agitating his heart and filling his eyes with tears, for he several times turned his head and wiped them away. And yet the more he watched in the direction of Nyack, the more restless and impatient he became.

The driver returned after an absence of ten minutes, accompanied by two sturdy fellows, both of whom affected to be in bad humor at being called on to ferry a traveller at that hour. With their hands thrust deep into their nether pockets, they moved reluctantly about, scanning the stranger from head to foot. "Couldn't stop this side till morning?" enquired one of them, in a grumbling tone. "I must cross to-night," replied the stranger, in a decided voice. "Cross to-night, eh? Well, it's a long pull across there now," muttered the man, blowing the ashes from his pipe and still affecting an air of indifference. Then raising his eyes and breaking a piece of tobacco between his fingers, he resumed: "Worth a matter of twelve shillin' extra—isn't it? Wouldn't mind a trifle like that—I take it."

"I must yield to your demands—of course. It is a necessity with me to get across as quick as possible," replied the stranger, and drawing from his pocket two Spanish dollars, he gave them to the boatman, saying: "We will settle the matter now. Here is your pay in advance."

The man took the money and at once became active and civil. "We must set the gentleman across, Tom," said he, addressing his comrade, and exposing the silver, "this makes it all right."

The stranger now dismissed the driver with an extra dollar, for which he considered himself lucky, for he had not kept his promise to reach the ferry by sundown.

The boatman who acted as spokesman, in attempting to lift the valise from the wagon, let it fall to the ground, such was its great weight. "There's somethin' more nor clothes in that," said the man, shaking his head and raising his hands in an attitude of alarm. Then, with an inquisitive look at the stranger, he continued: "Hadn't no connection with them are Kidd Discovery Company folks? They was swindlers, they was."

"Never heard of such a company before. Get my things aboard, and let us be away," replied the stranger, in a tone of command.

It required the strength of both boatmen to carry the valise comfortably; and when they had got it aboard and the stranger seated in the stern, for he said he could steer, they pulled away for the opposite shore. Not a word was spoken for several minutes. At length the stranger broke the silence. "How pleasant it seems," he said, "to get back on the old Tappan Zee. Everything looks so familiar—"

"You have been here before, then?" enquired the man pulling the stern oar, and who had acted as spokesman.

"Yes," returned the stranger. "My home was just out of Nyack not many years ago. I may find things changed there now. Do you know many people over there?"

"Why yes—nearly everybody—"

"Dominie Payson—is he living?"

"If he didn't die since yesterday. He was over here yesterday."

"And Doctor Critchel—you know him, I suppose? Is he alive?"

"Why, help you—he never intends to die."

"And you know, I suppose;" here the stranger hesitated, and his voice thickened; "you know, I suppose, Hanz Toodleburg—and his—. Are they living?"

"Living! That they are—and right hearty, too. They tried to get the old man mixed up in the Kidd Discovery affair—but they didn't." The boatman bent his head approvingly.

"There was a Chapman family—are they still in Nyack?"

"They're there—but its not sayin' much for Nyack. They went to New York proud, and as folks thought rich, for Chapman had his finger in schemes enough to get other people's money; but he com'd back poor as a crow, they say."

The stranger's mind seemed to have been relieved of some great anxiety by these answers, and he at once became more cheerful and talkative. He at the same time avoided saying anything that might discover who he was.

This caution excited the boatman's curiosity to such a pitch that he resolved to make a bold push to uncover the stranger.

"Wouldn't take it amiss, would you?" said he, "if a man like me was to ask what your name was? Needn't mind if there's any cause o' keepin' it a secret."

The stranger smiled, hesitated, and stammered in reply: "Hanz Toodleburg is my father."

"Well, well! Just what I expected. Didn't say nothin' you see; but I thought as how you was him," exclaimed the boatman.

"I have been over three years away from home," interrupted the stranger.

"Then you are Tite—the old man's son," resumed the boatman, "well, well!" Turning to him who pulled the bow-oar: "Stop pullin' a bit, Tom," said he, "stop pullin'."

The man now rested his oar, and rising from his seat, extended his hand to the stranger, saying: "There's a hard old honest hand that welcomes you safe back. John Flint is my name—called old Jack Flint generally." And he shook Tite's hand again and again. "A heap o' people round here reckoned how you was dead—they did. I can't tell you how glad I am to see you, my boy. Its fifteen years since you and me sailed comrades on the sloop. Bin all round the world an' aint above shakin' the hand of an old fellow like me. That's what I like." Again and again the old boatman shook Tite's hand, and gave expression to such sentiments of joy as showed how true and honest was his heart.

"Yes, this is me, Jack, and I am as glad to see you as you are to see me. But I wanted to get across without being recognized."

"Wouldn't take it amiss, would you," said he, "if a man like me was to ask what your name was?".

The old boatman felt in his pocket, and drawing forth the two Spanish dollars, insisted on returning them. "Them goes back into your pocket," he said, shaking his head, "Never shall be said Jack Flint charged an old comrade a sixpence for settin' him across stream."

"Keep it, keep it, Jack. I have enough for both of us," replied Tite, motioning his hand for the boatman to return the money to his pocket.

"Well, if you insist—an' I have to accept it, you see, it'll be out of respect and to please you." And he looked at the money doubtingly, shook his head, and reluctantly returned it to his pocket.

The man now resumed his oar, and they proceeded on with increased speed. In less than half an hour from that time, they had landed at Nyack, and proceeding up the road had reached Bright's Inn, the two boatmen carrying the valise. Here they came to a halt, the men setting the valise down, while Tite seemed in doubt what to do next. Bewildered with the position he found himself in, hesitating and nervous, almost overcome by anxiety, his throbbing heart beat quicker and quicker the nearer he reached his home. But there was now a more violent struggle going on in his feelings. It was a struggle to decide between love and duty. Now he looked up the road in the direction of his home, and advanced a few steps. Again he paused and looked up enquiringly at the house. The old boatman had told him that Chapman lived there, when all the embers of that love he had so long cherished for Mattie seemed to kindle again into a living fire. And yet what changes might have taken place since he left? If, however, she still loved him, and was true to him, how could he pass the house, even at that late hour, without at least letting her know he was in Nyack?

It was indeed late, and there was still a mile before he reached the home of his parents. He could have more time in the morning to meet Mattie, to unfold his heart to her, and to give her an account of the many strange things that had happened to him since he left.

There was a bright light in two of the upper windows, but below the house was nearly dark, and Bright was in his bar-room, settling up the business of the day. Suddenly the light in the windows became brighter, then the shadow of a female figure was seen crossing and recrossing the room every few seconds. Tite watched and watched that flitting shadow, for he read in it the object of his heart's love, read in it the joy that was in store for him, perhaps—perhaps the sorrow. The figure was Mattie's, and it was her shadow that was causing him all this heart-aching. Now the figure took the place of the shadow, and stood looking out at the window, as if contemplating the moon and the stars, for nearly a minute. Yes, there was Mattie, watching and wondering what had become of the man who was at that moment contemplating her movements. Then the figure and the shadow disappeared, but it was only to increase Tite's impatience to see her.

The three men now proceeded to the door and the bell was rung. A moving of chairs and unlocking of doors indicated that the house had not gone to bed. The door was soon opened by Titus Bright, in his shirt sleeves and slippers, and holding a candle in his hand. "What's up, Flint?" he enquired, for he saw only the boatmen; "what brings you over at this time of night?"

"There was a shillin' to be made, you see, Bright, and a passenger what wanted settin' over, you see," said the ferryman, his face beaming with good nature. "Know you'd like to see him, you know, Bright, and to make him as comfortable as you could for a night or so. Tom and me pulled him across." Tite now advanced towards the inn-keeper, who gazed at him with an air of astonishment, and held the candle above his head to avoid the shadow.

"Come in, come in," said Bright. "We will make the gentleman as comfortable as we can."

"You have forgotten me, I see," said Tite, smiling and extending his hand.

"God bless me!" exclaimed Bright, grasping his hand in a paroxysm of delight; "if here isn't Tite Toodleburg cum home. Come in, come in. Welcome home." After shaking him warmly by the hand and leading him into the parlor, the inn-keeper ran and brought his wife, who welcomed the young man with the tenderness of a mother. The good woman would have had a fire made and supper prepared, and indeed entertained him for the rest of the night, expressing her joy over his return, had he not told her how great was his anxiety to see his parents.

"I know who it is the young man wants to see," said Bright, touching him on the elbow and nodding his head suggestively. "And there'll be a flutter up stairs when it's told her you're cum home."

The boatmen had remained in the hall. Bright now invited them into his bar and filled mugs of ale for them, and joined them in drinking the health of the young man who had been round the world. He then dismissed them, saying he would take care of the young gentleman's baggage; and stepping up stairs, tapped gently at Chapman's door. "We were all retiring for the night," said Mrs. Chapman, opening the door slightly, and looking alarmed, for Bright was in a flutter of excitement, and it was nearly a minute before he could tell what he wanted. At length he stammered out: "There, there, there—there's a strange gentleman down stairs, mam—and he would like to see Miss Mattie, I am sure he would."

"Mr. Bright," replied Mrs. Chapman, tossing her head and compressing her lips, "he can't be much of a gentleman to come at this hour of night. My daughter has no acquaintance who would presume to take such a liberty. Etiquette forbids it."

Mattie now made her appearance, with a book half open in her left hand, and looking anxious and agitated. Then resting her right hand on her mother's shoulder, "Mr. Bright," she enquired, in a hesitating voice, "what does the gentleman look like?"

"A nice gentleman enough, Miss—"

"Is it any one you know?"

"Why, Miss," resumed Bright, with an air of reluctance, "wouldn't intrude at this house, but I know you'd like to see the gentleman; and wouldn't be particular about the time."

Mattie fixed her eyes on Bright with a steady gaze, her agitation increased, her face changed color rapidly, her heart seemed to beat anew with some sudden transport of joy. "Oh, mother! oh, mother!" she exclaimed, tossing the book on the floor, "I know who Mr. Bright means. It's him! I know it's him! He has come back!" She rushed past her mother, vaulted as it were down the stairs and into the parlor. The young man stood motionless. He was so changed in dress and appearance that she suddenly hesitated, and for a moment drew back, as if in doubt.

"It is me, Mattie," said Tite, smiling and advancing with his hand extended. The thought suddenly flashed through his mind that she might have expected some one else. He was mistaken, for she met his advance like one whose heart was filled with joy. In short, the words had hardly fallen from his lips when they were in each other's arms, and giving such proofs of their affection as only hearts bound together by the truest and purest of love can give.

"I knew you would come back to me—yes, I knew you would. There was an angel guarding you while absent," she whispered, looking up as he kissed her and kissed her. And as her eyes met his her face brightened with a smile so full of sweetness and gentleness.

"I knew what would happen," said Bright, opening the door apace and looking in. "Knew there would be just such a scene." Just at that moment Mrs. Chapman brushed past the exuberant inn-keeper, and stood like a massive statue, looking at the scene before her with an air of surprise and astonishment, for Mattie was still clasped in the young man's arms.

"My daughter! my daughter!" she exclaimed, raising her fat hands, "enough to make a mother faint to see a well-brought-up daughter so familiar? It shocks me, my daughter. I am sure I am glad to see the young man home. But familiarity of that kind's not becoming. Your father never would have married me if I had allowed familiarity of that kind."

"You must blame me; it was all my fault," said Tite, handing Mattie to a chair, and advancing toward Mrs. Chapman.

"You have been away a long time, haven't you," said the lady, receiving his hand in a cold and formal manner. "You are very much changed—the effect of the sea-air on the complexion, I suppose? We shall be very glad to see you at any time, Mr. Toodleburg. It was so late we didn't expect visitors, and were not prepared for them. You said you had not seen your aged parents?"

"Not yet," replied Tite, "but I shall proceed there soon."

"It was very kind of you," resumed the lady, "to pay us this compliment. How very anxious they must be to see you."

"And I am equally anxious to see them," he replied; "but I could not pass without seeing you—just for a few minutes." Then turning to Mattie, he exchanged kisses with her, kissed her good-night, to the great distress of her mother, who was compelled to look on. He also promised to call early in the morning, spend most of the day, and give an account of his voyage.

A minute more and he was seated in a wagon beside Bright, and proceeding over the road toward Hanz's little house.

When he was gone, and the Chapmans had retired to their room, "Ma," said Mattie, her face coloring with feeling, "it was very unkind, even cruel of you to treat the young gentleman so coldly."

"Done to balance the familiarity, my daughter—the familiarity! Needed something to balance that," interrupted the lady, bowing her head formally. "Young man looks respectable enough. He may have come home and not a sixpence in his pocket—who knows? In these matters, my daughter, it's always best to know where the line is drawn before building your house."

"He might have come home penniless; it would not have made a bit of difference to me, mother, I would love him just as much," replied Mattie. "But I can forgive you, ma, for I know you did not mean what you said." And she kissed her mother, and retired for the night, the happiest woman in all Nyack.

CHAPTER XXXIV.

HE BRINGS JOY INTO THE HOUSE.

All was silent and dark in the little house where Hanz Toodleburg lived, when the wagon containing Tite and the inn-keeper drew up at the gate. A dull, dreamy stillness seemed to hang over the place, and the little, old house was in the full enjoyment of a deep sleep. The two men alighted, and Tite stood for a few minutes viewing the scene around him. How strange and yet how familiar everything seemed. He was at the opposite side of the world only a few months ago, and time had sped on so swiftly that it seemed as if he had gone to bed at night on one side of the globe, and waked up in the morning at the other. Then he was on an island almost unknown to the rest of the world, surrounded by scenes so wild, so strange and romantic, that the reader would not believe them real.

Here now was the old lattice gate, the vine-covered arbor leading through the garden to the cracked and blistered-faced front door, the stack of hop-vines in the garden-corner, and the rickety veranda where, when a boy, he used to sit beside his father of a summer evening, for it was here Hanz welcomed his friends and smoked his pipe. It was here, too, that Angeline, the spirit of whose sweet face had been with him in his wanderings, used to sit at her flax-wheel, spinning thread that was famous in Fly Market.

Could this be a sweet dream, a beautiful delusion, a spirit-spell that moves the soul with pictures of love and enchantment, and from which some stern reality would soon awake him and dispel the charm? No, it was reality, appealing more forcibly to all that was true and kindly in his nature, and filling his eyes with tears.

The inn-keeper noticed the effect it was having on his feelings, and made an effort to divert his attention. "Looks kind o' natural after bein' round the world doesn't it, Tite?" he enquired.

"Yes—seems like home again," was the quiet reply.

"Zounds!" exclaimed the inn-keeper, suddenly; "but there's somethin' heavy in it." In attempting to lift the valise from the wagon it had fallen to the ground under its great weight. The inn-keeper shook his head and rubbed his hands. "Had a lucky voyage, I reckon," he concluded.

"More than eighty pounds of solid gold in that," returned Tite, coolly. The mention of so much gold astonished and delighted the inn-keeper.

"There'll be such a time when the town hears that!" said he. "There'll be enough o' them that'll call you their friend."

"Left three times as much more in the city," resumed Tite. "And there's enough on an island in the Pacific to buy a town as big as Nyack. And I know where it is."

"Eighty pounds of solid gold!" said the inn-keeper, looking enquiringly at Tite, then stooping down and testing the weight of the valise with his hands. "It's so. I always did know you'd come home a rich man."

They now carried the valise into the veranda, knocked at the door, and listened for footsteps within. The big old dog had been growling and barking fiercely for several minutes. Now he recognized the friendly voice of the inn-keeper, and barked them a welcome. He then ran to the little room where Hanz was sleeping, and only ceased barking when he got up.

Soft footsteps were heard inside, a dim light shone through the little window opening into the veranda, and a voice inside enquired: "Who comes t' mine house sho late?"

"Open the door, friend Toodleburg," replied the inn-keeper. "Shouldn't have disturbed you at this hour; but there's a gentleman here would like to see you—an' I'm sure you'd like to see him."

The old man opened the door at the sound of Bright's voice, and stood gazing at the visitors with an air of bewilderment. "You prings me goot news, eh, Bright?" he enquired. "Yes, I am shure you prings me shome news ash ish goot."

"Father, father," said Tite, advancing with his right hand extended, "you don't know me?"

"Ton't know mine own Tite? Mine poor poy Tite!" exclaimed the old man in a paroxysm of joy. "Yes I does." And he raised his hands, and threw his arms around Tite's neck, and wept for joy. "Ton't know mine own Tite," he repeated, raising his head and looking up in Tite's face, "yes I does. Yes, I shay mine Tite will cum home; an' he cums home—and mine poor old heart he pees sho glat. Yes, he pees you, mine Tite. You prings shoy into mine house. Mine poor Tite—he com'd home t' mine house. Tar pees no more shorrow now in mine house." The old man was overcome with joy. The idol of the house was home again, and true happiness reigned under that little roof.

"You ton't go away no more, mine Tite," he continued, patting him on the shoulder and pressing his hand.

Angeline heard Tite's voice and came rushing into the room frantic with joy. "Thank God! thank God!" she exclaimed. "He has brought our boy safe back to us." And she embraced him, threw her arms around his neck, and kissed him again and again.

"And I am so glad to get back to you, mother," he replied, returning her affection, and pressing her to his breast fondly. "It is so good to be in my old home, where I can receive your blessings, and be good to you."

And Angeline looked up in his face with such a sweet smile, as she patted him on the shoulder, and their tears mingled in the sweetest of joy as she invoked God's blessing on his head. Truly, God had heard their prayer, had blessed them, and had again made their little home bright with joy.

"I wish Chapman could look in here now," said Bright, "there'd be a lesson for him on what happiness is worth." And he shook Tite by the hand, told him to remember that his house was always open to him, and left for the night.

Even the old dog seemed anxious to join in welcoming the young gentleman back, for he would look up affectionately in his face, draw his body close to his feet, and lay his huge paw on his knee.

And now a fire was lighted, and Angeline prepared supper for Tite, for he had eaten nothing since morning. The chair that had stood empty so long was filled now, and the happiness that reigned under that little roof was such as gold could not purchase.

CHAPTER XXXV.

HOW HE GOT AWAY FROM THE ISLAND.

When supper was over, Tite proceeded to give his parents an account of the voyage, and the manner of escaping from the island with the treasure. The reader has already heard that portion which carries the story up to the death of old Dunman, the pirate. It will be only necessary then to give that part of it which relates to what took place afterward.

"Poor old Dunman," said Tite, "he was so kind to us all, and tried so much to relieve our sufferings and make us feel contented that we all liked him, and felt his death was a severe loss to us. There was something so terrible in the story of his life that we used to talk about it at night, and fancy all sorts of strange spirits haunting the place where his money was buried. It was this that made us all impatient to get away from the dreary place. Three or four days after we had buried him, we removed the stones he said the gold was buried under, and there found, as he had told us, bags and boxes of gold and silver, in bars and coin of various kinds, heavy silver and gold ornaments that had been plundered from churches and convents, with pearls and diamonds and other precious stones, enough to fill two iron chests two feet square and two feet deep. There was the thought that it was the price of so much crime. And what good after all was this gold and silver to do us, if we were to die on the island, like old Dunman? We divided it among us, just as we would something of little value, not caring which got the biggest portion. Then, after keeping out what we thought we might want, each buried his part in separate spots, and marked the places with piles of big stones.

"I always had a presentment that some vessel would come along, and afford us the means of getting away; but after several months of disappointment my companions began to despair, and saying they might as well die one way as another, fitted up the boat, and with sails made of prepared seal skins, and such scanty provisions as they could obtain, set sail in search of an island described by old Dunman to be two leagues distant, inhabited, and a place where whalers had been known to touch. Each took two bags of gold with him, promising that if they were successful they would return and rescue me.

"I felt, and told them they were undertaking what was sure death, and bid them good-bye, never expecting to see them again. Week after week and month after month passed, and nothing was heard of them. I was alone, and nothing but the animals old Dunman had domesticated to keep me company. As a means of attracting the attention of any vessel that might be passing, I built a hut on a high hill near the coast, and used to go there at night and build a fire as a signal. There wasn't a sail came near. I had never feared death before; but to have to die on this unknown island, with everything so strange and mysterious around me, and never be heard of again by my parents and friends, excited all sorts of curious fears in me. And the more I thought of it the more I wanted to get away.

"Well, it was five months since my companions set sail. Poor Ryder, poor Doane; these were their names. They were both young men from Cape Cod; and as brave and true-hearted as ever lived. I got up one morning to renew my signal-fire, and was wondering what had become of the poor fellows, and saying to myself how foolish they were to anticipate death. It was just in the grey of daylight. Happening to cast my eye down the coast, I espied the dim figure of a sail advancing quietly up the coast. I shouted for joy at the sight, not thinking or caring whether it might bring friends or foes. The wind was light, but fair, and the little craft, which turned out to be a taunt-rigged schooner of about a hundred and twenty tons, came gliding along like some white-winged thing of life, for she had a square sail and fore and main gaff-topsails set.

"Just before reaching the cove she furled her square sail and took in the gaff-topsails—a proof that she was making port. I hastened down to the coast, for it was broad daylight now, and watched her every movement. She stood into the cove, rounded to, hauled down her jibs, and dropped her anchor. The men in charge of that vessel handled her as if they were familiar with the place. An hour passed, and no attempt was made to land. Men appeared on deck, moving about in the quiet discharge of their duty, but no attention was directed to the shore. Then a man stood on the quarter with his glass raised, and scanned the shore from point to point. Then there was an aggravating pause, and the rest of the men seemed to disappear below. Then an increased number appeared on deck, and began clearing the lashings from the stern boat. That was a joyful moment, for it was a proof of their intention to land. Then the boat was lowered away and pulled alongside, when two oarsmen got in, and were followed by two men who sat in the stern sheets, and who turned out to be my old companions, Doane and Ryder. Deliverance had come at last.

"After being at sea three days and nights in the boat, they were picked up by a New Bedford whaleship, and landed at Honolulu, where they chartered the schooner Lapwing and returned for me. Thinking it necessary to keep our discovery a secret, lest it might excite the cupidity of the crew, who were all natives, we had to proceed cautiously, and disguise our movements as much as we could. It was decided to leave at least half of the treasure until we could find a more secure means of removing it, as well as one less liable to excite suspicion at the points we would be compelled to land at on our way home.

"We got what we agreed to take away quietly on board during the night, having filled Dunman's big old chest with shells and buried it among them.

Then each swore on oath that he would be true to the other, and that he wouldn't make an effort to remove what remained except by mutual agreement, and for the benefit of all equally. We disguised all our movements so well that not even the captain of the schooner, who was an old Spanish coaster, accustomed to suspicious transactions, mistrusted what we were doing.

"When we got all ready, we bid adieu to No Man's Island, and set sail for Honolulu, feeling as if we had been set free from a prison. We were on the way home now, and that was enough to lighten our hearts. We were three weeks getting to Honolulu; and had to remain there two months. We wanted an American ship homeward bound, to take passage on. But as none came, we shipped on board the British whaleship Rose, of Halifax, Nova Scotia, with a full cargo homeward bound. We got there after a long and stormy voyage, working our way as sailors before the mast. We were looked on as poor, shipwrecked whalemen; and no one on board thought we had an extra dollar in our pockets. At Halifax we found a vessel ready to sail for New York, and took passage on her, and here I am now, home again, and glad to get home." It was long after midnight when Tite concluded his story; and having received once more the caresses of his parents, he retired to the little room he had occupied when a boy, to sleep and dream of joys that were in store for him.

CHAPTER XXXVI.

AN INTERESTING CEREMONY.

The little sleepy town of Nyack had hardly waked up on the following morning, when the news of Tite's arrival was rung in it's ears. Marvelous stories, too, were told concerning the amount of money he had brought home, and the different countries he had visited. The inn-keeper declared at the breakfast table, intending that Mrs. Chapman should hear it, that he could say of his own knowledge, that the young gentleman had brought gold enough home to build a castle, have a coach of his own, and live like a gentleman in the city all the rest of his life.

"Has he really brought home so much money?" enquired Mrs. Chapman, raising her eyes and looking at Bright with an air of astonishment. "The young gentleman never mentioned it last night. Well, after all, there's nothing like young gentlemen of his class seeking their fortunes away from home. To say the least, it will give the young gentleman a fixed position in society."

"Yes, my dear," rejoined Chapman, "I always had a good opinion of the young gentleman. I always knew he would distinguish himself if he had a chance—"

"Good opinions are always plenty enough," interrupted the schoolmaster, who was a boarder at Bright's that week, "when a man has money and don't need good opinions."

Chapman made no reply. Indeed he was not prepared for such a thrust from so poor a fellow as the schoolmaster. He understood, however, what was meant by it, for he had gone into court only a few weeks before and given such testimony as showed himself a knave and a hypocrite, though it saved Hanz Toodleburg from ruin.

Mattie noticed the impression made on her mother by what Bright had said, but preserved a dignified silence. She felt that she had gained the price due to her constancy, had risen above the vanities and temptations designed to distract and mislead her, and by following the dictates of her own clear judgment would soon secure both happiness and fortune.

Breakfast was scarcely over at Hanz Toodleburg's before the neighbors, one after another, began to drop in to shake Tite by the hand, and welcome him home, and say "God bless you." Many of them brought little presents, to show how true and heart-felt was the friendship they bore him. And when he went down into the village he found himself surrounded by friends, all anxious to shake his hand, and to welcome him back, and to hear something concerning his voyage. In short, he was an object of curiosity as well as respect, for at that day there was a mysterious interest attached to a young man who had been a voyage round the world, it being associated with spirit and daring of a remarkable kind.

But it was not these friends Tite stole away and went down into the village to see. It was Mattie, at the mention of whose name a blush always colored his cheek. The two lovers had arranged for a morning walk, and were soon seen coming from the house together, smiling and happy. Mrs. Chapman had condescended to see them to the door, and her ponderous figure quite filled the space. "Don't forget, my daughter," she said, as they were leaving, "don't forget to bring the young gentleman back to dine with us. We can't promise him anything very nice; but he is welcome, you know, and must try and accommodate himself to our changed circumstances."

There is to me nothing more beautiful to contemplate than the picture of two young lovers brought happily together after years of trial and disappointment, themselves representing what there is good and pure in the human heart. It is then we seem to see the heart liberate itself from guile, and truth and right rejoice in their triumph over wrong. There was just such a picture presented by Mattie Chapman, the true-hearted American girl, and the active, earnest, persevering, and modest, American boy, just at this moment.

The day was bright and breezy, and there, high up on that hill overlooking the Tappan Zee, under that clump of trees, with their embracing branches forming a bower, in the very spot where they had liberated their hearts and pledged their love, and bid each other a sad adieu on the morning Tite sailed on his voyage, the young lovers were seated again. Hour after hour passed, and still they sat there, for Tite was recounting his adventures; telling Mattie the story of his strange voyage, and listening in return to her recital of what had taken place during his absence. Indeed, so earnestly were they engaged relating what had happened since they had been separated that they quite forgot dinner; and on returning to the house, found Mrs. Chapman in a state of great anxiety. It was not that they had been absent so long; but the young gentleman would find things cold and unsatisfactory. The truth was, Mrs. Chapman had dressed herself with a view to a little display, and was a little disappointed at not having the opportunity to make it before a full table. Mr. Bowles, too, had been ordered to appear bright and nice, in his new livery and top-boots, to wait on the family at dinner, and show, by his attentions to the young gentleman, that he was a well-brought-up servant. In fine, the lady so embarrassed the young gentleman with her attentions, that he was glad when dinner was over. I ought not to forget to mention that Chapman, though he was less demonstrative, took several occasions to assure the young gentleman of the high respect he had always held him in—especially on account of his father and mother.

Tite went home when dinner was over; but returned again in the evening, for there was an attraction there he could not resist. And it was then that Mrs. Chapman joined their hands, invoked a blessing on their heads and called them her children.

"I always did like the young gentleman—I am sure I always did," she added, with an air of condescension. "My daughter knows I always did. It was not on the young gentleman's account that I entertained a little misgiving (just a little) in reconciling the family connection." Pausing suddenly, the lady turned to Mattie in a somewhat confused manner: "My daughter, my daughter," she returned, "you must overlook a number of little things. You will—won't you? Now, don't say I am vain. But it was such a queer—yes, such a vulgar and very common name to carry into society."

"There's just one favor I have to ask, my daughter. I am sure the young gentleman won't object to it—I am sure he won't." Again Mrs. Chapman paused, and seemed a little confused.

"Certainly, ma, certainly," replied Mattie, with a pleasant smile, "anything to please my dear mother."

"Well, then," resumed Mrs. Chapman, mildly: "There'll be no harm in changing the name a little—just a little, for the sake of the effect it will have on society. The young gentleman, I am sure he will (he has got the means to do it, you see) set up a nice establishment in the city, and (looking forward a little, you know) you will have a set of society of your own. Things change so, you see. You wouldn't mind changing the name so that it will read Von Toodleburg? T.B. Von Toodleburg would be so much nicer."

I may mention here that such was the name the family took and flourished under at a subsequent period, as will appear in the second series of this work.

"Fix things, name and all, to your liking, my dear mother," replied Mattie, laughing heartily. "I don't believe Tite cares anything about it."

"Never was ashamed of my name," replied Tite, with an air of indifference, "never was. But it doesn't matter much what a man's name is. They used to call me all sorts of names at sea."

"Another little harmless request," resumed Mrs. Chapman, with a condescending bow. "You see there is Bowles. Bowles is such an excellent servant, and so very respectable. He has such a presentable appearance when in his livery. I have great respect for Bowles—he understands me so well. You won't have any objection to his having a fixed position in the family, will you?"

Mattie blushed, and drawing her mother aside, whispered in her ear: "We can settle such matters, my dear mother, when others of more importance are disposed of."

"But you know, my daughter," she returned, with an air of great seriousness, "he has done so much to make these common country people understand what our position was in the city."

Two weeks were passed in making preparations for the wedding. And now the day was come, and that ceremony that was to unite two loving hearts for weal or woe, which was to seal their fortunes in one bond, was to be performed in the little old church, quietly and unostentatiously, by Dominie Payson, for it had been settled after some reluctance on the part of Mrs. Chapman, that the job could be done by that worthy divine, and the world think none the less of the young people.

Nyack, my reader must know, was in the best of humor that day, and when it was four o'clock, appeared in a smiling face, and dressed in it's best clothes. Chapman, I may also mention, forgot his misfortunes, and for once appeared neat and tidy, and in a happy mood. Indeed he had kissed and congratulated his daughter several times during the day. He had also unburdened his heart by telling her how happy he felt that the family had escaped disgrace in the city. He had, indeed, something to be thankful for, since Gusher had been taken back to New Orleans, tried, convicted of his crimes, and sent for two years at hard labor in the penitentiary.

Mrs. Chapman, remembering that such events did not occur every day, resolved not to be outdone by any of them. She was sure a little display would not be wasted; and had spent four hours "getting herself elegant." She had more than half a suspicion that there would be some New York people present, and it would not do to be outshone by them in magnificence of toilet. Nor must I forget Bowles, who appeared shortly after breakfast in his new livery, with a tall hat half covered with a band and buckle, white gloves, and bright new boots and breeches. Bowles was a figure of immense importance, and contemplated himself with an air of amusing gravity, as he moved up and down in front of the house, much to the amusement of the visitors at Bright's Inn. A bunch of flowers had been provided for his button hole; and he was to drive the happy couple to and from church, an honor he seemed to appreciate fully.

There was an interesting scene, too, at Hanz Toodleburg's little house. Instead of making bridal presents of costly jewelry and works of art, as is now done, the worthy settlers sent the groom's father presents of a very different character. Hanz had found enough to do during the morning in receiving these presents and thanking the donors. There was a pig from farmer Tromp, a barrel of apples from neighbor Steuben, a big cheese from farmer Van Beuskirk, a ham from the widow Welcker, a pan of new-made sausages from farmer Deitman, and a bushel of dried apples from Dominie Payson. In fine, one sent a cow, another a sack of wheat, another a barrel of cider; and in that way they had well neigh stocked Hanz's larder for the winter.

It was now nearly time for the ceremony. Neatly, but plainly dressed people were seen treading their way toward the little church, while around its door a number of bright-faced children, all dressed so neatly in white, and with their hands full of flowers, stood ready to greet the bride and bridegroom. In short, the worthy settlers had come from all directions to witness the ceremony. There were rustics, in their simple attire, sauntering through the old church yard, or leaning listlessly over the paling. And there in the old belfry sat Jonas, the ringer, with his bald head and his weeping eyes, ready to ring out a merry peal as soon as the bride and bridegroom came in sight.

A laughing, happy throng of people filled the little church as soon as the door was opened. Then Dominie Payson took his place at the altar; and Hanz and Angeline, representing age beautified by simplicity, walked slowly up the aisle, and took their place on one side, followed by Critchel, the inn-keeper and the schoolmaster, who stood just behind them. A few minutes later and Mrs. Chapman, arrayed in all the majesty of her best wardrobe entered, accompanied by her meek little husband, and took their places on the opposite side, presenting such a contrast of characters. The picture only wanted the central figures now.

A few minutes more, and there was a sudden, anxious movement on the part of those inside. All eyes were turned towards the door. The bridal party had arrived. Old Jonas was ringing his bell. The children at the door were tossing flowers at their feet; and their voices were heard singing a sweet and touching song. Then the bridal party advanced up the aisle, the bride dressed in simple white, and with flowers in her golden hair, and looking so sweetly. And as they took their place before the altar, there was something so full of love and gentleness, of truth and purity, in that sweet face as Mattie looked up and calmly surveyed the scene, that it seemed as if earth had nothing to compare with it.

And as the simple, but impressive ceremony proceeded, and the young lovers once more pledged their love, and made that solemn vow never to separate until death comes, and knelt in prayer to sanctify it; and as the Dominie blessed them, and pronounced a benediction, and as the soft rays of the setting sun played over and lighted up that beautiful face, it seemed as if some gentle spirit, sent from on high, was hovering over the scene and whispering Amen.